YOU WILL BOW

USA TODAY BESTSELLING AUTHOR

RACHEL LEIGH

You Will Bow is the second book in a three part series. It is highly recommended to read book one, We Will Reign first.

Please advise, this is a dark college, why-choose romance with content that may be triggering

This book ends on a cliffhanger and picks up in next book of the trilogy: They Will Fall.

For the girls who like their
book boyfriends a little psycho.

BLURB

My first year at college has been anything but ordinary.
After spending so much energy trying to protect my secret, I
failed to realize it's not the past I need to fear—It's my future
that's at stake.
I've finally found someone who doesn't judge me for my sins
and stays by my side while I trudge through the shadowy
corners of my past.
The only problem is, his friends have other plans.
One watches me day and night—painting a picture of a
disturbed life together.
And the other is hanging my secret over my head as leverage
to aid in his own scheme.
But everyone has a weakness, and that weakness will be
mine.

There once was a sicko,
who watched me day and night.
His invisible leash,
never let me out of his sight.
His friends were unlike him,
one a monster I feared.
The other bled crimson,
with a heart that was pure.

Playlist
Listen Now on Spotify
I Will Not Bow by Breaking Benjamin
Careless Whisper by Seether
Yellow by Coldplay
Black by Pearl Jam
Daylight by Shinedown
Disappear by 12 Stones
My Sacrifice by Creed
Falling Away From Me by Korn
Crawling In The Dark by Hoobastank
Welcome To The End by 12 Stones
Cold by Crossfade
Send The Pain Below by Chevelle
Prayer by Disturbed
Enemy by 12 Stones
Monster You Made Me by Pop Evil
CHECK OUT THE PINTEREST BOARD

PROLOGUE
LEV

Fourteen Years Old

SLIDING my left arm into my dad's old black blazer—same one he wore to his junior prom—I beam with excitement. "My dudes, this dance is gonna be fucking lit."

Ridge drops down on Maddox's bed, already dressed for the dance. He's clad in a pair of holey jeans and a garbage band tee shirt, but at least he's wearing dress shoes—sleek black ones that don't match his getup at all. "Shelly Macomb's gonna be there." Ridge waggles his brows at Maddox. "You finally gonna make your move on the goody-two-shoes?"

Shelly's the preacher's daughter, and Maddox has had his eye on her since the end of summer, when his parents started dragging him and Ridge to her father's church.

Maddox buttons the top of his polo shirt. "Nah. She's not interested in me."

"Did you see the fucking rack on her, though?" I jiggle my hands against my chest. "Girl had a major glow-up since eighth grade. If you're not gonna shoot your shot, I might try her on for size."

I watch as Maddox's face flushes bright red, and it's the exact reaction I was looking for. I wouldn't really go for Shelly, knowing Maddox is interested. But sometimes, all it takes for a person to fight for what they want is knowing someone else might fight for it first.

"The hell you will. I'm gonna talk to her...tonight."

"You better," I tell him. "You have just as good of a chance as any other guy."

"Are we done here?" Ridge jumps to his feet. "You assholes are taking forever."

I scoff. "Maybe that's because we're actually getting ready for a semi-formal dance, versus whatever the hell you got dressed for."

Ridge lifts one foot. "I'm wearing the damn shoes Maddox's mom bought me."

"Yeah," Maddox says, "but you're missing the rest of the outfit."

Three years ago, Maddox's parents took over guardianship of Ridge when his mom passed away. Their families were neighbors and their moms were always really close. It was a tragic time for Ridge, and I truly didn't think he'd ever be okay. But he's resilient, and instead of getting weaker each day, he only got stronger. Ridge loves hard and never holds back on expressing himself—except when talking about his mother. The subject of her is too raw, and we don't dare touch it.

"Hey," Ridge says to Maddox, "think your ma's got any booze in the cabinet?"

"None worth taking. Remember, we filled the bottle of red stuff with Kool-Aid."

"Shit. That's right." Ridge snaps his fingers in disappointment, right before his eyes light up. "I got an epic idea, boys. You in?"

The excitement in his tone is terrifying. Any *epic* idea Ridge has always ends up either an epic failure, or a whole lot of trouble. Being the thrill seeker I am, I naturally say, "I'm in."

"I'm out," Maddox quips, and it's no surprise to either of us.

"Yeah. Okay." Ridge chuckles as he pulls open Maddox's bedroom door.

Maddox says he's out, but that means he'd need to leave our side, and he never does. The three of us do everything together. Always have. Always will.

Ten minutes later, we're all inside Larry's Liquor Market. Maddox is at the front of the store distracting Larry, the owner, and I'm covering Ridge. We're only fourteen years old and we don't know what to grab, so Ridge just goes for a random bottle of clear liquor. He stuffs it down the front of his pants and pulls his shirt down. Glancing back to see that Maddox still has the owner talking, Ridge and I leave as fast as possible.

Anxiously, we wait for Maddox down the alley. It's been a good ten minutes since we walked out, and he's still not showing. I pull my phone out of the breast pocket of my blazer and look at the time. "It shouldn't be taking him this long."

"Quit stressing," Ridge says. "We're solid." He pulls the bottle out of his pants and holds it up and reads it. "Everclear. One hundred ninety proof." His eyebrows lift. "Sounds good to me."

I'm unsure what any of that means, but when he twists the top off, the smell alone makes my stomach turn.

"That shit stinks. What is it? Pure rubbing alcohol?"

Ridge shrugs before taking a small drink. His forehead wrinkles and he gags. "That's nasty!"

I snatch the bottle from him. I'm my own worst enemy, but I need to see for myself. I take a sip and immediately mimic his same reaction. I cough and gag, then spit out whatever bit I didn't swallow. "Screw that. I'm not drinking that shit."

Maddox finally appears at the end of the alley and Ridge and I breathe a sigh of relief.

"Sorry, guys. Larry was asking how my grandma's doing since my pawpaw passed away, and I couldn't just leave. Felt too suspicious."

I narrow my eyes. "So we're good?"

"We're good."

"Hell yes!" I beam, slamming the bottle to Maddox's chest. "Try that shit."

I'm surprised when Maddox actually takes a drink, but I'm not surprised at all when he curls over and almost throws up.

We all take one more drink during the walk to the dance, trying to get a little buzz going before we go in. Maddox needs all the liquid courage he can get if he's gonna make a move on Shelly tonight.

When we arrive at the dance, we give the ticket collectors our tickets and step into the gym. A disco ball spins from the ceiling, and with every step we take, we kick the red and black balloons covering the floor.

"You guys want any more of this?" Ridge asks as he pats the bottle under his shirt.

"Nah. I'm good," I tell him, and Maddox says the same.

Ridge walks away, returning five minutes later. "I just dumped half the bottle in the fucking punch bowl." He laughs.

Maddox's eyes widen. "Fuck, man. There's no way no one's gonna know. That stuff is potent."

Twenty minutes later, everyone is talking about it. But when we see Maddox dancing with Shelly, Ridge and I have no regrets.

Although, something isn't sitting right with me. There's an unease in my stomach. I don't feel sick, just uneasy. I approach Ridge, who's talking to a couple of girls in our class, and rest my hand on his shoulder. "Hey. I'm taking off."

"What?" He huffs. "Why?"

"Not feeling too good. Call me after the dance. I'll come over and play some video games with you and Maddox."

He nods in response and I see myself out.

The walk home on the desolate street feels longer than it should. This is the same walk I make every day, going to school and coming home. But something feels off tonight. I'm not sure if it's the shots of alcohol stirring in my stomach, or if I'm coming down with something.

As I turn onto my road, I stop in my tracks when my phone beeps with a text. Pulling it out of my pocket, I read the text from Ridge.

> Ridge: Dude! You're not gonna believe this shit. Cops are at the dance. Maddox and I are hauling ass down Aero Drive. We're coming to your house.

I look over my shoulder, wondering how far behind they are. But when I don't see them, I keep on my way.

As I'm walking, I read a text that was sent earlier, while Ridge and I were in Larry's.

Dad: Be safe tonight. Make good choices. Most of all, have fun. Love ya, son.

I smile at the message. Most people have best friends that are their own age, and I do. But I also have a best friend that is twenty years older than me, and that's my dad.

Sticking my phone back in my pocket, I walk up my paved driveway toward the house. As I approach the door, my stomach twists into knots again.

The front door is wide open, which is odd, but I guess someone just forgot to shut it. I take the first step, then the second. When I hear the small whimpers of Alana, my three-year-old sister, I jog up the rest of the steps and hurry through the open front door.

Everything stands still. Time. Life. My heart. The world.

I freeze. Unable to comprehend what I'm looking at.

Lying in a pool of blood, six feet in front of me, is my mom. She's face up, her eyes glazed over. To the left, I see more blood—and my dad lying face down. "Emery," I shout. "Alana!" I'm not sure how many times I scream my sisters' names, but it's pointless because no one responds. All I have to go on is the muffled cries of Alana, so I follow the sound and fall into the doorframe when I see Emery, my nine-year-old sister—dead.

"Levy," Alana cries from her small toddler bed. "Levy. Help."

She's tucked peacefully in bed with her unicorn comforter wrapped around her on all sides, just the way she likes it. Her hands go in the air. "Hold me, Levy."

I hurry to her side, thankful to see that she's okay, and scoop her trembling body into my arms. The moment when I realize Alana is not okay, I do my best to remain calm, for her. "It's okay, sissy. Everything's gonna be okay." I want so badly to believe the words leaving my mouth, but the truth is, everything is not okay. My entire family has been shot. They're gone. Dead. Nothing is ever going to be okay again.

With a shaking hand, I call 911, and while I hold the phone to my ear, I hold tighter to Alana as she slowly slips away, falling deeper and deeper into her forever sleep.

CHAPTER 1
LEV

RILEY WALKS toward me down the hall, her head hung low, shoulders slumped. I can't help but feel superior to the girl. Not that I should feel otherwise. The level of intimidation I hold over her is not only empowering, but it also turns me the fuck on.

Of all the babes in this school, I'm pretty damn disappointed in my dick for getting hard for the one girl that should be off-limits. Ridge has made it abundantly clear he's obsessed with her, and Maddox has now caught feelings, too.

It's just my luck that Riley is the only person in the whole damn world to wake up emotions inside me that have been dead for so long. It's a foreign feeling, considering indifference is the only thing I've felt since the day my world was turned upside down.

Riley crawls under my skin like a thousand spiders, scratching and biting at my nerves. She has this insatiable power over me, driving me crazy with the desire to be near her just so I can explore what else I'll succumb to in her presence. It's like she's playing some dark game, and I'm just a willing pawn. But no one will ever know the hold she has on me. That secret is mine alone.

"I'm already late for class, Lev. What the hell do you want now?" Riley hugs her bag to her chest like a shy schoolgirl. But one with sass and annoyance written all over her face.

"Just making sure we're on the same page, that's all."

Her bag drops to her side and she straightens her back. "We're not even in the same book, asshole—"

"Hey," I snap, eyes narrowed. "Don't you fucking talk to me like that. You're under my thumb now, Trouble. When I say jump, you ask how high. When I say bow, you fucking bow."

"Mmmhmm," she mumbles with sarcasm. "Gotcha."

"Drop the attitude. Now."

"I'll drop my attitude when you end this madness. You can't really think Maddox and Ridge are going to accept our newfound friendship."

"Fuck Maddox and Ridge. This has nothing to do with them. This is about you and me. Now bow."

Her eyebrows draw together in a frown. "Excuse me?" she says, her voice rising with indignation.

"You heard me. Bow."

She makes a tsking sound as she walks past me with her nose in the air. "Fuck off."

I throw an arm out, catching her by the waist. "Ending the arrangement so soon?"

Her audible exhale ignites an inferno through my veins. I fucking love her defiance. My dick twitches, anticipating just how satisfying it will be when she does as she's told.

She rolls her eyes at me. "What the hell do you want me to do, Lev?"

"Exactly what I said. Bow."

Jerking herself out of my hold, she slaps my arm like an irrational child. One hand rests on her waist and the other drops to her side as she bends over, bowing in a way that would disgrace even the most impotent person. When she straightens her back, she scoffs, "I hate you so much."

Those words would offend most, but I hold them to a high honor. "Thank you. I hate you even more."

"Can I go now?"

I think for a minute, just to torture her. Then I drag it out for another thirty seconds. "This all stays between us, remember."

"Yes, Lev. I remember."

"Good. Because if you tell anyone, including *my* friends, you will be punished."

She huffs and puffs, her frustration growing wildly erratic.

"You can go."

I watch each step she takes with careful precision. She's a hot girl, I'll give her that. Got a nice rack on her and a tight ass. I've always been into blondes, even though it's been a while since I've found anyone attractive. She could lighten up on the makeup a tad. I prefer a natural look, and I've got no doubt that beneath the façade, she's even more beautiful. Her attitude could use some work, but once again, I crave her noncompliance.

Oh, Trouble. It won't be long until you're begging me to do the dirtiest things to you. You can hate me now, but one day, you're going to bow willingly.

Riley yanks open the door to her class, glancing in my

direction before stepping inside. Her expression is laced with disdain, and it's my new favorite look on her.

She steps inside and closes the door. I give it a good minute or two before I follow behind. She's not getting rid of me that easily.

"GOOD MORNING, BEAUTIFUL." I press a chaste kiss on Riley's cheek as I take the seat beside her in psychology class.

Gnawing on her bottom lip, she lifts her head, cracking a smile. "Morning."

"Rough day, so far?" I pull my laptop out of my bag and set it on the table in front of me then twist to hang my backpack on my chair. This is my only class with Riley. Our schedules don't align up until this part of the day, so it's the first I've seen her today.

"No," she says point-blankly. But I know better.

Riley and I are taking things slow. Much slower than I'd like, but I know it's for the best. Ridge is still in love with her. I doubt there will ever be a time when he's not. And, I can't help but wonder if Riley has started to catch feelings for him, too. It's a fucked-up situation. So yeah, slow is best, even if I want to dive in headfirst, without coming up for air.

Swinging my arm over the back of her chair, I lean in.

"What's really going on?" My other hand rests on her upper thigh, fingers grazing gently over her bare leg.

Her mouth opens to speak, but before she does, her eyes trail toward the open door, her thighs clenching and shoulders tightening. When I follow her line of sight, I see the reason for her bout of tension.

"What's he doing here?" My words come out in a mutter as I try to piece together why Lev would be coming into a class he's not taking.

My eyebrows lift, questioning him. I assume he's just dropping by to see me for whatever reason, but when he turns his gaze and drops his bag on the table beside Riley, I think otherwise. Lev pulls out a chair and sinks onto it and Riley rolls her lips together, averting her gaze from him. No comment. No questions. It's as if she was expecting him.

I lean over the table, looking around her. "Since when are you in this class?"

His chin is to his chest while he taps into his phone. "Since today."

Riley stiffens in her chair and I fall back in my seat, watching her. "Did you know about this?"

"We'll talk about it later," she deadpans, eyes locked on the whiteboard at the front of the classroom.

"It's a simple question—"

"I said we'll talk about it later," she snaps before relaxing a bit. To me, it's an attempt to hide her tautness, but it's not working. Something is going on with these two. Not sure why, or even how, considering I've never seen them interact before.

Lev slams his phone on the table, his arm now stretched across the chair where mine just was. "She knew." He confirms my suspicion with a mischievous grin. His fingers swipe across her cheek, and she flinches. "Isn't that right, Trouble?"

I grab the back of Riley's chair, jerking her closer to me. "What the fuck are you doing? Don't touch her!"

Riley swallows hard. "It's fine, Maddox."

"It's fine?" I ask in exasperation.

Lev chuckles, his fingers now running down her arm—an act of defiance, because Lev always does the opposite of what is asked of him.

Riley reaches over and rests her hand on my leg, pushing down with pressure as it dances with agitation. "Don't," she says, finally looking at me. I can see the distress in her eyes and it confuses the hell out of me.

Why is she protecting him?

I've always tried to be understanding of Lev's situation, and his state of mind, knowing he's got a lot going on that he's working through. But that doesn't give him the right to tread into my territory like the lion he claims to be. We might be best friends, but he knows this girl is different. Some might see me as a golden retriever, but all dogs have the ability to bite, and I will fucking bite if Lev thinks he's going to touch *my* girl.

The more I think about him touching her and intimidating her this way, the quicker all the blood in my body rushes to my head.

I spring to my feet and my chair goes flying back, bumping into the table behind us. All eyes in the class are on me as I smack the table and look at both Riley and Lev. "Do we have a problem, Lev?"

"Mr. Crane," Professor Atkins calls out from the front of the room. "Return to your seat."

Scoffing, I do as I'm asked, but not without shooting Lev a look of warning.

He doesn't even acknowledge me as he taps his pencil on the table repeatedly, his mouth curled upward. "We don't."

I draw in a deep breath, eyebrows knitted as I slump in my chair.

Professor Atkins's lecture proceeds to slip through my empty ears. All I can think about is getting the hell out of here and talking to Riley, so she can tell me what the hell's going on.

There's only five minutes left of class when Lev stretches his arm out around Riley's shoulders, again. He pulls her in, and I watch intently, waiting for her to defend herself before I have to step in, but she doesn't. When his mouth ghosts her ear and he whispers into it, she allows it.

I grab her arm, pulling her toward me, expecting some sort of compliance, but she pulls back and listens to whatever he's saying.

"What's he saying to you?"

It's as if I don't exist when she nods in response to whatever he's saying. There's a muffled, "Okay," before she returns to her position in her chair.

His arm drops and she straightens her back, her unease restored.

I lean in and whisper in her other ear, hell-bent on getting answers. "What did he say to you?"

She shakes her head. "Nothing."

"Bullshit!" The word comes out louder and harsher than planned. I lower my voice, knowing I won't get anywhere if I don't calm myself down. "Tell me what's going on. Why is he bothering you?"

Still, she says nothing. Her silence only fuels the fire

inside me. I'm ready to fucking explode. Jealousy isn't the issue here. If it were any other guy, maybe. But this is Lev. He doesn't feel emotions or have the emotional capacity to swoon a girl.

No. This isn't a matter of jealousy. Lev is up to something. Chills skate down my spine at the possibility of what that something could be.

Lev is many things, but if I had to choose a word that best describes him, it would be heartless.

MADDOX IS hot on my trail as I walk down the hall, attempting to put as much space between that room—specifically Lev—and us, as I can.

"You need to tell me what's going on, right now."

I keep walking, still not confident we're far enough away. My fingers grip the strap of my messenger bag so tightly, my knuckles turn white.

Turning down another hall, Maddox keeps on pressing. "Riley! Would you stop walking and tell me what's going on?"

I steal a glance over my shoulder to make sure Lev isn't following, and when I'm sure he's not, I stop.

"'About damn time," Maddox grumbles, dropping his bag to the floor and letting his head fall back. His fingers run through his dusky brunet hair and I can tell he's worked up. When he looks at me, I gulp, prepared to feed him whatever he wants to hear because the truth won't suffice. "Please don't tell me you've got yourself tangled in Lev's web. Please just fucking tell me that."

My lips roll together. Shoulders tight as I lean against the wall. The chilled brick cools my legs and actually feels sort of nice. "I'm not." It's a lie. Possibly the biggest one I've ever told, but I can't tell him what's really going on. I can't tell anyone. Lev made me a deal, his lips are sealed if mine are— and that includes telling Maddox and Ridge.

The truth is scratching like nails inside my head.
The sound drowns out the lies I shouldn't have said.
It's hard to be honest with so much at stake.
So I'll feed him dishonestly and I'll be the snake.

I'm not sure how long this will last, but I have to do whatever Lev says. He's going to help me, but I have to help him, too. The thought makes my stomach turn because our ideas of helping each other are not the same thing.

"Since when do you and Lev even talk to each other?"

"Just recently. He approached me and was kind, helpful even. Offered to help me with an assignment." I take Maddox's hand in mine and pull him close. "You're worrying over nothing. Everything is fine."

"No." He shakes his head, casting his gaze downward. "Nothing is ever fine when it involves Lev. And helping with schoolwork? That's laughable."

"Maddox," I chuckle, "he's your best friend. You, of all people, should know he's not that bad."

His eyebrows shoot to his forehead. "Not that bad? Ry, he's a fucking animal. You need to stay away from him. The guy doesn't have an empathetic bone in his body. Ridge and I are the only people in this entire world he's got because he doesn't let anyone else get close enough to see inside his darkness. We're the only ones who have seen it and refused to turn our backs on him."

"Welllll," I drag out the word, hating what I'm about to

say. "Maybe it's time someone else helped carry that weight. I think he needs another person in his life who cares."

"And you think you're gonna be that person? Not a chance. No way in hell."

I inhale deeply and drop Maddox's hand as I step around him. "In all honesty, that's not really your call. I can be friends with whoever I want."

"Friends?" He laughs. "If you seriously think you and Lev are going to be friends then..."

His words fall short, but I finish for him. "Then I'm, what? Crazy? Insane? Maybe I am. Or maybe I'm the one who needs more friends I can relate to. I'm not the virtuous person you've made me out to be in your head, Maddox. In case you've forgotten, I've..." I lower my voice to a whisper before saying, "I've killed someone."

"Not the same thing."

"Has Lev done that? Has he taken another life? Probably not. You make him sound like this murderous man. Yet, I'm the one who's done the unthinkable. Maybe I'm the one who the world needs protection from, not him."

Saying those words out loud has me questioning who I even am. This isn't me. I know I'm not a monster.

Nothing Maddox says will make me break because I have to do this. But I also know him and Ridge are not going to make this easy. Maddox is spot on when he speaks of Lev. He really is a monster. A sadistic man with no regard for human life. I don't doubt for a second that Lev would throw me under a bus just for the hell of it. I don't trust him at all, but my options have run dry. My life is on the line. From one sinner to the next, Lev and I are both fighting to survive.

"You're upset." Maddox reaches for his bag. "That

wasn't my intention. I just don't want you trusting someone who may not have your best interest at heart."

I get it. He's looking out for me, and I can't be mad at him for that. What I'm most concerned about is how Ridge is going to react. I know Maddox will run to him and tell him everything, and that thought scares the shit out of me. Maddox gets upset, while still remaining calm. Ridge doesn't. Not when it comes to me.

———

"You've gotta be kidding me," I mumble under my breath as I read the text message Ridge just sent me.

> Ridge: Stay the fuck away from Lev.
> Nothing good can come from you two
> 'hanging' out.

I shake my head in annoyance as I walk to the round table in the student center, where I usually have lunch with the guys. For a while, we were meeting outside, but the temperature is quickly dropping as we approach the end of fall. Most of the time it's just Ridge and Maddox—sometimes Lev. Today, Lev isn't around, and I can only assume that's Maddox's doing.

All eyes lift to me as I approach the table. "Got your text," I tell Ridge as I set my bottled lemonade on the table and unwrap my ham sandwich. I pull out a chair and sit down beside Maddox, crossing my legs under the table.

Ridge is directly across from us, his eyes piercing me like daggers. His mouth is a thin, colorless line, and I can feel the tension radiating from him.

Before either of them can say anything, I begin, "I'd like to know why either of you think you can tell me what to do?"

"It's for your own good," Maddox tells me, but his words only piss me off. I knew he'd go straight to Ridge. I knew they'd both try and convince me to stay away from Lev.

I think it's sweet they want to protect me, and it makes me feel good knowing they care. But I'm not a girl who likes being told what to do.

"How do you know what's good for me?" I set my sandwich down on a napkin, my appetite suddenly gone. I look at Ridge, who is still silently scowling at me. "I'm talking to both of you."

Ridge licks his lips, expression stoic. "We can always bring Scar into this. I'm sure she'd have a few choice words."

"You leave Scar out of this." My heart is pounding in my chest. I prepared myself for this. I know Scar will eventually have something to say about it, but I will let that happen on *my* time. The more I'm scolded, the angrier I get. Last year I would have let anyone and everyone dictate my life—not anymore. "If I want to be friends with Lev—a guy who both of you are friends with and live with—then I will be his friend."

Ridge rises from his chair slowly, its legs screeching against the linoleum floor. His muscles are tense, and his gaze never wavers as he comes toward me with purposeful steps. "Do you hear yourself right now?" He crouches down beside me, but I look away, not willing to give him the satisfaction of my eyes as he lectures me. "You obviously don't know Lev at all because anyone who uses his name and friends in the same sentence is delusional. Lev doesn't have friends. He has playthings and I don't want you getting your hopes up."

I roll my eyes at him. "What about you and Maddox?"

"Lev isn't our friend; he's our brother. We've known him our entire lives, which is exactly why I am telling you to stay away from him. For your own safety, you *have* to."

"No." The word pops out of my mouth with no thought process behind it.

"Babe," Maddox says, reaching for my hand, but I jerk it away.

I slide my chair back, causing Ridge to spring up. Snatching my drink and sandwich, I walk toward the exit because I have no desire to stick around for a pointless lecture.

I'm almost out of the student center when Lev walks into me. His chest presses to mine, walking me back a few steps. "Where do you think you're going, Trouble?"

I look around him, my sole focus on getting out of here. "Not right now, Lev. I have somewhere to be. Maddox and Ridge are at the table."

"I'm not here for them." He takes my hand, forcing me to turn back around and walk the way I just came. "I'm here for you."

I swallow hard. My chest rises and falls rapidly, and there's no doubt Ridge and Maddox notice my disdain.

Pull yourself together, Riley. Show them this is what you want. Fool them the same way you keep trying to fool yourself.

Everything is fine.

In two seconds flat, Maddox and Ridge are on their feet coming toward us. Two protective beasts ready to rescue me.

"This is a bad idea," I mumble to Lev as he keeps walking me toward them.

"I think it's gonna be a fantastic fucking time," he says, a wicked grin on his face.

Being over six feet tall, Lev towers over me. When he looks down, his mesmerizing blue eyes pierce into mine, and my breath hitches. "You see, Trouble. You're already getting me excited for what's to come. I knew you'd be the best person for this job."

His fingers glide across my cheek as he watches his own movements. "I've lived in the darkness for years. Unable to see the light. Unable to feel the heat of the sun. Like a vampire, I was cursed with existence and destined for doom. I've been clawing my way out, trying to break free from the shadows of my past, and when I touched you earlier, something woke inside me, and I haven't stopped thinking about the next touch. This is proof that hope is not lost. You are going to save me from myself, Trouble. And in return, I'm going to keep your secrets."

My body quivers. How does he speak like the poems I write in my journal? It's like I can feel him and his yearning for emotions deep in my soul. My words stutter as I struggle to respond. "I don't have any secrets."

"You're a terrible liar. We've been over this, Trouble. I know you killed the governor. I also know you're being framed for Zeke's death, amongst others. And every time you disobey me, I will make things worse for you."

I have no doubt in my mind, Lev will make things much worse for me if I don't do as he asks. So I don't fight him. Instead, I follow his lead and meet Ridge and Maddox in the center of the open space.

Ridge steps up to us, his gaze wandering to my hand Lev is gripping, then back up to my eyes. "Someone better tell me what the hell is going on right now, or I'm gonna lose my shit."

Maddox joins my side and places his arm around my waist, pulling me toward him, but Lev only tightens his grip on me. His fingers squeeze so forcefully, my bones crush together.

I wince at the pain and attempt to jerk my hand away without drawing attention to my action. It's lackluster at best, and Lev doesn't relent.

"I don't see what the problem is," Lev says, his head held high and a permanent grin on his face. "Riley and I are good friends now. Nothing wrong with that, is there? After all, you guys are her friends, too."

"Let her go," Maddox demands of him, playing tug-of-war with my body. He pulls me by the waist, while Lev squeezes my hand.

Lev looks down at me, the scent of sweet mint from the gum he's chewing invading my senses. "Is that what you want?"

It's a test, so I say exactly what I know he wants me to say. "No."

I'm gnawing nervously on my bottom lip when the tang of blood hits my tongue. My heart is imploding inside my chest, and the tension between the four of us thickens with each passing second.

Maddox takes a perplexed step back, his eyes blinking rapidly. "You're lying."

He's right, I am lying. My palms are sweating, my heart still rapid firing, while at the same time, it's breaking, because I'm allowing three best friends to be pinned against one another.

Lev's nostrils flare as he walks me past the guys. He has to know their level of possessiveness.

I subtly pull back, hoping he'll let go, but he doesn't. He gives me a firm squeeze and glowers at me, gritting, "Quit fighting this."

"They're going to make a big deal out of it. You know they will."

"Why?" He huffs under his breath. "Because they think I'm not good enough for you? Is that what you think? Do you think you're better than me?"

"No. Not at all." My voice is a whisper between us. "But they've told me things about you..." I'm putting my foot in my mouth. I need to just shut the hell up before I really mess things up. Lev is a ticking bomb, and the last thing I need is for any one of them to make a scene.

He stops walking abruptly, jerking my hand along with him. "What things?"

I gulp, now at the center of all three of them again, because Maddox and Ridge are hot on our trail.

"Come on, Angel," Ridge takes my other hand, pinning Lev with a hefty scowl as he says, "Let her go."

"Can't do that," Lev tells him, his defiance on display. "Riley was in the middle of telling me something." His eyes skate to mine, causing goosebumps to break out on my arms. "Go on."

I shake my head slowly. "I don't know what I was saying. Can we all just get out of here?" My eyes dance around the open space, where a few students are watching us inconspicuously. "People are looking at us."

"Riley was telling me that you two said some things about me to her? Any idea what she's talking about?" He watches me as he speaks to them, seeing if I'll react. All the while, knowing how much I hate being in the middle of this.

My back steels, while Maddox and Ridge share a glance before they both look at me, too. Once again, I'm the center of attention. I hate being put on the spot. Should have kept my damn mouth shut. Now this is all going to be put on me. I'll be forced to rat on Maddox and Ridge, telling Lev what they said.

I open my mouth but stop when Ridge pipes up. "She was probably referring to me warning her to stay away from you. Told her you were a fucking maniac, which we all know to be true."

My eyes soften, and I thank Ridge with a slight smile.

"Ah." Lev taps his chin. "As opposed to you being sane?"

Ridge pats Lev on the shoulder. "Never claimed to be sane." His hand slides up, landing on Lev's neck. With little pressure, his fingertips sink into his skin. "Let her go."

Lev tips his chin. "Fuck off."

"Dude, just let her the fuck go!" Maddox snaps, before wrapping his arm around my shoulders. He pulls me into him, but Lev still doesn't concede. "You see, this is exactly why you need to stay far away from him."

"I'm fine," I tell Maddox. Another lie sewn on my sleeve. It's obvious I'm not fine. Ridge is choking Lev because he won't let go of my fucking hand. I squirm and jerk and pull, but the animal refuses to unleash me.

I watch as Ridge strangles him harder, cringing at the sight because there is nothing gentle about the way he's manhandling Lev.

"Jesus Christ! Would you guys stop this?"

Lev growls, his teeth grinding brutally, but he doesn't fight back or fend Ridge off. His lack of reaction only eggs

Ridge on further, causing him to squeeze with all his might, likely cutting off Lev's air supply.

I pull my hand, fighting to get free, so Ridge will let him go before he passes out.

Seconds later, Lev lets me go.

Ridge drops his hold on him and takes a step back, while I rub the marks on my hand from where Lev was gripping me.

"Shouldn't have had to go this far," Ridge tells Lev, and I'm in complete agreement. None of this has to be this way. "Just stay the fuck away from her and all is fine."

"Oh really?" Lev scoffs. "So, you two fuckwads can do whatever you want with her. Pass her around, toy with her, make her believe you're saints. But I'm the bad guy here?"

Ridge quickly takes it upon himself to lead me away. We pass by the group of students who were watching the situation unfold. Whispers flow among them, but I pay them little attention. It's only a matter of time before everyone is gossiping about me. The guys have taken care of Cade. Apparently, they forced him away and told him to never show his face again. Since Cade is the one who was framing me for crimes I didn't commit, I know I'm safe in that respect. However, my secret is spreading far and wide, and now it's fallen into hands that want to punish me.

One wrong move, and Lev will turn on me. I have no doubt in my mind. Leaving with Ridge is bound to piss him off, and later, I fear I'll be faced with the consequences of this decision.

When I glance back and catch Lev's stare—his hands are fisted at his sides and a sinister smile's on his face—I'm certain he knew exactly what he was doing just now.

LOVE IS A FINICKY THING. Makes you do crazy shit. Oftentimes, I sit back and watch Ridge as he carries out a plot of destruction. Be it a midnight visit to his angel, a senseless fight with a stranger who pegged *his girl* with the wrong look, or even something as miniscule as sharing the air she breathes. Today it was choking our best friend with an audience. He didn't give a damn who saw. He came to her defense while I stood idly by, never once stepping in because I didn't know whose side to choose.

I've always wondered what goes through Ridge's mind in these moments. Does he feel an ounce of remorse for the things he does? Is there any weight of regret hanging heavy on his mind?

More often than not, the answer is no. Why? Because he does it all for her.

How will I ever outshine him in Riley's eyes when he's willing to go to the depths of the earth for her?

With Ridge, it's not his victims who feel the wrath of his disgruntled behavior, it's himself. Now here I am—mimicking the same behavior. I'm doing this for Riley, but it will be the one bad deed I've done that she'll never know about. Therefore, Ridge is still her hero.

It's true that I always try to do the right thing. I believe karma gives sinners what they deserve. But lately, I find myself questioning what the right thing is. My entire life I've hung on to my dad's every word, assuming he's always right. He knows everything. In my eyes, he can do no wrong. Now, I'm starting to realize what he thinks is right for him, might not be the same thing as what's right for me.

I'm sitting across from Cade, on babysitting duty until Ridge gets here. He drugged our girl before he committed heinous acts to her body. So, naturally, we kidnapped him.

All in the name of love.

Maybe I'm crazy for thinking this thing with me and Riley could ever work. Even if I do love her, Ridge's morbid love for her will always exist, and I don't have the guts to go to the extremes he does. So does that make me unworthy of her?

"Do you believe in love at first sight?" I ask Cade, who's bound and gagged in the chair in front of me. He can't answer, but his eyes are telling—wide and alert, the epitome of horror-struck. "I don't either." I stand up to pace in front of him, tapping my chin as I bide time until Ridge gets here so he can interrogate him again. "In fact, I'm a believer that the whole love at first sight thing came from fairy tales, and well, we all know fairy tales aren't real. You have to know the person to fall in love with them, right?"

Cade drops his chin to his chest, beaten and defeated. He doesn't give a damn what I have to say, and I really don't care if he listens or not. It's just nice to think out loud sometimes, and he happens to be in my vicinity. Even if he doesn't have a choice.

This place is depressing as fuck. There's colorful graffiti covering the cement block walls from trespassers that entered before Lev acquired the building. Every wall is embellished with an array of artistic designs and scribbled curse words. The concrete floor and lack of insulation make it colder than the Arctic. Fortunately there's a small space heater, but it only helps if you're standing directly in front of it.

The warehouse, that's been abandoned for years, is set in the middle of a field not far from campus. The only comfort in this building is the room Lev had remodeled for his appointments with his therapist. The fucker bought the entire building, just so he could use that one room and have the privacy he desperately needs during his sessions. I don't fault him for it. Hell, I'd do the same thing if I had the emotional incapacity that Lev does. I've never witnessed one of his sessions, but from what I gather, there is a lot of screaming on his part, and oftentimes, he breaks shit as well.

Ridge had the grand idea of utilizing the extra space in the warehouse for a fight club, which I think is a fantastic idea. I'm sure there are a lot of students on campus who would love to have a place to go to let out some of the aggression we're forced to hold in, due to being in The Society. We're not like normal people. In fact, we're the complete opposite of normal, and fuck if it isn't enough to make someone crazy. It's been almost five years since I stepped into my role as a Blue Blood—the start of junior year at The Academy. Now being a junior at BCU, I've seen enough to know that we're all going to be in dire need of therapy for years to come.

A triple knock at the door—our code for entry—has me snapping out of my thoughts, and Cade lifting his head. "Sounds like your dinner is here." I approach the door and click the deadbolt. "Better hope Ridge is in a pleasant mood today."

Before I have a chance to turn the knob, it comes flying open, causing me to jump back.

My eyes slide over to Cade's cautious ones as Ridge enters, the large space suddenly feeling small in his presence.

As soon as the door closes, Ridge clicks the lock, and the tension thickens. We haven't talked much lately. It's been two weeks since Riley and I started hanging out more. I wouldn't say we're 'dating,' but we're getting there. It's also been two weeks since we brought Cade down here. In that same amount of time, all conversations between Ridge and me have been focused on Cade and our plans for him. For a while, I was concerned Ridge might kill him. Ridge is unpredictable in that way. Not to mention, Cade hurt Riley, and that's a death sentence in Ridge's eyes. And maybe even mine too.

But something is stopping him, and I'm not sure what it is. Either way, I'm grateful because I'd rather not be an accomplice to murder.

Ridge chucks a paper lunch bag that's rolled up at Cade. It hits his chest, then rolls into his lap, almost falling to the floor. "Eat, fucker."

"How's he supposed to do that?" I scoff. "His hands are tied behind his back."

"He seems like a resourceful kinda guy. He'll figure it out."

The bag hits the floor, and my eyes roll as I grab it.

Reaching in the bag, I scowl at Ridge, while pulling out a squished sandwich that's not even in a plastic baggie. I hold it up, displaying the contents, when I realize a bite's been taken out of it.

Ridge shrugs his shoulders nonchalantly. "Got hungry on the walk over."

"Dipshit," I mumble under my breath, but the nudge to my shoulder confirms he heard me loud and clear.

"Why the fuck do you care if this bastard eats? In case you forgot, he took advantage of our girl."

"*Our* girl?" I laugh. Funny how he says it that way, considering it wasn't long ago that he scolded me for referencing her the same, when he was certain she was his and his alone. "Not our girl." I spin around to face him, sandwich in hand. "My girl."

I watch as his blood pumps faster and faster. Jaw locked, fists clenched, and the reddening of his face is impossible to miss. "What the fuck did you just say?"

"You heard me," I tell him, not feeling an ounce of regret for saying what I said. "My girl. Not ours. Not yours. Just *mine.*"

"Yeah?" His eyebrows lift. "If she's your girl then tell me where she's at. Do you know? Is she safe?"

"She is *my* fucking girl," I shout. "We've got the guy who was tormenting her, so she's safe. Now mind your own damn business."

"And Lev? Do you just not give a shit that he's worming his way in on *your* girl?"

My hand sweeps through the air, a mixture of frustration and defensiveness brewing inside me. It's not me I feel the need to defend; it's my relationship with Riley. Ridge is never going to allow me to get comfortable in it. "Lev's not gonna hurt her."

"How can you be so sure? You know what he's capable of." The confidence in his tone is unnerving. Riley will never be safe as far as Ridge is concerned. There will always be a threat, and I'm starting to think I'm the threat he sees right now.

"How about you let me take care of Riley, and mind your own fucking business." Generally, when I feel myself getting worked up like this, I walk away. But not this time. If I ever want to feel good enough, or be good enough for Riley, it's time I stand up for myself and our relationship. There's no doubt in my mind that Ridge and Lev look down at me. I'm the good guy. The pushover. The weak link.

Ridge bumps his chest into mine, his shoulders tight, nostrils flaring. "Riley *is* my fucking business." He steps into me again, and I stumble, falling onto Cade's lap.

I'm back on my feet in two seconds flat, hands flying to Ridge's chest. "Not anymore, she's not. She made her choice, and it wasn't you, so back the fuck off."

A roaring laugh ripples through Ridge's vocal cords, the sinister sound echoing off the brick walls surrounding us. "You gave her no choice. You put on a good show for a vulnerable girl and played your holier-than-thou act. This is only temporary, Maddox." He shoves me so hard, I fly back onto Cade, tipping the chair over and taking us both to the floor. "Don't get comfortable."

"You son of a bitch!" I push myself up and charge at him, teeth bared. My arms fly out, and I grab him around the waist. As soon as his back collides with the cement floor, so do my hands, scraping against the hard surface. Ridge curses and shouts, screaming monstrous words that only a psycho like him would ever say.

"I'll fucking kill you if you ever try and stand between us," Ridge roars. "I will literally slice your chest open and pull your heart out with my bare hands before freezing it and using it as an ice sculpture at mine and Riley's wedding."

One of his hands grabs at my face, palming it and turning it to the left, while the other whales at my shoulder, punching repeatedly, but I feel no pain.

I reach out and grab his throat. "Do it, you sick fuck. Go ahead and rip out my heart because I'm not giving up on her. I'll fight, and when you try to push me away from her, I'll come back and fight even harder."

A triple knock at the door has us both halting. I look at Ridge's angry eyes before my gaze slides to the door. In a swift motion, Ridge shoves me off him, and just when I think he's trying to take the upper hand, ready to pummel my ass, he pushes himself up. With a stern finger jabbed into my chest, he seethes, "This isn't over."

"You're right, it's not." Could've probably said something harsher, but it's better than silence. I refuse to let Ridge have the last word, but I also don't wanna stir up any more problems right now. We've got enough shit to deal with.

Getting on Ridge's bad side is never a good idea, though I'm certain I'm now on it. We always talk about Lev being the loose cannon, but Ridge is a ticking time bomb.

When Ridge opens the door, Lev comes inside with his typical heavy scowl. He nods toward Cade before slamming the door shut. "This fucker's still alive?"

My questioning eyes land on Ridge because I'm pretty surprised myself.

"He is. It's not time yet," Ridge tells him, and it's the

assurance I needed that he does have a plan. Which is good, because I sure as fuck don't. Really didn't want any part of this in the first place, but my loyalties lie with Lev and Ridge, even if they both piss me off daily.

"Hey," I say to Lev. "You checked this asshole for his phone, right?"

"Yep," he replies. "He said he didn't have it on him. I patted him down and didn't find it. What the hell are you doing here, anyways? Thought you were sitting this one out?"

"That was the plan, but apparently, plans change, and our prisoner needed a babysitter, while Ridge was out doing whatever the fuck Ridge does."

"Whatever the fuck I do?" Ridge mocks me. "How about looking after the girl you say is yours, while you're doing whatever the fuck you do."

"Maybe I would've been with her if you didn't send me here. Or was that all part of your plan to distract me?"

He wears a cocksure grin on his face as his shoulders waggle. "Maybe it was. Or maybe I don't need a plan because I don't give a fuck what you think about—"

"Shut the fuck up!" Lev howls. "Both of you. Is this chick really worth it? Are you willing to destroy a lifetime of friendship for a piece of ass?"

If that isn't the pot calling the kettle black. "Isn't that exactly what you're doing, Lev?"

"Nope. Not looking for a fling, or a piece of ass," Lev retorts as he hovers over Cade.

Ridge elbows Lev out of the way, then he grabs the chair and tips it back up. In one fell swoop, he gathers the tape over Cade's mouth and rips it off.

Cade gasps before spitting out the balled-up handkerchief in his mouth. It lands on his lap, all slobbery and gross. His tongue drags across his cracked, bloody lips. "Please. Please just let me go. You've got the wrong guy."

"What the hell are you doing?" Lev growls. "He doesn't deserve to fucking talk." He snatches the roll of duct tape from the metal table that resembles one you'd find alongside a hospital bed.

Ridge grabs the duct tape from Lev through a game of tug-of-war.

"This was my fucking plan," Ridge seethes. "Don't come in here and try to fuck it up."

"Your plan? Thought we were all in on this together. One goal in mind. Make this fucker pay?"

While they're having their little quarrel, I use this time wisely. "Look at me," I say to Cade sternly. "Tell me why the fuck you did it."

Cade shakes his head, tears rolling down his face as his legs bob up and down, as much as they can with his ankles bound to the chair. "I didn't do it." His dry lips smack together, a string of thick saliva stretching between them. "Whatever you're all accusing me of is false. You've got the wrong guy."

Out of nowhere, Lev's hand comes from behind me, his fist landing on Cade's face, which causes his head to fly back and a gush of blood to jet from his mouth, landing in a splatter at Ridge's feet.

"Liar," Lev roars. "If I had it my way, you'd be dead by now. I've got no idea why Ridge is keeping you alive, but you better thank your lucky stars and hope like hell you get to live to see another day."

I'm taken aback by Lev's passion for the situation, considering Riley isn't of importance to him. He said so himself—he's not looking for a fling or a piece of ass. Unless he really does want some sort of friendship with her. Maybe Lev cares about her, after all.

No. Impossible. Lev doesn't care about anyone.

My phone pings with a text, so I take a couple of steps back, letting them deal with Cade.

> Riley: Change of plans. I'm not going to be able to study tonight after all. I'm not feeling too well. Probably going to eat and go to bed early.

Shit. I forgot all about our plans to meet at the library. I've been so caught up in everything else happening that it completely slipped my mind.

> Me: No worries. I'm pretty busy, too. Rain check for tomorrow?

> Riley: Can't. We're decorating the campus square for Halloween.

> Me: Ok. Get some rest and I'll call you later.

After a minute has passed with no more text messages, I stick my phone back in my pocket.

When I turn around to see if things have settled with everyone, I find them all looking at me. Even Cade, who has tape back over his mouth.

"What?" I huff, curious as to why I'm getting the death stare from both Lev and Ridge.

"Where is she?" Ridge quips.

"At her dorm. She's not feeling well."

His eyebrows hit his forehead, as if he's pained just by the thought of her being ill. "She's sick?"

"Probably not. Just said she wasn't feeling well. She'll be fine."

His head shakes in frustration as he staggers toward the door. "You see. That right there is what I'm talking about. She deserves better."

Ridge's fingers wrap around the door handle as he shoots us a look over his shoulder. "Make sure that dickwad eats, then double-check the ropes before you leave. I'll come back tomorrow."

As he pulls the door open, I holler, "Where are you going?"

"Where you should be going, but aren't."

He steps out and slams the door closed.

My gut wrenches because, once again, I'm the worthless piece of shit who will never be good enough for his precious angel. I could go after him. Stop him and go instead, but it's useless. Ridge does what Ridge wants, and what he wants is to always be with her.

"I'm out, too," Lev says.

"Hell no. I was down here for an hour before you two showed up. I'm not dealing with him a second longer." I look at Cade, who seems to have fallen asleep with his chin snug to his chest.

"Shove that nasty sandwich in his mouth and leave then."

Without another word, Lev goes, too.

And the pushover stays.

THE LAST THING I want to do is lie to Maddox, but this thing with Lev is a battle I will not win, no matter how hard I fight.

As he walks toward me with a slow swagger, the corner of his lip curled, my insides shiver. Only a complete idiot would meet a guy like Lev in a graveyard. The sun is veiled by a thick blanket of clouds, cast over the graves as it begins to descend. In minutes, we will be greeted with darkness. Leaving the spirits of the dead as the only witnesses to what Lev has planned for me.

"Nice to see you, Trouble."

I cringe at his voice. "Why are we here?"

The space between us closes, and once he's directly in front of me, his finger rests underneath my chin and he tilts my head upward. "I'm impressed. Didn't think you'd show."

"It's not like you gave me much of a choice."

"Very true. But you chose to obey, nonetheless."

"Let's just get this over with." I slap away his hand,

angered by his touch. "I have better things to do than hang out with you in the cemetery."

"Oh yeah?" His eyes perk up. "Like what? Fucking Ridge, or fucking with Maddox?"

My chest quivers. "I don't have intentions of doing either of those things."

"But you have, right? You fucked Ridge and now you've moved on to our best friend."

"Did we meet here just so you can ridicule my poor choices?"

"So you're saying you regret it?"

"Regret what?"

"Fucking Ridge."

I scoff. "How do you even know that I *have* fucked Ridge?"

"Because I saw you. Ridge isn't the only one who watches you. Actually, I watch you often. I'll never forget the look in your eyes when he gave that final thrust that sent you over the edge."

"You're sick, you know that?" My cheeks burn with shame and anger, knowing he witnessed me losing my virginity.

"I do. But you're sick, too."

"I am nothing like you."

"Oh," he hums softly, "but you are. A sane person doesn't murder someone."

Silence engulfs us because it's true. Everything Lev is saying is accurate. I did fuck Ridge. I am falling for Maddox. And I did murder someone. But I didn't murder those other guys. Not the ones that Cade framed me for killing. Fortunately, that's in the past. My only concern now is protecting my secret. Which is exactly why I'm here, doing what Lev wants, just so I can have some semblance of a life.

He steps around me, my back now to him. "You killed a man, Riley."

I'm not sure he's ever referred to me as anything but Trouble, but I'm not complaining. What I am getting really fucking annoyed with is his need to keep bringing up my past. "Yes!" I blurt out. "We both know I did. So what the hell do you want from me?" I turn around, surprised to find that he's so close. Our chests collide, and when I take a step back, he pulls me right back in with a hand pressed firmly to my hip.

"Do you regret what you did?"

I gulp, not wanting to revisit that day. "No." It's the truth. I don't regret killing the governor. I saved the world from a heinous man.

"Then why do you shiver every time I bring it up?"

"I don't wanna talk about this."

His hold on me tightens and I'm forced to breathe in the scent of his mint gum that smacks between his teeth. His other hand wraps around me and his fingertips dig into my ass. My head turns, neck tilted back as I avoid looking at him. "Let me go, please."

"Not until you tell me why this conversation makes you so nervous."

"Because!" I spit out. "Because it's not a conversation that I care to have. Yes, I took a life. No, I'm not proud of it, but I also don't regret it because it had to be done. I didn't kill those other men, though."

"I know you didn't. Never thought for a second you did. But here's the thing, Trouble..." *There it is again. That stupid nickname.* "I know who you are. I know who your family is.

And I know what you're capable of. I'm not talking about murder in the first degree. I'm talking about your position in The Society. You're a Guardian, right?"

I bring two hands to his chest, ready to push him back if need be. "How do you know that?"

The vibration of his chuckle rattles against my breasts. "Don't you know by now that the only way secrets are safe is to not have any?"

When I don't respond, his hands dig deeper into my ass.

"Answer the question."

His lips ghost my ear and goosebumps trail his breath on my neck. "Do you know what my position is, Trouble?"

I swallow hard, shaking my head in response.

"I'm a Punisher and if you fuck up, I'll make sure I'm assigned to you when you're banished from The Society for killing all those men."

Lev's a Punisher? I had no idea. I would have never even guessed that was his role in The Society.

"But. I didn't..."

"Try telling them that as the evidence keeps stacking against you."

My breaths hitch as I struggle to breathe. "Cade did it. He set me up."

"Did he, though?"

"Yes. He did. He did it and Ridge took care of him. He sent him away, so it's over now. There's nothing to punish me for. Case closed."

"The case will close when I'm ready for it to close." His teeth drag across my lobe before he sucks it into his mouth, biting with enough tenacity to make me shudder. "And I'm not ready for it to close."

Tears sting the corners of my eyes, threatening to break free. "Why are you doing this to me?"

My eyes widen with horror as Lev grinds his erection against me, proof that he's turned on by my misery. "Because my body reacts to you, and that hasn't happened to me in a very long time. I want you to slice me open, Trouble. Show me what it's like to feel alive again."

I'm still not sure what that means. Lev seems to think I can bring back the emotions he's suppressed all these years from whatever traumatic experience he had that shut them down, but I think he's got the wrong girl.

"I'm not sure what you expect me to do, but I'll fail, Lev." My voice cracks as I exhale the words. "I'm barely hanging on myself. I don't know how to save us both."

His back straightens, and when he looks into my eyes, I wince because I know whatever he's about to say is not what I want to hear.

"A deal's a deal."

I close my eyes and fight my body like it's my own worst enemy as I nod in response to his statement. When I open them again, he's grinning, and I ascertain that my nonverbal acceptance is equivalent to signing my name in blood. Lev will hold me to this deal, come hell or high water.

"Good."

His hand slides gracefully up my arm, the skin beneath my bubblegum pink knitted sweater prickling. It's an old sweater and I thought wearing it might make me feel more like me again. The truth is, I still don't know the person under these layers. She's more of a stranger to me than the guy who's pushing me down on my knees.

"Have you ever sucked cock before, Trouble?"

I wince at his words as I lower myself to the ground,

head hung low in shame. "Yes," I tell him, truthfully. It was only once and I had no idea what I was doing, but it was enough for the guy to come within three minutes, so I must have done something right.

"Then you'll have no problem now."

I listen intently to the sound of his zipper coming down. When his jeans drop, pooling at his ankles in front of me, I draw in a deep breath and fill my lungs in preparation for what I'm about to do.

As much as I don't want to do this, I know I have to. Lev made it very clear that I will be his *pet* if I want my secret safe. Apparently, this fucking asshole thinks that *this* is the way to fix the broken parts of him.

Reaching down, Lev lifts my chin until I'm looking right at his erect cock. My eyes widen in surprise when I see not only how big he is, but also the three silver barbells on his shaft. I've never seen a guy with his dick pierced, and it's actually really sexy. I should've known he'd be pierced and hung like a horse. Someone with such a big mouth would have a large dick decked out in jewelry. His girth is astounding. I might not even be able to wrap my fingers around him. He's at least 8 inches in length—maybe more. He's cleanly shaved, which is nice. I'd hate to be pulling one of his curly black pubes out of my teeth later as a reminder of this shameful act. One might think they'd be blond, but the black stubble leads me to believe the hair on his head is colored that way. It's funny he picked white, being such a contrast to his black soul.

"Well," Lev grumbles as he strokes himself in front of my face. "You just gonna stare at it, or you gonna put it in your mouth."

"Just this once? Then never again?"

He chuckles cruelly, ice-cold eyes regarding me. "No, Trouble. This is only the beginning."

Lord have mercy on me. I should bite the fucking thing and run, or better yet, yank on one of those barbells. Temptation gnaws at my insides. But I can't do that. He'd catch me. There's not a doubt in my mind. And once he did, the consequences could be far worse. I'm not opposed to sucking him off. It's degrading, but it's better than letting him between my legs. So I'll suck it up—no pun intended—and I'll do this in hopes that he feels absolutely nothing and realizes what a stupid fucking plan this is.

Before I can even take it upon myself to put him in my mouth, Lev grips my cheeks with tenacity, forcing my mouth open. Guiding me toward him, he continues to stroke himself. Then he pushes until my lips part far and wide, and he slips the head inside.

"That's right. Open big for me, Trouble."

My stomach twists and turns until it feels like a hollow organ.

An audible gasp escapes him and his legs tremble in front of me. Lev thinks I'm the antidote to his illness—to his lack of empathy or emotion. I don't know how or why, but it has me wondering how long it's been since he's had any sort of sexual interaction with a girl. In a way, the thought of me being the first in a very long time is gratifying. Like I really am his chosen one.

My hand lifts slowly, shaking as I wrap my fingers around his girth, taking care not to graze his piercing.

"Does that hurt?" I muffle around him. I'm not sure why I asked, or why I even care.

"No." His voice is husky.

As predicted, my fingers barely touch when they're

wrapped around him. He is so fucking big. As his head swells even more in my mouth, I pray that he's at his full erection. Bobbing my head back and forth, I suck on the shallow end, dragging my tongue with each movement. My hand glides with my saliva coating his silky cock and I repeat the motions, hoping it's enough.

His piercings graze my tongue as I explore the metal with my mouth. It's a different sensation, both strange and thrilling.

When he steps one foot out of his jeans, then the other, spreading his legs wider, I pick up my pace in hopes of hurrying this along.

Give it all you've got, Riley. This will be over soon enough.

His fingers rake through my hair and he gets a good grip before forcing me to move faster. I can barely keep up with his rhythm.

Not a word is spoken from him, but when a low growl escapes from the back of his throat, I'm certain he's enjoying this.

At least one of us is.

Dragging my teeth along the corded purple veins of his cock, I suck in a breath. The salty taste of precum dabs against my tongue and to my surprise, my stomach doesn't curl. I assumed Lev's bodily fluids would make me vomit at his feet.

Lev bunches my hair in his hand and groans. "Fuck." Rocking my head back and forth, he glides himself in and out of my wet mouth.

I clench my thighs at the sound of his voice. So masculine and raspy. Even though it's *him*, I can't help but feel some sort of satisfaction, knowing I'm the one making him feel good. This monstrous man, who claims to feel nothing, is moaning over the pleasure *I* am bringing him. It's the drive I need to finish the job.

Unaware my hands are even on his ass, I use them as cushioning and squeeze harder. I take all of him. Every inch, until he's hitting the back of my throat, and when I feel like I'm going to gag, I choke it down and take even more. My mouth is completely stuffed with Lev's cock when he holds the back of my head, not letting me take him out. I gulp and try to release him, but his hips rock repeatedly. Rolling and pushing as he fucks my mouth.

"God damn, your mouth feels so fucking good."

No matter how hard I try, he continues to hold me in place, to the point of my heart feeling like it might implode in my chest. No longer able to stop myself from gagging, I do it right around his girthy cock.

The next thing I know, he's pushing me until my back hits the ground. I prop myself up on my elbows to get a better look at him. But as he takes two steps toward me, I lay back down. All I can see are his hung balls and his sizable dick coming toward my face.

Lev climbs on top of me and I turn my head. "What are you doing?"

He grabs my cheeks, squeezing my jaw until it pops open.

To the left of me is an old tomb that reads Glenda Morris 1902. *I'm sorry you have to witness this, Glenda.* It's obvious this place doesn't get many visitors. The graves themselves are covered in grime, mud, and mold.

Lev draws the head of his cock around my lips then smacks my cheek with it. "I'm not finished yet."

Filled with uncontrollable loathing, I screech, "You are such an asshole! The epitome of evil."

"That I am. Now open up."

The confidence in his tone, knowing that I'll do what he says, annoys the hell out of me. He's done a complete one-eighty from the time I greeted him here, transforming back into the despicable guy I know he is. This must be part of his thrill. He must like a fight. Maybe that's what makes him feel alive. So, I give him the fight he's looking for. In one swift motion, I raise my hand and slap him hard across the face. "Fuck you, Lev."

Cold fingers wrap around my throat as he juts my neck up, forcing my eyes on him. "Oh, I'm going to. I'm gonna fuck your pretty mouth, Trouble. And, you're gonna keep your eyes on me while I do it. Understood?"

I glower at him, feeding him what he needs, because Lev is hungry for noncompliance. He doesn't want me to obey. Not yet. He wants me to disobey so he can feel powerful when he puts me back in line.

The space between his feet widens, then he kneels beside my head. Still holding my throat, he lifts my head up then feeds me his cock once again. I spit and spatter and growl around him as he fucks my mouth like it's his gateway to sanity.

I watch him. My eyes never leaving his as the sun disappears into the night and the moon slowly rises.

He uses my mouth for his own pleasure. And before long, I get into it. My body tingles with its own desires because hormones are a bitch. It's in this moment of being used that I realize, I'm actually turned on by Lev's degree of aggression.

I'm as sick as he is—maybe more so.

I grab his hips and squeeze, while he does all the work. His hips gyrate as he slides in and out of my mouth.

I fall under a spell, locked in his gaze. My pussy throbs with desperation, and if I could, I'd touch myself right now. Hell, I might even let him do it to me.

No one will ever know how much I loved this. No one will know the darkness inside me, or that I am so fucking aroused by this man right now that I'd do just about anything to have him get me off.

Lev's head swells inside my mouth, his cock pulsating against my tongue. Without any verbal warning, he shoves himself as far back as he can go and pauses, letting a thick stream of cum shoot down my throat.

Once every drop is out, he pulls back, leaving my mouth open and full of his release. I don't move. I wait to see what he wants from me.

Slowly, his hand moves to my chin, and he pushes my mouth closed. "Swallow," he orders.

I hesitate, not immediately listening. It's not until his fingers dig into my chin that I finally give him what he wants. In one gulp, I swallow down the bitter liquid. I could swear Lev shivers as he watches my throat bob. "That's a good girl." He pats my cheek like I'm an obedient pet before standing up.

I drop my head back onto the ground, still on a high of my own.

CHAPTER 6
LEV

IT WORKED. My insides are literally screaming with enthusiasm because it actually fucking worked.

Listening to her moan and gag around my thick length while her fingers brushed my piercing had my legs shaking so hard, I had to move her to the ground.

The second she dug her hands into my hips, I could almost smell the arousal on her. It was like she had to hold on just to stop herself from touching what I'm willing to bet is now a very swollen clit.

A smile creeps onto my face, a genuine smile, and I find myself turning away from her before she can see it. I don't know what it is she's doing that makes her different, but I plan to stick around and find out.

The high fades all too quickly, and as the light at the end of the tunnel fades to black, I'm left with the only emotion I've known for the past seven years—vexation.

"Get up," I tell her. She's just lying there like she's settled in for a nap, a bead of my cum drying on her chin.

"Give me a minute."

"We don't have a minute. I've got somewhere to be."

I fully expected her to get up and run after I finished. Yet, here she is, as comfortable as can be, lying in a cemetery in the pitch-black night. Maybe I miscalculated the intensity of her depravity. At first glance, she's simply a weak link— one easily pursued. But deep down, I think her mind is as fucked as mine is.

"What the hell are you doing?" I howl into the chilly air.

Finally, she pushes herself up, elbows propped behind her and her ass still on the damp ground. "How long has it been since you...did that?"

My cheeks wear my surprise as they flood with heat at her ridiculous question. One I have no intention of answering. "Did what?" I play dumb, even though I know exactly what she's asking.

Is that what she's been lying there thinking about? How long it's been since a girl sucked my dick?

I can tell she's uncomfortable, but oddly curious. Her mouth opens to speak but she closes it again before decisively saying, "Never mind."

"Good. Because my business is none of yours. Now get your ass up, or you can walk outta here alone."

The truth is, it's been a very long time. So long, that I don't even masturbate anymore, because I didn't think my body knew what it was supposed to do. Not only is my mind completely fucked, my dick is, too. At least, it was.

What just happened is proof that I need her. For whatever reason, my soul reacts to this girl. She's the only one who can save me from myself, and I'd be a fool to let her get away.

After a few grumbles and curse words, she's on her feet.

"Quit being so damn dramatic. It was a blow job, not a marathon."

"It was the most shameful thing I've ever done in my life with the person I hate more than anyone."

"There's the dramatics again." I scoff. "More than anyone? Come on now. You shot a guy." I slap my hands to my chest. "And here I am still standing, so we both know that's not true."

"Is that an invitation to put a bullet in your chest? Because next time you drop your pants in front of me, I'd be more than happy to shoot you, too."

"There she is. The girl who pretends to have remorse, but really doesn't hold an ounce of it. I don't fault you for what you did. I think it's about time you start owning that shit."

"Owning that shit? I killed a guy, Lev. There is no part of me that wants to own up to that." Her voice drops to a near whisper. "It's been almost a year and I'm still trying to convince myself it was a bad dream."

Not in the mood to try and make someone feel better for an act I don't give a shit about, I shove her from behind. "Did you miss the part where I said I have somewhere to be?" I don't care what the fuck Riley does. All I care about is what she can do for me.

She stumbles forward a few feet, then catches herself and growls. "Then maybe you should have been there instead of wasting time with me."

"Oh, this time was not wasted, that's for sure."

I give her another shove as we walk toward the wrought-iron gate. The black coating is rusted with corroded surfaces smeared with moisture. It's distressed and chipped and does nothing to keep trespassers out, especially since it's always open, welcoming any deranged psychopath who cares to enter.

"You can leave me now," Riley pipes up. "I know my way back to campus."

"I'm sure you do, but there's only one road there, and it's the one I'm on, so unless you wanna go three miles out of your way, keep walking and keep your mouth shut."

She gripes and huffs, dramatically making her annoyance known.

Little does she know, her tantrum only has me itching for more of it. I love getting under this girl's skin, and there isn't much that humors me these days. I find myself biting back a smile, and a strange feeling floods through my body. It's unlike anything I've felt in a very long time. It's like an array of hope mixed with dread. I'm unsure if it's an emotion I like feeling, but it's something other than sheer hatred, so I count it as a win.

Leaves crunch in the distance and the snapping of a branch has Riley right at my side. It's hard to see her face in the inky blackness with the dim moon as our only source of light. I don't need to see her to know she's startled, though. Over the past couple weeks, I've watched her from afar, noticing how the feeblest sounds have her pulse beating visibly beneath her skin.

Toying with her, I stop walking, putting one foot behind me. "I think you were right. I'll let you find your way back. I'll take the long way."

"No!" she blurts out, her voice shaking. "It's fine. We're almost there anyway."

Internally laughing, I shrug my shoulders and keep on at her side. So predictable, yet so fun.

Riley doesn't say anything, nor do I. We walk in silence

until the lampposts surrounding the campus square come into view. Minutes later, we're back on campus.

Bypassing my dorm, I keep walking with her. I'm not sure why, but I do. She doesn't draw attention to my shadow, so I don't bring it up either because I'm not confident my response wouldn't make me appear desperate. Although, that's what I feel when I'm near her. Desperation, temptation, and a tinge of lechery. The desire to be in her presence is insatiable. I want more than anything to hold on to the emotions that surface when she's around—only her. No one else has this effect on me. Then there is the sick part of me that wants to be the sole reason tears pool in her eyes. It's a satisfaction I can't explain and I can only surmise it's because I want to be the one to also dry them.

Strange things are happening to my mind and body, but at least it's something. So, once again, I'll count it as a win.

Riley keeps on walking until her foot lands on the first step of her dormitory. She doesn't turn around, just stares straight ahead at the double doors. "Goodbye, Lev." Her tone is barren but stained with irritation.

I don't say goodbye because I hate the word. It's too traditional—too formal, and I can promise her, this is not goodbye.

SHOULD'VE FUCKING KNOWN. My muscles quiver as I throw the paper bag in my hand against the side of the Willamette House. The bowl collides with the concrete and the lid pops off. Broccoli cheese soup painting the brick. *Her favorite soup.*

My pounding heartbeat is no match for the heat flushing through my body. Anger ripples through my core as I watch the light in her room come on.

She lied. Not to me, but she told Maddox she wasn't feeling well. My first thought was, 'I'll do anything to make her feel better,' because the thought of Riley being ill is unbearable. I searched everywhere. Called her over a dozen times and each time I got her voicemail. Even listened to the entire recording each time just to hear her voice, then left a message in hopes hearing mine would brighten her night. Until the last couple, when worry began setting in. Each message was more and more aggressive, loaded with threats and insults because I was mad. I immediately wanted to get into her phone and erase them before she listened, but now, I'm calling her again to tell her I have no regrets.

"Answer the fucking phone," I mutter as I watch her shadow dance behind the shear curtain on her window.

Rage engulfs me when I get her voicemail again.

"Hey, it's Riley. I can't get to my phone right now, but if you leave a message, I might call you back. Or I might not."

Beeeep.

"Why the fuck were you with him? What did you do? Where did you go? Why are you ignoring my calls?!" I take a deep breath, attempting to compose myself as I lower my tone. "Angel, Angel, Angel," I tsk. "You're testing me." Then when I see her beside the window, looking down at her phone and still making no attempt to call me back, I lose it and grip the phone with both hands, screaming into the speaker, "Quit fucking testing me!"

Her head pops up quickly from being within earshot of my outburst, and she pulls back the curtain. Hurriedly, she shoves the windowsill up. She looks beautiful, as always. A sense of calm washes over me, but it's short-lived.

"Ridge!" she snaps. "What in the world are you doing down there, and why are you shouting?"

One glance at her hand confirms she saw my call come through and chose to ignore it. My chest rises and falls at warp speed, my jaw aching from the tight clench of my teeth. "I'm coming up."

Before she can respond, I round the building and jog quickly up the cement steps. The doors don't lock until midnight, so I'm able to enter without using the key I stole.

I'm met at the staircase by Riley. Her hair is down, the natural waves showcasing her highlights, and the streak of purple in the front. Wide eyes greet me as she stops halfway down. "It's late, Ridge. Please just go home and we can talk tomorrow."

I keep walking up, closing the space between us one step at a time, until I'm standing on the one just beneath her. I reach out, touching her waist gently, and that's all it takes to pacify the fury inside me. "Tell me what he wanted with you, Angel."

I swear to all that is holy, if he laid one finger on her, I will chop all ten of his digits off before tossing them in the rubble of ash I've formed with the victims I've killed for this girl.

"We just went for a walk. That's all."

I've watched Riley long enough to know when she's nervous. The slightest flare of her nostrils. Her avoidance of eye contact. And when her gaze casts over my shoulder, I know she's lying.

"I thought you were sick."

Her lips roll—another nervous tic. "I'm feeling better."

I walk into her, forcing her to move up the steps, backward. My hands never leave her hips as I spin her around at the top and guide her toward her room.

"Please don't do this right now. I've got a massive headache."

"Go to your room, Riley." Her shoulders draw back at the mention of her name. By now she knows I only use it when I'm furious. "We need to have a little talk."

"I'm so tired..."

Not giving her a chance to fight this any longer, I push open her already ajar door and force her inside. Slamming the door closed, I go right for her roommate's bed and rip off the comforter to make sure we're alone. Once I'm certain we are, I walk briskly toward the center of the room, where Riley is watching me keenly.

My fingers graze either side of her pink cheeks. "Tell me everything."

Averting her eyes anywhere but on mine, she says, "There's nothing to tell. Lev stopped by and we went for a walk."

I can feel myself getting worked up again as her deceitful words slice through my heart. "You're lying to me, Angel."

Her soft blue eyes land on mine. "And what reason would I have to lie to you, Ridge? I don't owe you anything."

"Is that so?" I grumble. "Do you owe Maddox anything?"

She huffs like it's a moot question, but it's valid.

"Well. Do you?"

"Honestly? No. Maddox and I have been spending a lot of time together, but we haven't labeled what we have going on. I'm free to do whatever I want, and so is he."

"And what you want is to go for walks with a psychopath in the dark?"

"I can tell you what I don't want and that's getting grilled by one, alone in my dorm room."

Her words make me laugh. "Is that what you think of me? After everything I've done to protect you, I'm still just a psychopath?"

"Are you implying that you're not? Listen to yourself. You're totally obsessed with everything I do."

"You're right. I am and I won't deny that. My world revolves around you. You're the air I breathe and my favorite scent. I'm consumed by your existence. So tell me why I'm willing to lay my life on the line for you, but you can't even answer a simple fucking question without lying to me."

"Please don't say things like that. It makes me...uncomfortable." She takes a step back, freeing herself from my touch.

I drop my hands to my sides, scorned. "Does my touch repulse you? I thought we were beyond that. After all, I was your first and I better have been your fucking last."

"You're too intense, Ridge." She waves her hand back and forth between us. "*This* is intense."

"Love is intense."

"See," she jabs a finger in the air, the sleeve of her hoodie riding up her hand, "that's what I mean. All this talk about love and my scent and how consumed by me you are. It's crazy."

"That's because I'm crazy about you."

"Stop it!" She walks to the window that's still open. Fortunately, it was replaced last week so it's no longer boarded up. Her curtain blows with a gust of wind and she gathers it in her hand and pulls it to the side, giving herself a clear view of the outside.

"He'll eat you alive. Lev, I mean. He'll never treat you the way you deserve—"

"Shut up!" She spins around and the curtain falls from her hand. "I don't want Lev!"

Matching her tone, I shout back, "Then why the hell have you been spending time with him?"

"Because I have to." Her hand claps to her mouth as if she said more than she wanted to.

I peel it away, holding it tightly in mine. "What do you mean, *you have to?*"

"That's not what I meant. I meant, I want to."

"No." I shake my head. "I think you said exactly what you're thinking and now you're wishing you hadn't. What does Lev have on you? Is it in regards to the governor's death?" Her lack of surprise tells me she already knew I was aware, which also leads me to believe I'm right. Lev knows. The question is, who the fuck told him? "It is, isn't it?"

"You're hurting me." She pulls her hand away. I didn't realize I was squeezing so hard, so I let her go.

"Answer the fucking question, and this time, don't lie to me."

She gulps, her bottom lip trembling, and I'd love more than anything to take it between my teeth and stop it from shaking—to stop her from being afraid.

"There is so much more to all of this. Just please, trust me. Okay?"

"It's not you I don't trust. It's him."

"He's your best friend."

"He's also everyone's worst enemy. If Lev has something on you..."

"What? Just say it. If Lev has something on me, then what?"

"Then it seems my hands are fuller than I thought."

The trepidation in her eyes has me weeping inside. I wrap my arms around her, pulling her close, though she hesitates to allow her body to relax against mine.

"You never have to be afraid, Angel. It's my job to carry the weight of your fears. I'd never let anyone hurt you. Do you understand that?"

Her voice cracks. "What if it's not someone else hurting me, but it's me hurting myself?"

"Then you let me make it all better."

"I don't think you can."

"I can and I will. So quit fighting me. I am not the enemy."

I lean back so I can look at her beautiful face. Tears soak her cheeks, and her damn lip is still quivering. *Fuck it.* I press my mouth to hers, and an immediate calm settles over me.

Gripping her shoulders, I hold her in place, knowing that she'll surrender after a few seconds of resistance.

Our lips seal, eyes wide open and cemented to one another's. Hers are stunned with a bit of curiosity behind them, while mine clutch onto hope. Every touch, every word, every kiss is one step closer to the life I dream of. Every second of every day, with this girl.

Parting my mouth slightly, I lead the way, confident that she'll follow. My eyes close, unable to see her reaction, but only feel it against my lips. And when she grants my tongue entrance, I take advantage, sliding it in nice and smooth while my knees weaken.

God, she's fucking everything.

All the beauty this world needs. All I need. All I want.

A salty taste seeps onto my tongue and I disengage from my own thoughts, not allowing myself to wonder what it is.

Her body relaxes. She falls into me and I catch her. Our chests heaving against one another's, and it's the reaction I need to give her all of me, knowing she'll accept.

I walk her backward, until she's halted by the footboard of her bed. Slowly, I lay her onto her back on top of the perfectly-made bedding.

One may say I've manipulated her into this, and they'd probably be accurate. Love isn't black and white. At least not at first. It's an array of colors and distorted lines that have you questioning what you really feel. It's my goal to erase the confusion, until it's perfectly clear that her heart has always belonged to me.

It will be messy. It will hurt. But in the end, it'll all be worth it.

She can fool around with Maddox, thinking they have a chance. I don't mind at all, because once the dust settles and she realizes I'm the one who saved her from herself, I will own her. Mind, body, and soul. Maddox might not be so accommodating. He's a good guy with good intentions. But when he realizes Riley is allowing another guy to taste her body, he'll pull back, leaving her free for me.

Blanketing her body with mine, I drag my lips down to her neck, sucking on the thin skin with enough force to mark her.

She contests by straining her neck, trying to free it from the vise grip of my teeth, but I suck harder and harder, bruising the delicate nape of her neck, while making it painfully obvious to Maddox—and Lev—that she's mine.

"Stop it, Ridge. You're gonna leave a hickey on my neck."

Too late, Angel. Far too late.

But I stop, because my work here is done. At least, with her neck. Positioning my arm between us, I push my hand down the waistband of her leggings. I fully expect her to fight it, but to my surprise, I find that her cunt is swollen and wet.

"Did Lev touch my pussy, Angel?"

Her head shakes no, and a rush of relief washes over me.

"Good. Let's keep it that way."

I SHOULD STOP HIM. My mind says no, but my body says hell yes. I crave the feeling of his hands on me, and I ache to lose all my inhibitions.

I shut off all thoughts that tell me this is wrong and that I'll only make the situation with him worse. All I can think about is how badly I want this. The desire for his touch is so strong that it physically pains me. My skin is buzzing with pins and needles, my heart throbbing rapidly and uncontrollably.

I separate my shaky legs, inviting him between them. An audible gasp escapes me when his fingers enter me. They curl at just the right angle, penetrating deeply.

Lifting up a tad, his face lingers over mine, and he watches me, much like he always does. "Who got you so worked up, Angel?"

I pierce my lips in silence, not willing to tell him that it was Lev and his aggression toward me that turned me on. I was fully prepared to return to my room and get myself off because I was so fucking horny from our encounter.

"Don't lie to me." He shoves his fingers deeper, forcing my body to ride up on the mattress. I wince in response, but he must take my silence as more lies because he does it again. "Tell me. Now. Did Lev touch you?"

"No," I tell him, truthfully. "At least, not in that way."

"Did you touch him?"

I inhale sharply as he drives into me, his nails grazing my inner walls. "Yes," I moan out in response.

"Did you suck his dick?"

I'm taken aback by his question because it's so direct. Of all the things, why would he suspect that?

"No."

"Liar!" He adds a third finger and plunges them so deep, pain slices through me. "I tasted it on your tongue. Saw the grass stains on your knees. You sucked his dick, didn't you?"

Fear swallows me whole. The unknown of what Ridge might do if he knows the truth, though, it seems he already does.

"Answer the goddamn question."

"Yes," I blurt out through a raspy breath. Suddenly, fear is replaced by humiliation, and that humiliation is replaced by anger. I look him straight in the eye and grit out, "So what if I did?"

The heat of his breath hits my face as he exhales heavily.

I yelp as he adds another finger, pushing painfully into me.

"Please slow down," I beg him quietly, before raising my voice to a near shout. "You're hurting me."

But he doesn't stop. Instead, he growls deeply, still violently fingering me. "How could you do this, Angel? Lev? Really?" His voice cracks while his body shakes with anger.

"I can't even entertain the possibility. Just tell me this is all a lie."

As my body rides farther up the bed, I shove my hands to his chest, surprising myself with my own strength. He lifts up, snarling back at me. "Get the fuck off me!" I seethe, hell-bent on ending this right now.

"You want me to move? Make me."

Ugh, he's really grating on my nerves now. I was seconds away from having a fantastic fucking orgasm and then he had to go and ruin it with his asinine mouth.

My arm extends and whips forward, my hand smacking hard against his face.

He lets out a maniacal laugh, taunting me. "Really? That's all you've got?"

My long nails embed into the top of his shoulders, digging deep enough to pierce the skin. Like the animal he is, he lifts a smile in response.

Watching for a reaction that proves he feels pain, I drag my nails down an inch, peeling back a layer of his skin. Blood drips onto my fingers, but it doesn't faze me. All I care about is making him pull back.

"You can't hurt me, Angel. Nothing hurts me when I'm with you."

"Stop talking like that!" I dig deeper, but stop when I realize the pain I'm inflicting is only arousing him.

What the fuck is wrong with all of us? Ridge is turned on by my pain. Lev gets off on my submission. And I engage because I'm the twisted one who finds excitement in it all. Maddox is the only sane one out of all of us.

Lev told me earlier I needed to own what I did. Maybe it's time I do, but maybe it's also time I start owning this new version of myself. Not only my sexual awakening, but also my inner strength.

For years, I've been surrounded by people who want to take care of me and protect me from the world. They only see my weaknesses. They all treat me like I'm made of glass. But deep down, I know I have a resilience that far surpasses what any of them could imagine. It's about time I prove to them, and myself, how strong I really am.

My legs buckle under Ridge's weight, his body pressing down on me. Part of me wants to give in and just let him overpower me, but instead, I grit my teeth. With one swift motion, I manage to lift my knee up, pushing him off-balance. Mustering all my strength, I kick my leg out and feel his body leave mine.

"How's that for making you move?" I dust my bloody hands off, pleased with myself.

It's short-lived as he charges at me with growly teeth, taking me down on the bed. With renewed vigor, I whale at his chest. "You're insufferable!"

"You want me to be manageable? Then quit fighting this. Quit pushing me away all the damn time."

He grabs me by the throat with a lax hold, and I clench my thighs, hating the way it turns me on. "I have no choice but to push you away because you make it so damn hard to be near you."

Jerking my head, he forces me to look at him. "Get used to it, because I'm not going anywhere."

"I'm not who you think I am, Ridge. I'm not perfect, I'm flawed. And I'm certainly not an angel."

"You," he pauses, stunned speechless by my words of admission, "you are perfection personified, and every flaw only makes you that much more desirable. I want every bit of you. Forever."

I gulp, my throat bobbing against his palm. My mind swirls with thoughts and emotions as I close my eyes and take a deep breath. When I open them, his gaze is still on me, studying me intently as if he can see straight into my soul. His gaze alone is enough to make my heart skip a beat, but it's his words that have rendered me speechless.

Every time Ridge confesses his love for me, no matter how passionate, I shut him down. I don't know why I do it, but I can only surmise it's because I don't feel worthy of that sort of love. Not to mention, he's more than a little unhinged. Something always brings me back to him, though. Or him to me, rather. No matter how hard I push, he's always there.

His fingers leave my neck, moving to the side of my head, and he twirls my hair. "Say something, Angel."

I don't even know where to begin. No matter what I say, I'll come off as a hypocrite. I could tell him that I want him so badly right now it hurts. Or I could keep pushing him away, knowing he won't go far.

"I don't want to hurt you, Ridge." My heart sinks as the words leave my mouth because I've never spoken a truer phrase.

He's growing on me. I can feel it.

His face comes closer to mine. "The only way you could ever hurt me is by not existing."

The need to be honest with him is dire. The last thing I want is to lead him on, especially when my heart is being pulled in so many different directions. "This won't end how you want it to."

"You're right. That's because it has no end."

He cups my face in his hands and kisses me softly,

making my entire body tremble with anticipation. His lips are so soft and gentle, yet so passionate and full of emotion. I've never kissed someone with such sentiment. I knew that from the first time, in the hallway after class.

Two different men have hung me on the brink of arousal tonight, both in the same manner. So hostile and cruel. But nothing compares to the level of exhilaration I'm feeling right now.

Desire surges through my body as heat rushes to my core.

Even as blood runs down Ridge's arm, his flesh still rooted in my fingernails, I am unequivocally consumed by this kiss.

I refuse to overthink this. I won't let my thoughts control the situation because I'm not doing anything wrong.

My fingers slide over his chest as I trail my mouth down his neck. My trembling hand moves lower, tracing his abs through the fabric of his tee shirt. My breath catches in my throat as I rim the waistband of his jeans and slowly, teasingly, unbutton them.

Ridge breaks the kiss and looks at me with surprise in his eyes. "Really?"

I nod, biting back a smile. "You want to, right?"

"Fuck yes, I want to." He lifts off me and peels his shirt over his head, tossing it on the floor. With the light in the room on, I get a clear view of his bare chest. I've never seen him without a shirt before, and I try to hide my curiosity, but when he runs his hands over the pink bulging scars on his side, it's no use.

"It was nothing. Got jumped by a guy a couple years ago. I wasn't prepared, and he got in a few good slashes."

My gut wrenches, hurting for him. "He cut you?"

"Yeah. But he won't be hurting anyone else ever again."

I don't even want him to elaborate on that statement because there's no saying what Ridge did to that guy. If I had to guess, he's probably dead.

I run my fingers over his wounded flesh. "Must've hurt."

"Like hell." He retreats. And as he pushes his pants down, he crawls between my legs. "You sure you wanna do this?"

"I can't believe you're even asking my permission."

He quirks a brow. "Would you rather I didn't?"

Biting my bottom lip, I contemplate my response because there is part of me that wants to explore that side of myself. But it doesn't feel right with him in the same way it does with Lev. "No," I tell him, "I respect you asking."

His expression drops quickly. "Did Lev ask for permission when he put his cock in your mouth?"

There it is. Ridge will never be okay with anything I do with any other guy.

"Can we not talk about that right now?"

"But we *will* talk about it."

I nod in response, only because it appeases him. I want nothing more than to feel his skin against mine while his length moves inside me.

The next thing I know, Ridge is gathering the waistband of my leggings in his hand. His muscles strain against the skin of his biceps as he rips them in half.

My breath hitches, and the moment intensifies when he jerks them off the rest of the way, taking my panties, too. I don't even scold him for ruining my favorite leggings, because the knees of them are already destroyed. Besides, it was hot as hell.

He stands up, tall and confident with his eyes on me, and

when he tugs down his boxers, springing his erect cock free, I gasp.

Back on the bed, he crawls up until his face is settled between my legs. Anticipation has me shaking. His hands gather behind my knees and he lifts my legs up, immediately feasting on my cunt. I wince in delight as the rough part of his tongue drags up and down abrasively. He flicks the tip at my clit, setting my soul ablaze, then he repeats the action.

With my hands on either side of me, I fist the comforter.

Ridge moves up my body, tracing my curves with his tongue. Sucking, then kissing and licking. Every cell in my body tingles with delight. My senses are overwhelmed by the pleasure he's creating. He moves to my breasts, teasing, tantalizing my nipples until I'm a quivering mess.

"Fuck me, Ridge," I cry out in desperation. "Touch me. Kiss me. Anything."

"Someone's anxious tonight. I wonder why that is."

I swear on everything, if he takes this back to Lev, I will kick his ass out and pleasure my own damn self.

I twist and writhe, my body aching. I look down at him with pleading eyes. "Please, just do it," I whimper, desperate for relief.

His mouth lands on mine, violently. Sharing each breath, our tongues lap, and our lips smack. My fingers draw lines down his back, landing on his waist, and I squeeze with tenacity.

"I'm gonna fuck you hard, Angel. Is that okay with you?"

"Mmmhmm."

Yes. God yes.

His lower half slides up, and as it does, he easily slides inside me. My tense shoulders drop against the pillowcase, and I groan in delight as he pushes deeper, giving me all of him.

The sharp scent of his cologne climbs up my nose, and it's intoxicating. The woodsy smell blurs my senses with each deep breath that I take.

Ridge's hands grip my wrists, tightening their grasp and trapping me against the mattress. Pounding into me, he stares down into my eyes with a mischievous smirk, as if he knows I am wholly his to do with as he wishes. I'm powerless beneath him, my body quivering as every nerve in me tingles with anticipation. *Well-played, Ridge. Well-played.*

I'm caught off guard when Ridge pulls out. "On your knees."

I do as I'm told, getting on all fours for him, even as my pussy spasms with a dire need to be filled back up.

Suddenly, he's back inside me. With two hands on my hips, he uses them as handles and slams into me with a brutal force. Thrust after thrust, my body grows tighter with the fire he's building inside me.

"I think you were molded for me, Angel. In fact, I'm certain you were." He pushes deeper, earning a whimper from me.

I'm not arguing with him because, right now, I think he's right. The way he's making me feel is indescribable. And a sick part of me wants it to last forever.

He smacks my ass cheek and I jolt. "Tell me this pussy is mine."

"It's yours," I cry out, because at this moment, it truly is.

"Damn straight it is."

Each powerful thrust sends a shock wave through my body, driving cries of pleasure to echo off the walls. Just as

I'm about to come, Ridge halts his movements, and the intensity builds.

"Don't stop," I beg him.

He pants and groans, massaging my hips before rocking into them again.

Without warning, he slaps my ass again, and a surge of electricity shoots through me.

When his hand comes underneath me, and his fingers rub circles on my swollen clit, I lose it. My screams are so loud that I'm certain the students in the neighboring rooms can hear me. I attempt to muffle my sounds, but they are uncontainable as Ridge claims every ounce of my pleasure.

Breath held, fireworks explode behind my eyelids. "Fuck, Ridge!"

The pulse of him against my body, combined with his fingers playing with my clit, send me even further over the edge. Waves of pleasure wash over me as I exhale a pent-up breath.

"God damn, Angel," he croaks. A couple more rhythmic thrusts and pants, then he stops.

A slick trace of our mixed arousal drips down my inner thigh, likely landing on my comforter.

He hasn't even pulled out of me when I drop down on my stomach, forcing his exit.

Ridge collapses beside me, his chest still heaving. One hand rests on my back, stroking softly. "That was amazing."

He's not lying. It was so good, I wouldn't mind doing it again, right now. Ever since my first time with Ridge, I feel like I've been reborn. It's at this moment, I decide I'm ready to grasp the new me and love her because I am still *me*.

After my first time with Ridge, I deiced to play it safe

and get a prescription for birth control. Now, more than ever, I'm grateful I did.

I allow myself a few minutes to come down, then I go to clean up in the bathroom down the hall, and change into a pair of shorts with a tee shirt.

Once I'm ready for bed, I return to see Ridge still lying on the bed, his smooth skin exposed. A part of me wants to know when he plans to leave, but the other part of me doesn't want to ask, because I'm not opposed to him staying a bit longer. Slowly, almost reluctantly, I lie down beside him, leaving a decent amount of space between us. The air thickens with tension.

I'm not sure how to react or respond in this situation. I can sense that my feelings are beginning to change toward him, and that scares the shit out of me. I don't know what I want yet, or even if I have the courage to explore what could be between us. There's an apprehension that I can't explain. Ridge isn't like anyone else I've met before, but maybe that's why I feel so strongly toward him.

We lie there in silence for minutes, me on my side facing Ridge, and him on his back looking back at me.

He's so gorgeous. So often he tells me how perfect I am in his eyes, but I've never once told him that when I look at him, I truly see beyond his flaws. I've never complimented Ridge at all, for that matter. Never even thanked him for all the kind words he says to me. I'm not sure why I push him away like I do. Is it because I worry what people will say? Or because I'm scared he's unstable? Maybe a little of both.

I shift on the bed, moving so I can better see the scars on his chest. My thoughts go back to our conversation earlier, and how he said that person won't be hurting anyone ever again. I wonder what he meant by that.

"Ridge," I say his name with hesitation because what I'm about to ask is so ridiculous. But fuck it. I'm asking anyway.

He pulls the comforter underneath him, trying to get under it. "Yeah?"

"Have you..." I'm as crazy as he is by asking this. "Have you ever taken someone else's life?"

Oh my god, I wish I could take that back. It's not like people just go around killing others. Just because I shot someone doesn't mean he has. I'm so embarrassed. I cover my face with my hands and shake my head against the pillow. "Forget I asked that. It was dumb."

"I have," he says. The way his words come out, it's like the idea doesn't even bother him. Like it's just another fact about his life. And maybe, for him, it can be that simple.

Why can't I feel that way, too?

I move my hands away from my face and prop myself up with one arm. "You have?" I surprise myself by the calmness in my tone. Instead of overreacting and thinking the worst, I just watch him, hoping he'll open up about his situation.

Or, he might not care to disclose any details, which is understandable. I wouldn't want to revisit the night I took another person's life.

Now tucked under the blanket, giving me the impression he's not planning to leave my room anytime soon, Ridge turns onto his side, facing me. "I was eleven—just a kid who was protecting his mom." My heart swells at his admission. *He was protecting his mom.*

"Is she okay? You're mom, I mean."

His fingers drag through his hair and he sucks in his bottom lip. Seconds pass before he says, "No. I saved her that night, but I failed her only a few days later."

A lump rises in my throat, a sharp pain throbbing in my

chest. I can see the blame etched on his face, and I ache for him. Reaching out, I gently touch his arm. "You were just a kid," I say softly. "I hope you haven't been carrying that guilt all these years."

"It's a long story, and one day I'll fill you in, but not tonight."

For the first time, Ridge and I have common ground. And while it's because of devastating events, I feel like it connects us in a weird way. I understand him on a deeper level than ever before because he's experienced the same thing that turned my world upside down.

"Okay," I tell him.

More minutes pass as I lie there watching him. His eyes droop a few times and I can tell he's fighting to stay awake. I doubt Ridge gets a lot of sleep, considering he's always popping up here all hours of the night. Whether it's in my room, or outside my window.

I watch until his eyes close. Then mine do the same.

I CALL HER AGAIN, letting it ring until I get her voicemail for the dozenth time. Last night after Riley canceled our plans because she wasn't feeling well, I ran into Scar at the student center and she said Riley wasn't home. So I went there to see for myself, and sure enough, no one answered her door.

I keep telling myself she was probably sleeping, but after Scar saying she wasn't there, I knew in my gut she was out with one of them. It was just a matter of finding out which one she was with.

When I got back to my shared room with the guys, Lev was on the couch watching TV, and Ridge wasn't there. That's when I knew it had to be him she was with. Therefore, I knew she wasn't in harm's way.

I passed out waiting for him to come back, but when I woke up this morning, his bed was still empty.

"Fuck!" I jab my finger at the end button and stick my phone back in my pocket as I approach her door. I raise my fist to knock but stop with it in midair. *Do I really wanna know if he stayed here?*

Hell yes, I do. I need to know if she lied to me, and why. If our relationship is ever going to grow, I have to be able to trust her. Me being here now proves that I can't, but I'm hopeful Ridge won't be here, and this will all be a nightmare I manifested in my head.

I tentatively turn the handle, not expecting it to budge. When it does, I hold my breath and push it open with a painful slowness. Then I see them. Riley lying on her side, facing Ridge with her eyes closed in a peaceful sleep. Ridge's bare leg hangs out from under the blankets, and his clothes are strewn carelessly on the floor.

Frozen in the doorway, I watch them breathe for what feels like hours. Finally, I tear my gaze away and slip out of the room before they wake up and see me.

My heart drops into my stomach and my back collides with the wall, opposite of the door.

I can't compete with him. I'll never win.

———

Riley: Why weren't you in psych class today?

Riley: Is everything ok?

Riley: Can we talk?

Riley: Skipping lunch, too? Is it me, or are you sick?

Riley: Ok. It's obvious you're ignoring me so can you please tell me why?

I read the last one, sent only three minutes ago.

> Riley: I'm heading to the campus square to decorate with the Delta Chi girls. If you feel like talking, swing by.

I slam my phone onto my bed and it bounces in the air. "Dammit," I curse loudly. How could she do this to me?

It was only a couple weeks ago that she was certain of her decision, and she chose me. Ridge was even on board, then they pull this bullshit. Fucking around behind my back. I'm not even sure she's not doing the same thing with Lev.

The door flies open as I pace in front of the bed, stroking my chin deep in thought. My eyes lift to Lev as he steps inside.

"Where is Ridge?" is my first question. And when he strolls casually to his dresser in silence, I follow behind him. "And, what the fuck is going on with you and Riley?"

He pulls open his top drawer, where he keeps all his junk, and he drops his shit inside then closes it. "Haven't seen Ridge all day, if that's what you're asking."

"All right. Answer the second question."

"What do you care what's going on with me and that girl?" He raises a brow with a glassy stare. "If you were smart, you'd quit worrying so damn much about what I'm doing and start asking yourself what's going on with her and Ridge."

Little does he know, I'm well aware what's going on with her and Ridge. Saw it with my own eyes this morning. What I need to know is where Ridge is now. It's about time we set this shit straight.

I'm hot on Lev's trail as he walks to the mini fridge.

"Jesus Christ, Maddox." He spins around, glowering.

"Back the hell up. And if you're so damn concerned, why don't you call him, or send out a search party. Whatever the fuck you need to do, but get off my ass." He snatches a bottle of water from the fridge. "I've got a meeting. Then I'm paying Cade a visit. It's time we quit dragging this shit out. It needs to end. Soon."

I let him leave because every conversation with Lev is pointless. He's unreasonable and so damn private about everything.

Snatching my phone off the bed, I dial Ridge. But just like all my calls to Riley, it goes to voicemail.

"If you got this message it means I probably don't wanna talk to you. Leave a message and I'll decide."

My heart races through the beep, and when it ends, I unleash all my fury through the speaker of the phone. "Fifteen fucking years of friendship and this is how it's gonna end? Did you get it out of your system, Ridge? Are you done fucking with her now? You couldn't just walk away with your pride intact when she chose me, could you? You had to test the limits. Well congrat-u-fucking-lations, you won her and you lost me."

I end the call, internally screaming. Without another thought, I yank open the door and slam it closed behind me.

An hour later, I find myself at the top of the water tower a mile from campus. A bottle of whiskey in my hand and my feet dangling over the ledge of the elevated structure. I rest my chin on the bars and look out at the setting sun.

Never thought I'd be here. Not here, per se, but in this situation. Me and the guys are being torn apart. Riley is slipping away, and while our relationship was short-lived, I saw a future with her and this shit fucking sucks.

Gripping my phone in my other hand, it vibrates against

my palm. At first, I expect it to be Riley, but *Dad* pops up on the screen. Against my better judgment, given my intoxicated state, I answer it.

"Hey, Daddy-o," I sing into the speaker. "What's poppin'?"

"Are you drunk?"

I laugh at his question. "Nah. I'm not drunk. Are you?"

"Where the hell are you, Maddox?"

I take a long drink of my booze, relishing the burn as it settles in a pool of warmth in my stomach. I smack my whiskey-infused lips. "Around. Where are you?"

"Goddammit, Maddox," Dad explodes. "This isn't like you. Get your shit together and sober up."

I chuckle at his assumption that he knows me at all. "Really? What am I like then? A doormat? The weak link?"

"Where the hell is this coming from?"

"Oh, I dunno." I set my bottle down beside me and pull myself up, using the cold bars surrounding the top of the tower to aid in my quest to stand. Swaying to the left, I hold tighter and laugh at myself. "Maybe this is coming from a place deep inside me that's tired of everyone thinking I'm so predictable. What if I don't wanna be the good boy everyone thinks I am? Maybe I wanna fuck up sometimes. Maybe then I'd stand out against those guys."

"Listen, son," Dad lowers his voice, "I don't know what's going on out there, but you need to drink some water and go to bed. We'll talk tomorrow."

"What if I wanna talk now? Am I not allowed to call the shots on that?" My hand slips and I spin around, my back hitting the bar. Then I see the bottle at my feet. All alone. I lean down to snatch it up. "I wanna talk about this shit and drink until I forget we talked about it." I lift the half-empty fifth to my lips and take a long swig. Dribbles of the dark liquor slide down my chin, but I wipe them away with my forearm and lick it off, refusing to waste a drop of the only thing tethering me to this world.

"All right. You wanna talk? Let's talk. But you have to promise me you'll stop drinking for the night."

I look at the whiskey in my hand and pout. "Fine."

"What's on your mind, son?"

"For starters, you need to understand that I'm gonna fuck up sometimes."

"We all do. It's only natural, but as your father, I can only hope and pray your fuckups are minimal."

"Ohhhhh," I drawl humorously. "What we did is not minimal. But I'm not going to tell you, so don't ask. But," I emphasize the word, "I will be honest and tell you I haven't been doing a very good job at my task as a Guardian. Got no idea what's going on at the Kappa Rho House. Don't watch those fucking guys. I honestly don't even go there," I tsk. "It was a stupid assignment anyways."

"All right. You know you'll have to write a report to The Elders by the end of the semester and you have to have truthful knowledge of what's going on in that house. Just try harder."

"Forget that. It's not even important. I'll have plenty to report soon enough. Let's talk about your involvement with the governor. Why are you so hell-bent on investigating his death?"

His silence leads me to believe my suspicion of him having a personal interest in this case is accurate.

"Why are you asking about the governor? Did you witness something that you haven't shared with me?"

"Why are you deflecting? Just answer the question. It's easy enough."

"You're drunk, son. Get some rest. I'm ending this call. We can talk when you're sober."

"Don't do it." I deepen my tone. "Don't you hang up on me!"

The line goes silent, and I stomp my foot. "Dammit!"

I knew he was hiding something from me. Him hanging up shows his guilt. That's okay. I'll get to the bottom of this one way or another. I'll keep an eye on things as a Guardian, but it's not going to be who The Elders want my eye on. I always knew there were some crooked members in The Society. Just never imagined my dad might be one of them.

My phone pings with a text, and I assume it's my dad telling me to get to bed and sober up. But it's Riley. I hold it out in front of me. Nine messages from her today. All read with no response on my part. The effects of the booze are clouding my judgment, but I refuse to text her back. No matter what I say, it won't be good enough. Ridge will always come out on top.

I bring the bottle to my mouth and take another long swig before tapping the message to read it.

Riley: Don't move. I'm coming up.

What the...

I stagger to the left, and just when I grab the pole to catch my balance, my phone flies out of my hand, falling fifty feet to the ground and likely shattering on the concrete.

"Shit."

I walk around the head of the tower to the ladder and look down. "How'd you find me here?"

"Whoa, Maddox." She peers up at me with horror-struck eyes. "Stay still. Do not get too close to the ledge."

"Since when do you care what happens to me?"

She reaches my foot near the ladder shelving and I step back. She curls over and catches her breath once she's on the solid landing. "Holy shit, that was scary."

"Why are you even here?"

Her hand comes out, clutching onto my arm. "Are you drunk?"

"Yeah, I am drunk," I tell her. "Got a lot on my mind. Now are you gonna answer my question or you gonna lecture me like my dad always does?"

"I've been worried about you. Once I got done decorating, I traced all your steps today and Ridge told me—"

"Oh," I chortle. "Ridge told you? Was this pillow talk last night or this morning?"

Me and the guys come up here sometimes when we wanna get away, so I'm not surprised Ridge told her I might be here.

Tilting my head to the left, I look keenly at her neck. "Is that a hickey on your neck?" Her hand slaps over the bruised skin, and she presses her lips into a thin white line. "It is, isn't it?" I peel her hand away and get a closer look. "Did Ridge do that to you?"

When she doesn't say anything at all, I exhale sharply. "You know what? Forget about it. I know it was him."

"I'm sorry you have to see this." She covers the mark again. "I could slap him for doing it."

"But did you? Because if not, I sure as hell can."

"What has gotten into you, Maddox? Did something happen?"

It really fucking bothers me that she's gaslighting me

right now. Like I'm the one who has some explaining to do. "Don't act dumb, Riley. You know exactly what happened." I jerk my arm away and walk back around to the other side. The sun is now hidden behind clouds. The feeling of static in the air, mixed with the moisture, tells me a storm is coming. It's gonna make for a slippery climb down that ladder, but I'll deal with that when the time comes. Right now, I just need to fucking think.

I bend down, letting my forearms rest against the railing, and I close my eyes. Exhaling deeply, I let my head hang limply between my arms. It's a failed attempt at sinking into the silence of my mind, because she's right behind me.

Her hand rests on my back, but her touch feels like an itch I can't scratch. "Talk to me."

Normally, I'd welcome it. Hell, before this morning, I would have done anything for it. But now, I'm too hurt to even look at her. "Please, Maddox. Why are you so angry with me?"

My head flies up and her hand drops when I straighten my back. "You wanna know why I'm mad? Because you lied to me. You weren't sick."

She inhales deeply and bites her bottom lip. "I'm sorry."

"You should be."

I snatch the bottle back off the landing and bring it to my mouth, but she snatches it away and holds it up to observe the contents. "Did you drink all this tonight?"

"Like you care." I try to take it back but she extends her arm.

"I do care. I care so much about you. Look. I'm sorry I lied but..."

"But what? He made you lie? Or did you just prefer to

spend your night with him instead? You could have just fucking told me, Riley."

"I know. I should have. I just...I knew you and Ridge would overreact, just like you did at lunch."

"Whoa. Wait a damn minute. Who the hell were you with last night?"

I know it was Ridge in her bed this morning. There's no mistake about that. I'm confused as hell, though, because why would Ridge and I overreact if it's Ridge she was with.

Fuck. Maybe I'm misconstruing things. I am pretty damn drunk.

"I was with Lev. Isn't that why you're mad? Because I canceled our plans and hung out with him?"

"What the fuck?" I snap, my voice quivering with rage. "No! I thought you were with Ridge. Why the hell would you cancel plans with me and lie about being sick, just to hang out with Lev?"

Her hands fold into the sleeves of her shirt and she hugs herself. "I knew you'd be upset if I told you the truth."

"Well, you're right. I am upset. But I'm really fucking confused about how Ridge ended up in your bed this morning when you were hanging with Lev last night."

She takes a steadying breath, filling her cheeks with air, then exhales it all at once. "You saw us?"

I'm so damn tired of her avoiding every question I ask. With the bottle in hand, I stretch my arm back and toss it over the edge. Seconds later, I hear it shattering against the cement. "You know what," I wave my hand in the air, "forget this. It's a waste of time. Go fuck Ridge. Go hang out with Lev. I'm done."

I take a step away, but I feel her grip on my arm and hear her cries. "Maddox, wait. Please. I'm sorry." I continue to move forward, pulling her along with me. "Just give me a chance to explain."

"It's obvious you made your choice, Riley. I thought it was me, but I guess I was wrong." I jerk my arm again, this time freeing it. Then I head down the ladder, trying like hell not to fall.

"Be careful. Go slow." I hear her coaching me as she descends from above me.

When I reach the bottom, I stomp through the field, my thoughts running rampant. I'm not sure what happened with her and Ridge last night, or this morning. Don't even know what she and Lev were up to. She turns every question around and it's obvious she's hiding something. I want more than anything to stop walking as she pulls at me with tears in her eyes, but this will never work if she can't be honest with me.

"Maddox. Don't do this."

I keep on, and she does the same, not willing to just let me go.

"Please, just stop and talk to me. It's not what you think."

I spin around, our faces mere inches from one another's. "Then fucking tell me, Riley! What is this? What the hell is going on with you and Ridge? Do you have feelings for him?"

She sniffles and chokes, dragging her sleeve across her nose before her hands fly in the air. "I don't know!"

"It's a simple yes or no question, Riley. You either have feelings for him, or you don't."

"I..." she sputters. "I really don't know. Maybe. But I don't want this thing with us to end. I care about you so much."

"I'm glad you care about me, Riley. How kind of you. But

here I was planning a future with you, thinking I could be falling in love with you, while you're out fucking my best friend. Thanks for that."

Her hands slip out of her sleeves and she grabs my face, forcing me to look into her sad eyes. My heart splinters at the sight in front of me. The last thing I want is to make her cry, but she's brought all this on herself. I'm only reacting the way any guy would.

"You're falling in love with me?"

I shake my head, not willing to answer that question until she answers mine. "Did you fuck him last night?"

When her gaze casts down and she licks her lips, I've got my answer.

I shove her hands down and continue walking briskly. "Don't fucking follow me."

IT'S ONLY BEEN twenty-four hours since Maddox and I have talked, but my chest aches wanting to be near him. I've sent him so many messages with no response, so I gave up. I don't blame him for being mad at me. I've been so indecisive, toying with his and Ridge's emotions, while trying to come to terms with mine.

"Talk to me, babe," Scar says from across the picnic table in the courtyard.

I shake my head, not even sure where to begin. Picking at the splintered wood of the table, I decide to start at the beginning. "What do you think of Ridge?" I'm not sure why I'm even asking. I guess I just need to be sure my judgment isn't clouded by all the sweet things he says to me.

"Ridge, huh? Well, let's see." She pauses for a beat. "Yeah. Ridge is fucking intense. There's no denying that."

"Yeah. He is." My voice is solemn and I nod in response.

"But why are you asking me this, Ry. Maybe you should be asking yourself what *you* think of Ridge?"

Rose are red,

Violets are blue.
I caught feelings for a psycho,
and I don't know what to do.

"Yeah." I pick at the wood some more. "You're probably right."

"Well," Scar slaps her hand over mine and I'm forced to stop the nervous habit, "what is it? Do you like him?"

I shrug my shoulders. "Maybe."

"Oh dear God, Ry. Of all the guys, why him?"

"I don't understand it either. It's like one day he was just...there. Then he was always there. Then he got annoying. Then sweet." I find myself smiling the more I talk about him. "Then suddenly, he wasn't there as much, and I missed him." My hands fly to my face and I rest my elbows on the table. "I know it's crazy."

"Well, he was your first, so it's possible you're just clinging to that instead of having actual feelings for him."

I never really thought of it that way.

"Yeah," I say, stopping short when I move my hands from my face and I see him. Standing tall, about six feet away, talking with two girls I don't recognize. My heart quivers as jealousy has my chest caving in. Ridge doesn't interact with other girls often, so this feeling is somewhat foreign to me.

He hasn't even looked in our direction, so I'm led to believe he doesn't know I'm here.

A smile parts his lips, and one of the girls laughs. Ridge says something, while using his hands as he speaks.

"So, is it safe to assume the hickey you tried to cover on your neck is from Ridge?"

Her words slip right through my ears as I focus on the man in question.

Are those girls flirting with him?

One of the girls reaches out and squeezes his bicep, but he takes a step back, a look of annoyance now on his face.

I swing my legs over the bench of the picnic table and stand up.

Scar asks me what's wrong, but I ignore her, making a beeline for Ridge and his new friends.

"Don't touch me again," I hear him say to the girl.

"Oh, come on." She giggles, grabbing his arm again.

"Hey!" I shout, making my presence known. "Pretty sure he said not to touch him." My blood is fucking boiling to the point of explosion.

I stalk up to the group, my hands firmly on my hips.

"Who the hell are you?" the touchy girl asks with her nose in the air.

Not a fan of her attitude, I walk into her, bumping my chest with hers. "Who the fuck are you?"

"All right, Angel," Ridge puts a hand on my hip and attempts to diffuse the situation by leading me away, "they're just a couple nobodies. Don't waste your time on them."

"Nobodies?" The girl laughs. "I'm the headmaster's daughter, so I'm most definitely somebody." Her lip curls in disgust, while my fists clench at my sides. "Why don't you take your Barbie doll bitch away, before you both find out what I'm capable of?"

"Oh yeah?" I push toward her, ready to let my fist fly, but I'm pulled back by Ridge when his arms wrap around my stomach. "Bring it on, bitch. You and your fucking friend." Ridge lifts me and my sweater rides up, exposing my stomach, while my feet leave the ground. "Let's fucking go."

I'm being carried away when Scar appears out of nowhere, tearing into the girls. "Put me down!" I shout at Ridge.

"Not a chance in hell. You're better than that."

"The fuck I am." I wait for him to loosen his hold, then kick out, trying to break free. "Scar needs backup, now put me the fuck down." With my head turned, I see that the girls are walking away. I breathe a sigh of relief, now slightly more settled.

Scar has a bigger mouth on her than I do, much bigger. In fact, I'm not even sure where that defensive side of me came from.

Once we're back in the student center, Ridge sets me down.

My hands run down my chenille sweater, smoothing out the wrinkles. Standing up straight, I push away the strands of hair in my face. "What did those girls want with you?"

Ridge gives a cheeky smile as he scratches the back of his neck. "Were you watching me, Angel?"

"No."

"Yeah, you were," he teases, poking at my side and making me squirm.

"I was eating lunch and happened to see you. Don't let it go to your head." I grab his hand to stop him from tickling me, but once it's in mine, I don't let it go. We both freeze, staring longingly at each other. In awe, I just stand there—holding on to him while the world pauses around us. Students come and go, but it's only him I see.

The sound of my phone buzzing has me breaking from our shared gaze. "Sorry," I say, reaching into my back pocket and pulling it out.

Repulsion fills my stomach when my phone lights up with a message from Lev. "I, err...I need to go."

In an instant, Ridge tries to snare my phone from my hand, but I'm faster and hide it behind my back.

He bends and twists, but I keep turning as he attempts to steal a glance. "Who was it?"

I manage to slip it in my back pocket. "It was Scar asking me to finish lunch with her. Possessive much?"

"Me? What about you, Miss Ready to Attack the Head-master's Daughter Because She Touched My Arm?"

My cheeks flush with heat. "I was not going to attack her. I was simply helping you out of a sticky situation."

"Uh-huh," he hums, "say what you want, but I know you were jealous."

"Was not!"

"Who said the situation was sticky? Maybe I wanted her to touch my arm."

"Bullshit," I spatter, calling his bluff. "I saw you gnash your teeth and heard you tell her not to touch you. Admit it, you don't want any other girls to touch you but me."

It's highly presumptuous, and overly confident of me to say. But it's true, and we both know it.

"I'll admit it when you admit that her touching my arm bothered you. And you didn't want either of those girls thinking they stood a chance. Which they didn't, by the way."

"Fine." I lift my shoulders, letting them fall. "I didn't like it. Satisfied?"

A sly grin twists up the corners of his mouth, and his teeth graze lightly on his bottom lip. "Very much so," he says, his tone low and sultry.

"Good. Now that it's settled, I have to go find Scar." I grab my coat and slip it on. God, I hate lying. I hate it so damn much. These lies are bound to catch up to me, just like they did last night with Maddox. The reminder pains me, but I can't think about that right now.

"Want me to walk you?" he asks.

"Nah, I'll be fine. Thanks, though."

Ridge leans in and presses a chaste kiss to my cheek. "Can I see you later?"

Butterflies flutter through my stomach and I can't help the smile that draws on my face. "Sure."

"Great. Text me when you're back."

I am so screwed.

KEEPING A SAFE DISTANCE, I follow her down the wooded trail. Her black winter coat is fastened tightly around her, the white fur-lined hood bobbing up and down as she moves. Branches hang overhead, a mixture of autumn colors falling rapidly. Thankfully the sun is still hanging in the sky, making it easier to get a clear view of her as she moves away from campus, and deeper down the path.

My heart sinks low in my chest with each step Riley takes, and my eye twitches as her lie replays in my head. I fucking knew she wasn't being honest about that text she got. My mind wanders to who it could have been—Maddox, Lev, or maybe it really was Scar and they're both up to something.

Riley stops walking and I hurriedly slide behind a tree in the nick of time. My hands jam tightly into the pockets of my jeans and I flip the black hood of my sweatshirt up on my head. I press my back snug to the trunk, turning my head slightly and peeping around it. Once I see that she's walking again, I duck out from behind the tree and keep following her.

When she takes the turnoff onto the desolate road on the outskirts of campus, my pulse quickens.

"Where the hell are you going, Angel?"

Headed in the direction of the building where Cade is, my first thought is that she's going there and that maybe she's onto us. But when she passes by it, only stealing a couple small glances at the tall brick structure, my worries are put to rest.

We've had Cade bound for over two weeks now, feeding and watering him daily. I've been questioned countless times as to why he's still alive after what he did to my girl, and the truth is, I can't tell them why he's still here. I've drilled the guy repeatedly, hoping he'll crack, but he's held tight to his innocence. Claims it wasn't him that drugged Riley or pushed Zeke from her window.

Normally I wouldn't buy the sob story bullshit, but something in my gut tells me he's being honest. Cade's a fucking prick, to say the least. He's your typical jock, only worse. He's drugged girls and taken advantage of them. Parties like a fucking animal. He'd be the prime suspect in almost anyone's eyes, especially given his past encounters with Riley. But my intuition is pretty spot on most of the time and I fear that if I end him now, I might never find out who really did do this to Riley. And once I'm certain, mark my fucking words, they will pay—be it Cade, or someone else.

My phone buzzing in the pocket of my jacket has me bolting into the rubble on the side of the road. I steal one more glance at Riley, making sure she didn't hear or see me.

And when I'm sure she didn't, I crouch down near a bush and take my phone out.

> Maddox: 10-33

Son of a bitch!

10-33 is our code for an emergency, and fuck if Maddox doesn't overuse the stupid numbers. He, Lev, and I made a deal that, no matter what, if one of us texts that, we drop everything and go. The thing is, Maddox uses it for the dumbest shit. I can never tell if he's really in trouble or if he's just having a panic attack that'll pass by the time I get to him. He worries more than anyone I fucking know.

Instead of rushing to him, I send a text back to make sure this is legit.

> Me: If this is something ridiculous, I will hunt you for dinner.

I stand up and step around the bush, not realizing how long I've been down. Riley is nowhere in sight. With my phone in hand, I jog down the gravel road.

As I move quickly, trying to catch up before I lose her, I read Maddox's response.

> Maddox: Get the fuck here! NOW! I'm at the warehouse.

I slow my stride to a brisk walk, realizing I've already lost Riley. Then I look over my shoulder, seeing the top floor of the warehouse I just passed peeking through the trees. *What the hell is he doing there?*

"Dammit," I grumble as I spin on my heel and head back

in the direction I came, still pissed I missed where my angel was heading.

Me: You're timing is fucking impeccable.

Sometimes I feel like he does this shit on purpose. Always interrupting what I have going on. Especially when it involves Riley. Wouldn't surprise me if he saw us pass by from a window in the old building and came up with some lame excuse to make me turn around. He's lucky I'm a loyal friend.

When he left me that angry voice message, I was truly worried he was done with me. All those years of friendship, plotting to reign together, and hiding in the dark were close to being washed down the drain. But, in true Maddox form, once he sobered up, he came to realize I didn't do this to hurt him. Riley was mine first, and she will be mine—forever.

I steal a look over my shoulder. It's not often I lose her, but it's becoming habitual now that Lev and Maddox are in her life. Seems the closer I get to her, the farther they try to pull her back.

I quickly tap on my phone as I walk toward the property, sending a message to Maddox. The trees guarding the entrance of the old warehouse have multiple layers of no trespassing signs posted on them, and even more signs on the outside of the brick walls. This place is like an island in a grassy sea with the woods about thirty yards away from its four sides. No one else comes here, at least not that we're aware of. Which is odd considering it's so close to campus, and the perfect location for students to throw parties. It's sort of the reason I mentioned making use of the empty space.

Me: Are you with him?

Him, being Cade. It's a dumb question because there's no other reason Maddox would be at the warehouse. Lev is the only one of us who goes there for something else.

When he doesn't respond, I drop my phone back in the inside pocket of my jacket and tap in the code to unlock the door—1033. Once it buzzes, granting me entrance, I pull open the slate metal door. There's multiple entry points, but all the other doors are locked, and this is the only one we use.

The scent of wet cement floods my senses as I walk down the hall to the basement door. As I bypass the open rooms, I envision tearing down all the walls and opening it up to accommodate a large crowd. I shiver with excitement at the thought.

I open up the door to the basement, and immediately see Maddox at the bottom. Before I can even ask him what happened, I notice the panicked look on his face. "Get the fuck down here, now!" His chest is heaving and his hands are shaking.

I push the door closed in haste before taking the stairs two at a time. "What the fuck happened?" Maddox doesn't say anything, just starts walking toward the room where Cade is being held. "Answer me, dammit!"

Immediately, I notice the door is open, and when I follow Maddox inside, I can see that this 10-33 was necessary.

"Son of a bitch," I grumble as I approach Cade's lifeless body. He's lying on his stomach in a thick pool of blood. I kick him in the gut to make sure he's not faking it, although his glossy, open eyes make it clear he's dead. "I needed him alive a little longer. What the hell did you do?"

"Me?" Maddox gasps. "Fuck no. I didn't do this. I just got here and found him like that."

I crouch down, observing his corpse. "Think he fell over and hit his head?"

Maddox sprints out the door, and the sound of him upchucking assures me he didn't do this. Maddox doesn't have the balls, or the guts, to kill someone.

While he's emptying his stomach, I flip Cade onto his back. Immediately I notice one of his ankles has slipped out of the rope. He must've got one out and tried to free the other when he tipped over. It's the only logical explanation I can come up with.

"Yo," I holler as I pickpocket Cade in search of his wallet, unsure why we didn't do this in the first place. He claimed to not have his phone on him, and Lev did a quick search and said he didn't find it. "You heard from Lev at all tonight?"

"Nope," he hollers back.

Once I find Cade's wallet, I flip open the billfold and rummage through it, unsure what it is I'm looking for. I take out the cash that's inside and toss the wallet back down before counting out my payday. *Hundred and thirty bucks.* Not bad.

My eyes land on the wallet and I notice a small plastic baggie sticking out from one of the compartments. Slotting the cash in the pocket of my jacket, I pick up the baggie, pinching it with just the tips of my fingernails so I don't leave any prints on it.

Holding it up, I observe the six white pills inside.

I fucking knew this jackass was dealing pills.

I pick the wallet back up and shuffle through everything

inside, tossing credit cards and business cards on Cade's chest. One in particular catches my eye.

"Hey, Maddox. What's the name of Lev's therapist?"

He's still outside the door, and I doubt he's coming back in here anytime soon. "Ugh. Edmonds, I think."

"Yeah," I say quietly as I tap the card to Cade's leg, smirking—Dr. Eugene Edmonds's card. "That's what it is."

Why the fuck would Cade have Lev's therapist's business card? I stare at Cade, trying to make sense of it all. "What the hell were you up to?"

Lev and Cade had been rival cousins for as long as I can remember—there's no way that this is a coincidence. I can't imagine Cade did sessions with the same guy. There's definitely a reason Cade has it, and I'm gonna find out what that it is.

I add the other things to my pocket and stand up.

"We're gonna need to take care of this dipshit," I shout to Maddox.

Seconds later, he's vomiting again and it's safe to assume I'm going to be handling this myself. Lucky for him, I'm no rookie when it comes to disposing bodies. Can't promise he'll never be found, but I can guarantee he'll never be traced back to us.

"FOR THE LOVE OF GOD, Ridge. Pick his fucking head up." My stomach turns at the constant thudding of Cade's skull against the stairs. I turn away before I get sick again, unable to look at his lifeless face and the trail of blood behind us any longer.

"He's dead. He doesn't give a shit."

"Only you would say something as depraved as that."

I've hardly spoken to him since I found him with Riley. Even looking at him now is one of the reasons my stomach is so on edge. It hurts a lot considering me and Riley were getting closer, and Ridge knew it. In fact, he practically encouraged it. I would have never pursued her without his approval. So naturally, seeing them together was a punch to the gut.

Dragging Cade's feet behind me, I give it all I've got. It's not much, though, because as soon as we get to the main door of this warehouse, I'm out of here. Ridge can take care of the rest. This is too much. How I got myself into this situation is beyond me. A momentary lack of sanity is all I can presume.

We all fall into the pit of despair and loneliness at some point, right?

We reach the doors and I drop his feet behind me, still staring straight ahead. "You got it from here?"

"At least help me get him out the damn door," he says in annoyance.

I grumble as I push open the door, poking my head out, while subtly sweeping the area to make sure no one is watching. When I'm sure it's clear, I slouch down and grab his ankles again. "I'll drop him outside, then I'm outta here. Told you, I'm not dealing with this mess."

"I heard you, shithead. You're leaving it to me, and I didn't even get the satisfaction of torturing him to death."

Once again, Ridge's lack of morality is evident. He's fucking insane. It wouldn't be enough for Cade to just die for his sins; Ridge would have preferred he suffer a slow, agonizing death.

Too bad for him.

I walk through the open doorway and inhale a deep breath of fresh air, then I let him go. Just as his feet hit the ground, Lev comes strolling into view. I'm not sure where he's coming from, or why he's here, but it's perfect timing because I'm ready to bolt.

Lev catches Cade lying on the ground and he jogs in our direction, eyes wide and panicked. "What the fuck happened?"

"Why don't you tell us?" Ridge asks. It's an obvious accusation, but it's necessary for Ridge to approach this situation from all angles to weed out suspicion. It's what anyone would do if they came across a dead body.

Lev's eyebrows pinch together and his eyes dance from me to Ridge. "What the fuck?"

"Did you do it?" I ask him sternly. "Did you kill him?"

"I just got here. Are you fucking serious right now?" He walks over to Cade's body and crouches down. "No, I didn't kill him, but he sure as hell is dead."

"Yeah. No kidding. We just dragged his two-hundred-pound ass through the building."

"Would you two quit this shit," Ridge snaps. "We need to get him out of here. Anyone comes through here and we're all screwed."

"You better clean up all this blood." Lev peers up at me. "I've got a meeting here tomorrow morning."

"Why the hell do you keep looking at me? I'm not cleaning up shit."

Lev and Ridge share a look and I know exactly what they're thinking. That I'll clean it up because I'm a pushover. Always the one taking orders but never giving them.

"Screw you both. You can clean up the mess and get rid of the body." I walk past them, snarling. *Fucking assholes.* Why am I even friends with these guys?

Part of me thinks I need to just walk away from it all. Them, her, this. Sure would make my life a hell of a lot easier.

"Whoa, wait a minute," Ridge calls out.

I shoot him a glance over my shoulder. "What now?"

"We all need to talk about the shit I found on this fuck-er." He gives Cade a swift kick and my stomach tightens again. "Go back to the room and we'll meet ya there. And don't you dare tell a single fucking soul about this."

The fact that he has such little trust in me goes to show that our friendship isn't what it used to be. "Whatever." I turn back around and head toward the road.

I'm dragging my feet, kicking up gravel, when an eerie

feeling washes over me. I'll probably see Cade's lifeless face in my nightmares for the rest of my existence.

"Maddox."

My feet practically leave my shoes as I jump around to face the voice behind me. "Riley," I gasp, hurrying toward her. "Where are you coming from?" I look beyond her shadow, hoping like hell she didn't see anything outside of the warehouse. Then again, if she did, and she saw the guys, she wouldn't be walking down the road fearlessly right now.

"Just went for a walk. Why are you here?"

I put a shaky hand on her waist, leading her quickly down the road.

"I...umm. Same. Went for a walk." I look over my shoulder again, picking up my pace. "You need to get out of here."

The last thing I want is anyone to see her and assume that she had something to do with Cade's demise, if his disappearance and death should ever come out.

"Maddox." She chuckles. "What's the matter with you?"

"Nothing. Why?"

"You're acting like you just saw a dead body."

My eyes widen. "What? Why would you say that? I'm fine. There's no dead body."

"It was a joke. But seriously, is everything okay?"

"Everything's fine."

"Well," she drawls. "You're acting really strange, but I will say, I'm glad you're finally talking to me."

For a second, I forgot I was even upset with her. Truth is, I don't want to be. I hate avoiding her. I actually miss her. A lot. And being with her now gives me a sliver of comfort. If anyone can make me forget what just happened, it's her.

I dig up some of the gravel with the toe of my shoe. "Yeah. Me, too."

"Soooo. Is it safe to assume you skipped class today to avoid me?"

"Pretty much."

"Hmm." She bites her lip nervously. "Care to tell me why?"

My arms stiffen with my hands pushed deep in the pockets of my jeans. "I saw you, in bed, with Ridge."

"I know, you told me when you were drinking last night. I'm sorry, Maddox. We haven't labeled what we are and I... It's..."

I let out a strained laugh. "Not what I think?" I mock. "That's what they all say."

I pick up my pace, trying to remember back to when I was drunk last night. I remember going up to the tower, but I don't remember talking to Riley.

When I woke up with a shattered phone in my pocket, I briefly remembered the conversation with my father, but after that, it's blank. I don't even remember dropping my phone.

I only just returned from getting a new one when I decided to run by and check on Cade.

We make the turn onto campus, passing through the open gate. Low branches droop down full of colorful leaves. Thoughts of the approaching holidays enter my mind. Before long, we'll be going home for Thanksgiving. I can't help but think about my relationship with Riley. Would things still be *complicated* by then? Would we even be friends anymore? The thought of being anything less pains me.

"You like him?" I quip, holding my breath as I await her response.

She stops walking, though her gaze lingers past me. "I like you."

"That's not what I asked." I know Riley likes me. There's no doubt about that. Neither of us can deny the way we've connected over these past few weeks. I'm just not sure it means anything if she likes another guy more.

Her lips roll together and she inhales sharply. "Ridge is... confusing. The way I feel about him is even more confusing. I just...yeah. I guess I do."

I nod repeatedly before my feet move again. "Gotcha."

"Maddox, wait. I like you, too. So much." She jogs at my side as I pick up my pace. "Why are you giving up on us so easily?"

How the hell am I supposed to fight for her when she gives me no indication she wants to be fought for? When I told Ridge how I felt about Riley, he was willing to let me have a shot at winning her over, but he wasn't backing down either. I thought I might stand a chance, but it seems he's come out on top. I need to just walk away while my dignity is still intact.

Just as we are rounding the corner of Riley's dorm, she plants herself in my path. "Will you just talk to me?"

"Are you giving up on us?" I ask her, sounding as defeated as I feel in the moment.

"No." She doesn't even hesitate with her answer. "The idea of not having you in my life is terrifying."

Riley and I have been taking things slow—too slow, in fact. Maybe I'm just not satisfying her needs the way Ridge does. Lord knows I want to, but I was respecting her by not pushing things.

I grab her hand, encouraging her to follow me up the stairs and straight to her room. She opens her door without hesitation, practically pulling me inside with her.

When the sound of the lock clicks, I turn to her, caging her between me and the wall. "Prove it."

I HAVE every reason to prove to Maddox that I want him. I've planted so much doubt in his mind, and I'm willing to do whatever it takes to erase that.

I feel like such a whore for wanting Maddox so soon after having Lev's fingers inside me. Yet, here I am—desperation clawing at my skin that still holds fresh imprints of Lev's touch. I want to tell Maddox what I did, and that I had no choice. I wish I could tell him Lev is hanging my secret over my head. But, I can't. At least, not yet.

My fingers interlock behind his neck and I pull him closer. My cold lips press to his warm ones, and my hand moves down the contours of his tight stomach, tracing around each perfectly-sculpted muscle. Our tongues dance in unison and when I deepen the kiss, Maddox groans into my mouth. The vibration sends a rush of heat through my core.

Running my fingers along the waistband of his jeans, my heart thuds with anticipation for what's to come.

I push my hand down the front of his jeans, and I'm

pleased to be greeted with his engorged cock. It's the first time I've touched him, so naturally, my hand trembles as I wrap my fingers around his silky form.

Moving his lips hungrily against mine, he pulls me forward, walking toward my bed, while his hands roam my body.

His desire presses into me and he grinds himself against my hand. Tingles shoot through my body at his yearning for this, for me.

Maddox falls backward onto the bed, taking me down with him, while my hand slips out of his pants. The heat of his skin radiates through his clothes and I'm certain the same can be said for me.

With my legs straddling his waist, I lift up and pinch the button on his jeans. With a gentle tug, it releases from its hole and I pull the zipper down, hearing each metal tooth unlock one by one. I push them down and he kicks his feet lightly, ridding himself of his jeans.

Maddox caresses my upper thigh as he peers down at his boxers and waggles his brows. "Take those, too."

I grip the waistband of his boxers and slip them down. His cock springs free, and my teeth dig into my lip.

Lifting his shoulders off the bed, he sits up on his elbows as I move between his exposed lower half. He tugs gently on the hem of my sweater, and I raise my hands as he takes it off. His arms envelop me, and I tilt my head slightly to the left when he peppers my neck with kisses.

We stay like that for a while, kissing and exploring each other. There is something about his body against mine that makes my chest feel full. He switches between slow, soft kisses to hard, brutal ones. He nips and sucks at my skin, savoring every part of me with his mouth while my hands do the same to him.

Trailing his mouth downward, he kisses his way to my puckered nipple. I arch my back and roll my head as he sucks it between his teeth. Giving the same attention to my other breast, he cups it in his hand and rolls it between his fingers. My body floods with heat and want. I reach between us, taking him back in my hand, grazing my thumb over his silky head.

Maddox moves his way back up, sucking and kissing and biting, until he stops at my ear, dragging my lobe between his teeth. "I need to tell you something," he whispers.

Bemused, I crane my neck, so I can see his face better. "What is it?"

"Well." He lifts his shoulders and drops them. "I'm a virgin." The words come out of his mouth as a simple confession. There's no humiliation in his expression, no shame— and I'm grateful for that. Maddox has no reason to be embarrassed that he's a virgin. In fact, it has me all the more excited to be his first. But if we do this, there is no going back. I have to be all in with him. No more games. No more lies.

But that all feels impossible right now. Until I get the upper hand with Lev, I can't commit. But I'm willing to give him everything I've got, while still holding up my end of the deal with Lev.

"Are..." I stutter. "Are you sure this is what *you* want?"

His eyes wear his surprise, but more than that, I see pain there as well. "More than anything. Babe, if this is about Ridge..."

"It's not. Well, it is. But it's more than that."

"Look, Riley," he lifts my chin with his forefinger, "I like you, and I know you like me too. Let's just allow that to be enough right now. It's just us. No one else. Even if it's only for tonight."

I nod in response, liking the sound of that. "Okay."

There's no doubt I'm extremely drawn to Maddox. Everything about him is sheer perfection. His smile, his laugh, the way he can light up a room. Not to mention, he's sexy as hell. But not only that, he's so sweet to me. He makes me feel adored, just like Ridge does, but in a different way. Maddox adores me in a way I understand, and can actually relate to.

All my senses are heightened when Maddox flips us and gently lays me on my back. His lack of experience is concealed by his confidence, and when his mouth drags kisses down my stomach, I find it hard to believe he's never had sex. Then again, I never did either until a couple weeks ago.

Chills shimmy from my waist down, settling between my quivering thighs. Maddox pulls down my pants, inch by inch, while his eyes rest on mine. Once they're settled around my ankles, he yanks them off, then his hands travel back up my body to remove my lacey pink panties.

Motionless, he stares at the sight in front of him and I separate my legs, bending them at the knees, to give him a better view. Shyness isn't a friend of mine, and I have every intention of allowing Maddox to explore every inch of my body.

His breathing deepens as his fingertips trace the curves of my waist. Everything feels electrified as I lie there, naked and vulnerable. "Touch me," I tell him as I grab his hand and place it on my dripping center. My fingers move over the top of his, forcing pressure.

He licks his lips, gawking at my exposed form. "You're so damn sexy."

Once he gets into a rhythm of his own, I remove my hand and run my fingers down his chest. "Turn this way," I order him, needing to touch him while he touches me.

Twisting around, he kneels at my side while still playing with my pussy. I take him in my hand, pumping a few times before lifting off the bed and licking his head. A bead of precum lands on my tongue, and I swirl it around in my mouth before sucking the short end of his cock. It's a different taste than Lev—sweeter almost, which is fitting.

Maddox swipes his fingers up and down rapidly, while the sound of my arousal rings out as it pools against his hand. "Jesus, babe. You're so fucking wet."

My cheeks flush with heat, and I smile around his cock. Maddox isn't small, by any means, but he's not quite as endowed as Ridge and Lev. Still, he's a mouthful.

I take in more of his length, coasting my tongue up and down, while stroking his slippery dick in my hand to the same rhythm as my sucking motions.

Maddox's fingers work magic inside me. Curving at just the right angle, teasingly, before finding a spot that sends sparks of pleasure radiating throughout my body. I gasp, and my spine arches off the bed as he hits the sensitive area again and again. The agonizing plummet of his fingers forces moans of pleasure from my lips.

Bringing up my left hand, I cup his balls, feeling the prickle of tiny hairs against my palm. I massage them gently, and he shudders in response.

He pushes deeper and faster, forcing a lightning bolt through my veins that leaves me breathless. My hips rise of their own accord, meeting his fingers thrust for thrust.

Maddox pushes my head back, stopping me from sucking him off. "Stop, baby. Or I'm gonna come, and I'm not ready." I pull him out of my mouth and keep stroking him as I cry out, "Oh god." Squeezing his fingers inside me, I hold my breath and release, feeling light-headed and unfocused.

He keeps going, fingering me through my orgasm, and it isn't until I slap a hand over his that he stops. Immediately, he climbs on top of me. My legs separate farther, and he settles between them, sliding his dick swiftly between my folds. I gasp as he penetrates deeply, hitting my back walls. My fingers graze down his arms, my nails just scratching the surface of his skin.

"You're so damn tight, baby." His voice is hoarse and raspy, his breaths heady and labored.

Just as I come down from one orgasm, I find myself at the height of another. My voice is not my own as I cry out in ecstasy. Animalistic sounds slip through my lips, and I'm forced to lift my head, nuzzling into the nape of Maddox's neck.

His skin is so smooth and hot. Everything about him right now is driving me wild. I grip his biceps, squeezing with tenacity as the urge to combust overpowers me.

Maddox lifts my leg, letting it hang over his forearm, and he drives himself deeper and faster inside me.

"Fuck," he whimpers. "I'm gonna..."

Fisting the sheets with his free hand, he pants and groans, the symphony of his pleasure only arousing me further.

His body stiffens, and I feel him swell inside me. His breaths come in fast, short gasps, and his hips buck against mine as he thrusts one last time. Shuddering with pleasure, I feel his release deep inside me.

I tighten my walls around him, squeezing and milking his cock.

Dropping his head, he rests it on my chest. "Holy shit. That was fucking amazing."

My fingers trail down his back and I close my eyes, smiling. "Yeah it was."

Suddenly, the sound of an orchestrated clap has both our heads bolting up, eyes on the perpetrator.

Standing tall and cocky is Ridge, clapping his hands. "Bravo, my friend. Well done."

CHAPTER 14
RIDGE

IF LOOKS COULD FUCKING KILL, I'd be as dead as the body I just lit on fire.

"A virgin no longer," I sing to Maddox. "Congrats, brother. But..." I drag the word out. "I thought I told you to go back to *our* room so we could talk?"

"In case you've forgotten," Maddox says, unashamedly still on top of Riley, "I don't take orders from you."

As much as I wanted to head straight back to the room to tell the boys what I found, I had told Riley I would be coming by, and I needed her presence to help calm the fire raging in me. I'm so pissed I didn't get the answers I was looking for. I thought coming here would help. Instead, I now feel like my insides are molten lava.

Riley pushes Maddox off of her, then grabs the side of the comforter, pulling it as much as she can in an attempt to shield herself. "Ridge," she gasps. "What are you doing in my room?"

Meanwhile, Maddox is now on his feet, butt-ass naked, as if it's the most normal thing in the world. Not like I haven't seen his package before. Just never thought I'd see it in this room—with her. Shouldn't be surprised, though, considering they've been seeing each other.

"How was he?" I ask Riley. "You know it was his first time, right?" Lev and I have been busting Maddox's balls for years about being a virgin. He's fucked around with plenty of girls, but never actually fucked them. It's not that he didn't have the opportunity, because opportunities arose every weekend. But the noble guy said he was waiting for the right girl. The fact that Riley is that girl doesn't sit well with me.

"Can you please leave until we're...decent?" Riley asks me, but I don't. Instead, I drop down on the bed beside her, arms folded over my chest, ankles crossed.

"But why? I wanna hear all about it. Did he last long?" I chuckle. "My guess is three minutes, tops."

"Shut the fuck up," Maddox seethes as he tugs up his boxers. He snaps the waistband with a scowl on his face. "You shouldn't even fucking be here."

Riley tugs nervously at the edge of the blanket, trying to conceal her exposed chest. Her efforts are futile since I'm now sitting on top of said blanket. Every movement from her shifting the comforter only exposes more of her cleavage.

My eyes wander to the plump skin. *God, she's sexy as hell.* So much so that my cock is now straining against the fabric of my jeans, while my blood pumps furiously.

"You're a lucky guy," I say to Maddox, but my eyes are still on Riley's breasts. "So lucky that your dick got to swim in a pussy that's probably still soaked with my cum. Not to mention, those lips you kissed, well, they were wrapped around Lev's cock not long ago."

I hear Maddox's movements freeze beside me, but I don't look at him. Right now, I don't even care about him. My words aren't meant to piss him off, but rather to make Riley feel about two feet tall for what she just did.

"Ridge!" Riley snaps, flinging her legs over the side of her bed and taking the blanket with her. She gives one swift tug that sends me rolling over the side of the bed. I'm able to catch myself before I hit the floor, but damn, she must be pissed.

"Get the hell out!" She jabs a stern finger at the door. "How dare you!"

"How dare I?" I laugh. "How dare you? You're fucking three guys and telling us all three different things." My words are harsh, but valid.

She snarks, her tongue clicking on the roof of her mouth. "I've been honest with all of you. Never once have I down-played what I have with Maddox. And as far as me and Lev, that was unexpected."

"And what about me?" My voice rises with each word. "Huh? What about the way we connect and the moments we share together? Does that mean nothing to you?"

"Look," Maddox cuts in, now fully dressed. "I'm gonna go down the hall and take a piss and I'll give you two a minute. Sounds like you need one." He rounds the bed to where Riley is standing and kisses her cheek. "You were amazing."

"Fucking kiss ass," I mumble under my breath. How is he not pissed after what I just told him? Riley has screwed around with all three of us in the last forty-eight hours. I can easily forgive her, but Maddox isn't the type to just let that shit go. At least, he never used to be.

"Better yet," I pipe up. "Don't come back at all. It's gonna take more than a minute to hash this shit out."

Gripping the blanket with one hand, Riley throws the other in the air, fuming. "There's nothing to hash out!"

As soon as the door closes and Maddox is gone, I close the space between me and my girl. She takes a step back, halting me with her hand on my chest. "Don't!" Her gaze shoots to the left, avoiding eye contact with me.

I slide up to her with my arms on either side of her waist. "Don't be like that."

"You're unbelievable, Ridge."

"Unbelievably, madly, crazy in love with you." I nuzzle my face into the fold of her neck, and when she pulls back, I follow her lead. "Are you really gonna punish me for being jealous?"

"Jealous?" she huffs. "More like possessive."

"I won't deny that." I kiss her neck, feeling my heart beat faster as I explore her skin with my mouth. I move to her shoulder as my hands slide up to the top of the blanket. Tugging it softly, I hope she'll let it fall so I can see her beautiful body before she kicks me out of her room—which she will. Riley is a forgiving person, but her forgiveness takes time. Sometimes days. "Are you mad at me, Angel?" I pull the blanket again, my mouth still on her.

She hesitates before lifting my head, so she can look at me. "No. I'm not mad. Just disappointed. I understand you're jealous and you don't like seeing me with Maddox, but you have to remember, you gave us your approval."

"True," I quip, "but I also made it clear I'm not backing down. Not for him. Not for anyone. Ever."

"Yeah," she exhales sharply. "You've made that abundantly clear."

My eyes widen at her biting words. "Do you want me to back down?"

Have I ever mentioned how much I hate silence after asking a question? Fucking hate it. Silence tells me the person is conflicted. And by no means should Riley be conflicted with that question.

"Well," I press. "Do you? It's a simple fucking question, Riley."

In a torrent of anger, I grab the blanket she's lazily hanging onto and I rip it off.

"What the hell!" She bends over to try and grab it, ready to hide herself from me again, but I kick it behind us.

"You don't need that. Do you understand me? You don't need to hide from me!"

"Ridge," she says cautiously, "you're acting crazy again."

"Because you fucking make me crazy," I shout, fisting the sides of my head. "Now answer the goddamn question. Do you want me to back down?"

"No!" she shouts back. "I don't want you to back down, or give up, or walk away." Her voice drops to a near whisper and her eyes soften. "I'd miss you too much." She stops trying to shield herself from me and steps forward. "You may be a thorn in my side, Ridge Foster, but you're a thorn that's growing on me."

Trying to wrap my head around the emotions I'm feeling right now is impossible. Pretty sure my heart has just doubled in size. When I first laid eyes on Riley, she became my conquest. I knew one day she'd be mine, and I was willing to do everything in my power to get her. And the moment those words finally leave her mouth, it makes everything feel more than worth it.

I pull her close, enveloping her warm skin in my arms. Her tits press against my chest and I peer down at her. "You have no idea how much I needed to hear that." I kiss her fore-head softly, utterly consumed by this girl.

Her arms wrap around my head and she locks her fingers at the back of my neck. "I don't know what tomorrow brings, and I have no idea what I plan to do, so one day at a time is all I can offer any of you."

"One day at a time is good enough for me. As long as you're still there tomorrow."

I know Maddox is still in the picture, as is Lev, but I draw the line there. Anyone else who tries to get with her is fucking dead.

The door comes back open, and Maddox steps inside, closing it behind him. Riley springs forward and grabs the blanket, covering herself again. Ironic how that works.

"Everything cool in here?" Maddox asks as his eyes dance between me and Riley.

"Yeah," Riley tells him before returning her attention to me. "Listen, I know things are good between us now, but Maddox and I were sort of in the middle of something..."

"Say no more," I tell her. "I'll go. But I'll be back." I kiss her cheek and walk away, patting Maddox on the back on my way out.

"CHIPS, PLEASE." Riley holds out her hand, and I pass her the bag while she exchanges me for the cheese curls.

Chuckling, I swipe my thumb across her chin, wiping up the cheese powder. "You're a messy eater."

"Can't help it." She smacks her lips. "They're so good. I haven't eaten all day."

"Guess snacks in bed wasn't such a bad idea, after all."

Her lips press to my salty ones. "Not even a little bit." She retreats and stuffs her hand in the bag of chips. "Only thing that would make this better is a movie."

"Ah, let me guess. Chick flick?"

"Well, duh."

"And which one would you pick?"

She pops a chip in her mouth, chewing as she thinks. I never realized someone could look so cute eating.

"Hmm. I'd have to go with *How to Lose a Guy in 10 Days*."

"You would."

"All right, smartass." She crumples the top of the bag as

she folds it over. She places it on the end table, then she straightens her back and crosses her legs. Seconds later, her hand is back in the cheese curls bag. "Which movie would you pick?"

Giving her a side-eye, I click my tongue on the roof of my mouth. "*How to Lose a Guy in 10 Days.*"

Her eyebrows scrunch together in amusement. "Shut up." She laughs. "You like that movie, too?"

"No," I tell her honestly. "I like you, and if that movie makes you smile, then I wanna watch you smile."

Her crumb-covered fingers pinch my cheeks, and she plants a kiss on my lips. "You're too sweet for your own good, Maddox Crane."

An hour later, our stomachs are full of junk, and we're lying on the bed bloated as hell. Riley's leg is flung across both of mine as her head rests on my chest. One arm locked around her, I graze the skin of her upper thigh with my other hand. "Tell me a secret," she says, drawing lines on my stomach.

"A secret, huh?" I think hard on this one. There's so much I wish I could tell her, and someday I will, but right now, I opt for something less privileged. "Freshman year of high school, it was our first dance. Ridge was living with me at the time, and he was always a bit of a troublemaker."

"Nooo," she teases. "Not Ridge."

"Hard to believe, right? Anyways, my mom and dad had to work, so we walked to the dance with Lev. As we passed by the liquor store, Ridge had the grand idea of stealing a bottle of booze. We were only fourteen, and booze was booze as far as we were concerned. I distracted the cashier while Lev and Ridge stole the bottle. We all took a sip of it on the way and the shit was nasty as fuck. I literally curled over, certain I was gonna throw up. Well, twenty minutes into the dance, we decided to ditch the shit, and what better way than to share it with everyone else. So Ridge dumped the whole bottle into the punch bowl."

"No, you didn't! Did anyone notice? I mean, if it was that nasty, they'd have to, right?"

"Oh, they noticed, but no one told any of the chaperones. Everyone was gathered around the punch bowl at that point. Next thing we know, the freshman class is getting tipsy, and the preacher's daughter is throwing up on the principal's shoes. Cops were called and she and a few other students were given tickets for minors in possession."

"Maddox." Riley slaps my arm playfully. "That's so bad. Did you guys ever get caught?"

"Nope. No one ever knew it was us. Needless to say, Shelly Macomb's father did a lot of praying for his daughter."

"Well, your secret is safe with me."

"It was a night I'll never forget." I don't divulge any more information because what happened next isn't my story to tell. "All right," I roll onto my side, studying her eyes, "your turn. Tell me a secret." I tuck her hair behind her ears and sweep my fingers across her warm cheek.

"Hmm." She taps her chin, smiling coyly. "When I was thirteen years old, I was at a friend's slumber party playing truth or dare, and I got dared to streak and run down the street." Her cheeks tinge pink from embarrassment and it's cute as hell. "So I stood outside in the dark, took all my clothes off, and ran. The next thing I know, I'm bumping into our gym teacher who was out walking his dog."

"No way? What'd you do?"

"What any sane thirteen-year-old would do." She laughs.

"I turned around and ran, then skipped gym class for two weeks straight."

"Damn. That's funny as hell." I drag my fingers down her smooth leg. "Now a serious one?"

"All right. Well, you already know my big secret...but there's more to it."

"If you don't wanna..."

"No. It's okay. I trust you, Maddox. And it might do me some good to finally get this out." She swallows hard, giving herself a moment, while I massage her shoulder, letting her know I'm here for her. "I've never told anyone this, well, not in depth anyways. But, I don't feel bad for what I did." She clears her throat. "Killing the governor, I mean."

I nod in response, giving her every opportunity to express how she feels. I can tell by the look on her face she needs to do this.

"I know it was wrong, but I also think it was good. I'm haunted by that day, but I lack the remorse someone should have in my position. And what I really feel bad about is not feeling bad. Does that make sense?"

"Well," I begin, "your feelings are valid, no matter what they are. Don't ever feel like a monster for not having regret. You acted selflessly, and you saved a lot of people from an even worse fate. If anything, I think you should look at yourself as a hero."

I strain to keep the words fresh in my mind as I ignore my own lack of guilt for the terrible things I've done.

"A hero?" Riley chuckles. "I highly doubt that."

Pushing my own thoughts aside, I focus on her—the here and now. "No matter how you feel, or what inner demons you battle, I'm here for you. Always."

She smiles broadly. "I know."

We lie there for a few more minutes, engulfed in silence while holding each other. This moment is perfect. One I want to hold on to for eternity. There's no doubt in my mind that I'm falling for Riley. Her arms are like home and the sound of her heart beating against mine is my new favorite sound.

CHAPTER 16
RIDGE

I'VE CHEWED off half of my thumbnail as I pace this fucking room, and the other half isn't looking so well. It's been two hours since I left Maddox with Riley and he's still not back. Bet they're fucking again. I know the guy just lost his virginity, but Jesus Christ, give the girl a break. The thought irks me. As long as I don't dwell on it, I'll be fine. *Don't go there, Ridge.*

An hour and a bleeding thumb later, the door comes open. My movements freeze and my shoulders rise, but when I see that it's Lev, they drop in defeat. "Dammit. Thought you were Maddox." I swipe a stack of papers off the table aggressively. "What the fuck is taking him so long?"

"Where's he at?"

"Willamette House. With Riley."

Lev's eyes widen in surprise. "Is that so?"

"The fuck do you care?"

"Don't care at all. Just surprised considering..." His words trail off, and he smirks.

"Considering *what*?" I emphasize the word.

I already know Lev and Riley have been fucking around, and his sly remark just gave me an opening to tear him to shreds over it.

Lev doesn't fuck around with girls; he destroys them. And I don't want his sick interest anywhere near *my* angel.

He bends down and begins restacking the papers. Since when does Lev pick shit up?

I kick them out of his hand and they scatter around on the floor. "What the fuck has gotten into you?"

The fury in his eyes intensifies. He snaps his neck to the left, then right, before standing up. "The question is," Lev says as his hands plant on my chest and he shoves me hard, "what the fuck has gotten into *you*?"

I lunge toward him, reaching for his waist. Two arms wrap around him tightly as I drag us both to the ground. "You didn't give her a choice, did you? There's no way in hell Riley would suck your dick without being forced."

"She fucking loved it."

Rage consumes me as we grapple and roll across the floor, slamming into the legs of the table and knocking down chairs. No punches are thrown, but I won't hesitate if he says another degrading thing about her.

"What are you hanging over her head?" I howl into the room. "Fucking tell me!"

"Nothing!" he bellows. "Not a damn thing. Don't hate me because she's greedy for my cock after being left unsatisfied with yours."

"You fucking son of a bitch." I throw the first punch, hitting him square in the eye.

"I'll fucking kill you," he roars, flipping me onto my back. He raises his fist, but it freezes in midair.

"Do it, pussy. Fucking hit me."

He could. He has the advantage, and it's Lev. He never thinks twice about this sort of shit. Yet, here he is—not acting on impulse. And what I don't understand is how, or why.

"Eat shit," he grumbles as his hand unravels and he climbs off of me.

I sit up, knees bent and arms dangling over them. I study him for a moment as he staggers to his dresser, pretending to rummage through shit.

What the fuck just happened?

"Lev," I begin, but he raises a hand with his back to me. "Don't."

My hands rise then fall, smacking my knees. "All right." He doesn't want to talk, and I'm not even sure if I have the capacity to listen right now.

I get up, giving us both a minute to cool off, while I think about how I'm going to approach this situation.

Something happened to him. I haven't seen Lev act this humane in years.

Could it be her? Is she changing him?

I shake my head at that ridiculous thought. Nope. That's impossible. Although, she'd be the girl to do it. After all, she is an angel.

Maddox comes barreling through the door, making a bunch of racket. It isn't until I see him scouring the area that I remember he's been with Riley for fucking hours.

"Where were you?" I ask him, tone flat.

He snickers. "You know where I was."

"What took you so long?" He walks past me and I get a whiff of her scent. "Did you fuck her again?"

"Look, man," he plops on the couch and looks me in the

eye, "if this is ever gonna work, you need to stop prying so much. You're only gonna drive yourself mad."

He's right. It does make me mad.

I sit down beside him, confused as fuck about everything. I never imagined I'd be in this position—my two best friends after the girl of my dreams.

And Lev. I look at him folding his fucking shirt. "Dude. Since when do you fold your damn clothes?"

He's always just thrown them into his dresser, never cared to take the time to organize them, or anything for that matter.

His eyes shoot over his shoulder, his cheek still red from where I landed a hit and the scowl on his face reassures me that he's still an angry bastard.

Fuck it. I'll try and figure him out later, not that I ever will.

Shifting from one tense moment to another, I say, "There's something you guys need to know." I reach into my pocket and pull out Cade's wallet.

"You stole his wallet?" Maddox gasps. It's so like him to get worked up over something so miniscule.

"We just lit a fucking body on fire, and that's your concern?" I shake my head in disbelief. "It's not about the wallet. It's about what I found inside."

"I'm outta here," Lev says as he heads to the door. Before I can say anything, he swipes his jacket off the hook.

"Wait a damn minute." I jump to my feet and he freezes mid-step in front of the door. Furious eyes dart over his shoulder, settling on mine in a threat. "You need to see this."

In a fleeting second, he whips around and tears open the door with such force that it ricochets off the wall. Then he leaves and slams it shut.

Whatever momentary bout of humanity I thought I saw was certainly short-lived. It's like anytime he feels anything but anger, it quickly leaves and rage returns tenfold.

"What was that all about?" Maddox asks from the couch, while I stare dumbfoundedly at the door.

"We got into it earlier. Something's going on with him and Riley."

"Remember how I said you need to quit prying..."

"This is different, man." I spin around, dragging my fingers through my sweat-infused hair. "This is fucking Lev. He's not you. He's not good."

"For our own sanity, we just have to trust that she's making the right choice for herself, while making it abundantly clear that we're here if she needs us." Maddox leans forward, his elbows pressed to his knees. "Now tell me what you found in that wallet that's so important."

Sweeping away the thoughts of Lev and Riley, I return my attention to the wallet. I smack it a few times against my palm before saying, "Cade had some sort of connection to Dr. Edmonds."

"Lev's therapist?"

I nod. "Yup. Found the good doc's business card in Cade's wallet."

"That can't be a coincidence. Dr. Edmonds isn't even from Glendale."

"No shit. Hence why I said there's some sort of connection." Glendale is the small town where we all lived before we came to BCU. Dr. Edmonds became Lev's therapist years ago after Lev was kicked out of his aunt and uncle's home.

"Unless Cade was just being a nosy little shit, trying to see if he can get info on his cousin from Edmonds."

"That's a possibility. But I still think we need to investigate this."

"Well, The Sleuth is on the case. I'm sure you'll figure it all out." He's referring to my position in The Society.

"Fuck no. You're helping me on this one, Mr. High and Mighty Guardian."

He waves his hand through the air. "The Society's worst Guardian."

"Nah. I think Riley has you beat on that." We both laugh because it's true. Riley and Maddox both suck as Guardians. Hell, we all suck at our positions right now. But we're still young, we have a lot of time to grow. "What's our motto?" I ask him, my mouth tugging up in a grin.

"We will reign."

"Damn straight we will. And that means all of us. You, me, Lev, *and* Riley. And we can't reign if there is a snake on the inside. We need to make damn sure this doctor wasn't in cahoots with Cade."

"Agreed." Maddox stands up, his face drawn with stress, and I can't help but notice the shift in his demeanor. He lets out a deep breath. "While we're on the subject of weeding out snakes..." He rolls his shoulders before letting them relax. "I think my dad might have had some sort of connection to Governor Saint."

My eyebrows rise. "What makes you think that?"

"I'm pretty sure he's The Elder that's forcing this inside investigation. I think he put out the assignment for you to find out what really happened that night. Thank fuck it was you who got it; otherwise, Riley might have been banished by now. Or worse."

I think about that every day. All the what-ifs. If this assignment would have fallen into the lap of any other

Sleuth, she'd be screwed. They would've found out she was the one who killed the governor. I try hard not to let it linger on my mind, but it's impossible for it to not pop up from time to time.

"Well," I begin, "I guess we've got another case on our hands. Seems Lev is preoccupied with his own shit, so it's just me and you."

"Yeah. No shit." He blows out a heavy breath. "All right then. You dig up what you can on Edmonds, and I'll see what I can find out about my dad."

"You really wanna do this? You and your dad are pretty tight."

"If he's trying to wreak havoc on Riley's world, damn straight I'm doing this."

Seems we've got the same mindset on that. The thought of Riley falling for another guy rips my heart out, but if I had to choose the other guy in her life, it would be Maddox. We've both got her best interests at heart. Therefore, she'll always be protected.

CHAPTER 17
RILEY

MY MUSCLES ARE SCREAMING in agony. My sexual encounters with all three guys over the last few days have me feeling like I engaged in another mud wrestling match with Melody.

Each day Lev has tightened the invisible leash on me more and more, keeping me within arm's reach. Every time he texts me, things between us go further. There's a part of me that is scared of what he might do next, but another part of me yearns for the thrill he gives me. Butterflies erupt inside me with each degrading word, every time he forces me to obey him. Fighting Lev is like a game of how far I can test the devil before I end up getting burned alive.

Then there are times like now, when I look at him when he doesn't realize I'm watching. He appears human. Reading a page in his textbook, his eyebrows scrunched together, deep in thought. I steal a glance at the page number and flip my book to the same one and begin reading, trying to see what part he is at, just so I can try and guess what he's thinking.

It's actually an interesting topic about the human mind, although it's not the same subject we're currently studying.

He turns the page and I do the same, reading along with him. Every now and then, I steal another glance, and he's none the wiser.

Lev is so bemusing. He's the type of person who instills fear in others when he's not even trying. He walks around with a pissed-off expression all day, every day, and his fists are almost always clenched at his sides. His body looks like it's constantly on the defense, prepared to attack and protect at any given moment.

I should fear him. I should run as fast and as far as I can. Yet, I don't. Because he won't let me.

His eyes lift from the book and catch mine. I quickly turn away. My cheeks flush with heat as I resume reading, or at least, appearing to do so.

"What the hell are you looking at?" he asks with that pissed-off attitude I know so well by now.

"Hmm?" I raise my brows, playing dumb.

"You were staring at me. Why?"

Maddox is on the other side of me, oblivious to what's even going on right now and I'm grateful because the last thing I need is another spectacle in this class.

My head shakes in slow movements. "No, I wasn't."

"Yes, you were." His voice is a whisper amongst the silent room of students who are reading the passage we were assigned.

"Don't let it get to your head, Lev." I turn the page again, completely skipping over the whole section. "I'm just reading like everyone else."

"All right, class." I jolt at Professor Atkins's interruption, though I'm grateful for it. "Finish chapter eight tonight and we'll have a quiz on Friday."

Everyone closes their textbooks at the same time, shuffling to gather their belongings. But before I can close mine, Lev slaps a hand between the pages of my book and leans over to see what I was reading. His eyes slide to mine, and the perplexed look on his face tells me he knows I was reading the same thing as him.

My body flushes with heat, and when he pulls his hand back, I'm the first one in the class to stand, ready to flee this room and Lev.

Leaving Maddox behind, too, my feet move so fast down the hall that I nearly trip over them. There's an hour break between now and my next class, which is usually when I have lunch with Ridge and Maddox—and Lev, when he shows up. If I let Lev catch me, I have no doubt he'll force me to walk into the student center with him. Probably holding his hand with a smile, while pretending we have a budding relationship. *Gag.*

I turn the corner and crash into a group of guys—four or five of them. "Sorry." I keep my head down as I pass through their group.

"Are you?" I hear one of the guys say, and I whip my head around to find a tall, muscular guy coming my way. He's got caramel-colored, shoulder-length hair, and big brown eyes, with a hang-ten surfer vibe. My gaze drifts to his arm where he has a tattoo of a surfboard and waves. *Fitting.*

"Excuse me?" I say to him as he stirs to my side.

"Are you really sorry?" The cocky grin on his face grows wider. "Or did you do it on purpose to try and get our attention? Well," his eyebrows waggle, "you've got it, baby." His eyes slide up and down my body, stopping on my chest.

The other guys gather around, and before I know it, I'm in the center of a circle.

Turning to my side, I attempt to slide past two of them. "I have somewhere to be. So if you don't mind..."

"But I do mind," Surfer Boy says, his hand now on my waist.

I slap it down and scoff. "Get lost, creep."

"Oh, come on," he snickers. "I just wanna have a little fun with you. Give me a chance and I'll show you how fun I can be."

My stomach turns at this guy's abundance of arrogance. "Thanks, but I think I'll pass."

In an attempt to slip out of his reach, I fail. Both of his hands land on either side of my waist before he tosses me across the circle into the hands of another guy.

"What's up, pretty girl?" my new handler says.

I peer up at him and snarl. "Get your hands off of me."

And he does. By tossing me to a new guy. They all laugh, like I'm a ball to be thrown around—something they can play with.

"You guys are fucking disgusting," I spit. "Find someone else to mess with because I'm not your girl."

I'm tossed again, and this time, my hand swings back and my palm smacks hard against the stranger's face. "You fucking bitch," he seethes, squeezing my wrist so hard, I fear it'll snap in two. "You're gonna pay for that."

In a split second, the crowd parts, and I bolt through the opening, my heart pounding in my chest. But before I can get away, I crash into another guy. Just as I draw my fist back, ready to punch this shithead, I look up and see that it's Lev.

His jaw locks as one hand rests softly on my side. "Go to

the student center, Riley." He barks the order, though his eyes are held tight to the guy I just slapped.

"These guys were—"

"Go!"

Hesitantly, I slide around him, watching intently as he takes small strides toward the guy who appears to be his main focus. The others step aside, gasping. Lev may have the attitude down, but he lacks the brawn to take on any of those guys, much less a group of them.

It's not until I see what he's holding in his right hand that I understand why these built guys are all taking steps back, widening their circle.

A few feet away, I tuck my back into a corner and watch as Lev raises the handgun and brings it down on the guy's head with so much force I worry he cracked his skull. I choke on my breath, hand clapped over my mouth.

The guy drops to his knees, blood spilling down his face, and not one of his friends comes to his aid. Just seeing the gun triggers something inside me. The night I shot the governor flashes through my mind, and it's like my body is reliving the experience all over again.

Lev crouches down in front of the guy, and while I can't see his face, I can hear him. "I've got one bullet, mother-fucker, and if you touch her again, it's got your name on it." His head whips around and his gaze dances from one guy to the next. "That goes for any of you. Are we clear?"

Two of the guys take off and the others nod while they retreat from Lev, who's still holding the gun in his hand.

Before he can see that I was watching, I walk speedily down the hall, fighting to catch my breath.

I don't stop until I'm at the round table in the student center where Maddox and Ridge are. I drop down quickly into a chair, my eyes bolting over my shoulder every couple seconds.

"Running from someone?" Maddox asks teasingly, but I see no humor in it.

I can't tell them Lev has a gun, although they might already know. There's a saying...*friends don't let friends drive drunk*. Well, I think the same can be said in this situation. *Friends don't let their psycho friends own guns*. It's a recipe for disaster, and has me wondering if Lev has actually used it on someone. The thought terrifies me. *Guns* terrify me.

I open my mouth to speak, but I close it just as fast, knowing I can't say a word. Not when it entails Lev. I can't do anything to piss him off because he could turn on me in a split second. Then again, he just defended me, which is odd considering he doesn't even like me. Or so I thought.

"No," I finally say, my heart still exploding in my chest, "just really hungry."

Ridge side-eyes me, his eyebrow raised. "Where's your food?"

I force a laugh and smack my hands to the table. "Oh, right. Silly me. I was so excited to eat that I totally forgot to get any." I go to stand, but Ridge raises his hand, lowering it as he orders me back to my chair.

His chair slides back, the legs scraping against the waxed floor. "I've got you." His voice is soft, but strong. "What are you in the mood for today?"

"Umm. Chicken soup and crackers is fine."

"Drink?" He gets to his feet, towing over the table as he waits patiently for my response, but I'm too distracted to even process his question.

I look over my shoulder again and see Lev coming, so I turn back around quickly.

"Do you want anything to drink?" Ridge asks again.

"Sorry." I shake my head, trying to dislodge the thoughts racing through my mind. "I didn't sleep well last night. Water is fine. Thank you."

Maddox reaches over and places a hand on my leg. "You sure you're all right?"

I roll my lips together and nod. "I'm fine. Like I said, I didn't sleep well."

"Ridge?"

"No," I tell him, "Ridge didn't come last night."

It's not often he doesn't show up at some point in the night, but last night he never came. I'm not lying when I say I didn't sleep well. For some reason, I sleep better when Ridge is there. I feel safe knowing he's watching, and the steady sounds of his breathing lull me to sleep.

Before I even see him, I can feel Lev's presence as he approaches the table. My back stiffens and my shoulders draw back. Maddox massages my leg, watching me carefully. "You okay?"

"Fine," I quip, just as a shadowy figure appears beside me. Temptation gnaws at my stomach. The need to look and see if he's still clutching the gun is strong. Is it in his hand? Is it hidden on him? If so, where?

A hand plants to the table right beside me, and when I finally look, Lev's face is directly in front of mine. "What did those guys do to you?" he grits out, jaw clenched.

Maddox removes his hand from my leg and his chair inches back, though he remains seated. "What guys?"

"It was nothing," I lie. "A few guys made me the butt of their fun for a couple minutes. No big deal."

"I asked you if something was wrong when you sat

down," Maddox says sternly. "Ridge and I both did, but you said you were fine."

My hands rise then fall before resting on the table. "Because I am *fine*."

"She's lying," Lev says impassively. "When I found her, some fucker was holding her by the wrist." He grabs my arm and pushes down the sleeve of my cream knitted sweater, exposing the imprint of the guy's fingers. Lev tosses my hand back at me and takes a step back, his fingers dragging through his hair as he mumbles some words under his breath. "He fucking did that?"

I'm not sure why he even cares. I understand Ridge and Maddox being upset about something like this, but Lev doesn't give a damn about me, unless it comes to using me for his own selfish gain.

Maddox is now on his feet, drilling Lev for more information, when Ridge returns. Ignoring the two of them, he sets my soup in front of me, as if I'm really going to eat with all the commotion going on. I swear, all I want is one day where I'm not surrounded by chaos.

The next thing I know, all three of them are bickering, and it's all over me. All I can think about is Lev and the gun. The thought of him pulling that out in a fit of rage terrifies me.

I have to get out of here.

None of them even notice when I grab my soup and my bag, and walk away quietly. If they wanna pry into my business, they can do it without me.

Lately, I feel like a damn bone, and the three of them are a pack of wolves fighting over me. I'm not sure if I should be flattered or pissed, but I'm a bit of both.

"WHAT THE HELL has gotten into you?" Ridge snaps. "Your mood swings are making us all fucking crazy lately."

I chew on my bottom lip, trying to collect any bit of composure I've got, which isn't much. "Riley left class quickly and I told Maddox I'd find her and bring her to lunch. He agreed and left, so I searched the nearby halls. I found her in the center of a group of guys, one of which was strangling her wrist. I told her to get out of there, then I took care of him."

"Took care of him, how?"

"Knocked the fucker upside the head and threatened 'em all. Doesn't matter," I snap. "They're not gonna fuck with her again, but I wanted to know what else they did to her."

"Fuck," Ridge sighs, "I shoulda been there."

"I told you I handled it."

"I appreciate that, brother." He claps a hand to my shoulder. "As hard as I try, I can't keep my eyes on her twenty-four seven."

"Don't thank me. I didn't do it for you," I say sternly. I

don't even know why I did it, all I know is I needed to see someone bleed for causing that look in her eyes. Only I get to be the reason for that look.

Ridge scoffs, but it's the truth. I've got a really hard time not speaking my mind, and an even harder time letting people think I'm doing them favors. This wasn't a favor for Ridge or Maddox. In fact, it wasn't even a favor for Riley. Everything I do is for myself. Each day I find myself slowly changing, more and more, touching the emotional side of myself that once existed. But it's always so short-lived.

My hope is that one day, I can fully embrace it again. That's why I did it. Because Riley is my key to sanity, and no one touches what's mine—except Ridge and Maddox, but even that irks me to the core. I don't like to share, but if I have to, they're the only ones I'd ever consider sharing with.

Maddox pipes in and says he has to get to his next class, and Ridge says he's cutting out for the rest of the day to make sure there's no evidence of Cade left behind after the fire sizzled out.

I pull out my phone and send Riley a text, knowing she'll respond because she has to.

> Me: There's an old cabin down Ruddiman Drive. Sits back between two tall evergreens. Big red door. You can't miss it. Meet me there in twenty minutes.

If Ridge is going to check the arson spot, that means he'll be in the vicinity of the warehouse and the cemetery, so my meeting spot with Riley has to change for today.

> Riley: I have class!

Knowing she's upset only brings a smile to my face.

Me: Not anymore you don't.

I stuff my phone in my pocket and leave the student center, going straight for the main doors. If Riley doesn't intend to tell me what those guys did, then I'll have to force it out of her.

———

"This is new." She howls into the chilly air as she walks up to the cabin. She's pulled her hair up into a high ponytail since I saw her a half hour ago, and she's wearing her black winter coat and a pair of thick-knitted mittens.

With my arms crossed over my chest, I stand tall on the small front porch of the cabin. The worn wooden planks creak beneath me as I take one step forward, the toe of my boot teetering on the edge. "Options are currently limited, and we need to have a little chat."

Her eyes flicker from one part of the property to the next. When I purchased the warehouse, all the land, including this old cabin tucked in the corner of the fifteen acres, was part of it. It's nothing special, just a small cabin with a kitchenette, a living room, and a bathroom. There's a loft big enough to fit a queen-size mattress. I've only come here a couple times, so I don't even have the electricity turned on. There is running well water, though. Against the back wall sits an aged wood stove, but its use would require wood. I'm many things, but a lumberjack isn't one of them.

Riley comes toward me with slow steps, taking in the

scenery. "I've passed by this place a couple times, but never really stopped to look. It's...cute. And quaint."

"Just a cabin. Nothing to get too excited about." My lack of ability to see the beauty in the smallest things is something else I'm working on. So far, nada.

"Always such a downer," she grumbles as she comes up the two steps and passes by me.

"And you're always such a pain in the ass," I retort. Although she has caught my eye at this moment and I'm finding it easy to look past the anger that has been bubbling in my stomach.

"Go on in." My eyes roll. "Make yourself at home." My voice is laced with sarcasm. Leave it to Riley to not await instructions. Sometimes I swear the girl lives in her own little world.

I follow behind her, leaving the door ajar to allow some daylight to seep in.

I watch intently as her eyes linger on the peeling paint, and the moss that has started to take over the chipped wooden frame. Bypassing the living area, she enters the door beside a floral imprinted, dusty couch facing a cracked box TV. I stay close as she continues to look around, curious what's to be found in this place. I've owned it since my freshman year at BCU, but I've never inspected this cabin.

We enter a bathroom that looks like it hasn't been used in years. A small porcelain sink sits under a ghosted mirror, and there's a stand-up shower in the corner with rusted-out tiles. The toilet lid is closed and I'd prefer to keep it that way. There's no saying what kind of filth is underneath that thing.

"I love this place," Riley beams, and my neck cranes in confusion.

"You do?"

"It's like a tiny house with everything you need."

"That's because it is. It's a small cabin that's run-down and weathered. Nothing to love about this dump."

"Let me fix it up, Lev." She spins around to face me with her fingertips pressed together in a pleading manner. "This is the perfect thing to get my mind off everything else going on."

At first I think she's joking, but when her lips pout into a frown, I'm pretty sure she's serious.

"You wanna fix up this old cabin? For what?"

"I've always loved decorating, and I've got a good eye for it. It'll be fun."

I'd love more than anything to crush her spirits right now, but instead, I use it to my advantage. "Ya know. I brought you here because you lied to me, and all liars need to be punished." I slide up to her, my hands running down the sleeve of her winter coat. Slowly, I unzip it, sliding it off her shoulders and push it to the floor along with her mittens. "But I'll tell you what. You can do whatever the fuck you want to this place," I skim my lips across her earlobe, "...as long as I get to do whatever I want, to you."

Her voice shakes. "What do you want to do to me?"

My hands flex underneath her shirt, fingers stroking the warm, smooth skin of her stomach as I whisper, "So many dirty things."

"No deal," she quips, crushing my spirit. The pieces quickly reassemble when I remember that I'm the one with the power.

"I don't like being told no, Trouble." I slide my hands up farther, my fingers edging the cups of her bra.

Goosebumps break out under my touch, and she trembles. "Do I have a choice?"

"Nope." I slip my hands up, pinching both of her nipples.

She whimpers, and I'm hopeful that she'll put up more of a fight because I love it when she resists me.

I pinch harder, forcing a moan out of her before I remove her shirt and her bra in one swift motion.

"Tell me no again," I challenge her. The desperation inside me to hear the word falling from her lips has my cock twitching.

"Is that what you like, Lev? You like when I tell you no?"

"Do it. I dare ya."

"How about..." Her hands land on my chest and she shoves me until my back crashes against the bathroom wall. "...fuck no!"

Mmm. She wants to play.

I charge at her, outstretching my fingers as they go for her throat. They tangle around her delicate skin, and the more I squeeze, the more satisfying it becomes.

"Fight me, bitch."

Riley stretches her hand out and slaps me hard across the face. The sting stimulates something inside me. Not pain, but something deeper. Something I've been searching so long for.

I spin her around and pin her against the wall with my hand still wrapped around her throat. My other hand flips the button of my pants. In one fell swoop, I push down my zipper and they pool around my ankles.

I force her to her knees. "Suck my dick, you dirty little whore."

She gasps and moans as I stuff my cock between her lips. There is nothing gentle about the way I fuck her mouth.

Using her head to aid in my forceful thrusts, I rock my hips, crushing my pelvis against her nose. The way her tongue curls around the barbells of my piercings as she licks and sucks on my cock causes a sensation that starts in my balls and builds outward into a white-hot ball of pleasure.

"That's my girl."

It's a quick blow job, because I have every intention of finishing inside her. I haven't entered that territory yet, but I've been craving to know how her pussy feels milking my cock.

Fisting her hair, I jerk her head back. She wipes the back of her hand across her mouth, cleaning up the slobbery mess she's made.

"Crawl," I demand.

She gets down on all fours, and I lead her by her hair out of the small bathroom as I kick out of my pants. "Such a good little pet."

Once we're in the open space of the living room, I immediately tear off my shirt, sending it flying across the room.

I crouch down behind her and give her legging-clad ass a firm slap, before grabbing her hips and pulling her firmly against my erection. "I'm gonna fuck you, Trouble, and you better let me hear how much you like it."

CHAPTER 19

RILEY

MY SKIN TINGLES with anticipation as Lev yanks off my shoes and jerks down my leggings. I lift my knee and he pulls the pant leg off, followed by the other, while taking my panties along with them. I feel so exposed, but so turned on. I hate that I enjoy his dominance. It's highly stimulating, but also so humiliating.

Lev slides his hand between my thighs, parting them, and my body flushes with heat knowing he'll see how aroused I am. I can literally feel my want for him dripping down my leg.

With a swift tug of my hair, Lev yanks my head back. "Chin up."

I try to keep my head still, holding it high as instructed. Two fingers plunge into my pussy like a spear and an audible gasp slips through my lips. Knuckles deep, he prods and twists and turns. "So fucking wet," he rasps.

My body is not my own as I arch my back, granting him more access, while I push against his fingers. My traitorous pussy craves to feel more of him. I'm not sure what more he can give me, but I want it all. I'm one thrust away from explosion, but nowhere near ready. I want this to last an eternity.

I drop my head, resting it against the floor while biting down on my fist to drown out my cries of pleasure. "Oh god, Lev."

My heart is beating so quickly, I swear I can hear it thumping against my rib cage.

Just as I clench my inner muscles around his fingers, he pulls them out. I glance over my shoulder to see why he's stopped and see him fisting his cock, pumping it while massaging my ass cheek.

Mouth agape, he lines his head with my entrance before ramming inside me, forcing a harsh breath out of me. The initial feeling of the cool metal piercings is strange and unfamiliar, but as he glides deeper into me, the ribbed steel balls along the length of his shaft create a unique sensation that sends tingles through my body. I keep watching him, hungry to see the look in his eyes as his fucks me. The intensity building with each of his thrusts.

I bite my bottom lip, looking into his lust-filled eyes with eagerness as he stares back at me. A surge of pleasure ripples through me as his hands explore my back end. Sweeping his fingers between my ass cheeks, he pushes his thumb against my hole. "You ever been fucked in the ass, Trouble?"

I gulp, shaking my head no, while hoping he's not planning to change that tonight. "Good. You save that for me, understood?"

I nod in response while he speeds up, rocking into me with confidence and surety. My hips roll as I meet him push for shove, and the sound of my cries echo off the weathered log walls.

Leaning forward, Lev cloaks my back with his chest and puts his thumb in my mouth. I'm not sure what he wants me to do, but I do what feels right in the moment, and I suck it. It's not until my tongue travels down the ridges that I realize it's the same thumb that was just circling my asshole. *Too late to care now.*

With his chin pressed to my shoulder blade, Lev grabs my throat and groans. The sound of his pleasure has my nails digging into the chipped wood beneath me. Splinters embed under my nails and I wail as Lev moves faster and faster and faster.

My entire body vibrates against his. Unable to hold back, I release, screaming around his thumb. "Oh god. Fuck!" I bite into his skin so hard, I taste metal as his blood seeps onto my tongue.

Grasping my hip with one hand, Lev lunges deeper, settling in as far as he will go, and I can feel the pulsating of his head deep inside me as he releases. A few groans and short pants later, he stops.

He doesn't hesitate to pull himself out and get on his feet, while I drop to my stomach, giving myself time to come down. It may be nearly freezing outside, but my body is on fire.

I'm in a state of ecstasy when Lev tosses my clothes on my back. I don't make a move to get up, or get dressed. I just lie there on the dirty floor while my labored breaths steady.

"Sun's setting. We need to go or we'll be sitting here in the pitch black."

I roll to my side, looking down at my breasts and picking a piece of black fuzz off my nipple. Once I've got it pinched between my fingers, I realize it's not fuzz. "Gross." I jump up. "That's a fucking mouse turd." I toss it to the floor and quickly sweep off the rest of my naked, sticky body.

Lev busts out in laughter and I can't help but stop for a minute, taking in the sound. I can't even be mad that he's finding humor in my misfortune.

His eyebrows cave in and he growls. "Why are you looking at me like that?"

"Like what?"

He jabs a finger at me. "Like that. Knock that shit off."

"I wasn't even looking at you."

"The fuck you weren't. You were looking at me like I sang the world's worst tune."

"So dramatic. I was just listening to you laugh."

"Why?"

"Because I've never heard you laugh before."

"You don't listen with your eyes; you listen with your ears."

"Hence why my eyes weren't looking at you," I sing back, playful sarcasm lacing my tone.

I chuckle as I peel my eyes away and snatch my panties off the floor. I shake them a couple times then hold them up to make sure there's no mouse poop on them. "You're so paranoid, smartass."

"I'm the paranoid one? Look at you inspecting your underwear."

"There was mouse poop stuck to my fucking boob!" I shiver. "Ugh. Does the shower in this place work? I feel disgusting."

"Have you seen the shower in this place? I'd rather bathe in a clean tub full of mouse shit than step foot in that thing." He waves his hand toward the bathroom. "But have at it. Make it fast, though, or you'll be showering in the dark."

I look out the small, circular window in front of me, realizing the sun has almost completely set. There's no doubt it's going to be dark in that bathroom. "Will you come with me?"

"Fuck no," he scoffs, spinning around and walking over to the step ladder that goes to the loft. His hands rest on one of the spindles and he peers up.

"Please."

He shoots me a look of annoyance. "Are you serious?"

I nod.

"Jesus Christ, Riley. Get your ass in there." He steps away from the ladder, shoulders slumped as he swings his hand back and forth. "Hurry your ass up."

I know this is quite literally tearing him up inside, while it's lighting a flame in me. Lev is doing something kind for someone else, and that someone else is me.

My heart swells momentarily. That is until he says, "Wash Maddox and Ridge's scent off your pussy, too. Thought I smelt something stank down there." Then my heart shrinks back to size.

"Fuck you." I flip him my middle finger, but he grabs a hold of it.

"I intend to. Every single day until I'm normal again."

I should be mad at how abrasive Lev is with me. But when he says things like that, I can't help but feel sorry for him. "Who says you're not normal?" I'm taking a risk by prying because he's still holding tight to my finger. One wrong word and he could snap it in half.

To my surprise, he drops my finger and turns the handle in the shower. Rust-colored water expels from the showerhead and I shriek. "Get your ass in if you're gonna do this. We gotta go."

I give it a few seconds, waiting for the water to run clear.

I'm disappointed I didn't reach a breaking point with Lev. I was really hoping he'd open up to me, because it would have been monumental for this thing we have going on, even if it is just an arrangement. It would be proof that it's working, and I might be inclined to stop fighting him so much. But I don't think that's what he really wants.

After a few seconds, the water runs clear. And with nothing left to say, I step into the shower and close the worn fabric curtain. I'm surprised to find the water is warm. There's obviously no soap or shampoo, so I just let the water run down my body, rinsing off the dirt and potential mouse poop that was on me.

"I say I'm not normal," Lev says from the other side of the curtain. "That's who."

My eyes widen and I'm stunned speechless. Is Lev actually revealing his inner thoughts to me?

I'm not sure what to say because I don't want this to go south. So, I decide to speak from my heart.

"Just because you feel things differently than most people, doesn't mean you're not normal."

He huffs. "Tell that to your boyfriends."

"What do you mean? Ridge and Maddox are your best friends. They love you."

"Maybe so. But that doesn't mean they think I'm good for anything. Last night I stood outside our door and heard Ridge tell Maddox," he mocks Ridge's voice in a masculine tone, "this is fucking Lev. He's not you. He's not good. If my best friends can think that about me, then why wouldn't I feel that way about myself?"

My chest tightens. Never would I have imagined I'd feel Lev's pain, but I do.

I run my fingers through my hair, then turn off the water.

Pulling back the shower curtain, I see him standing with his leg kicked up behind him against the wall. His arms are crossed over his chest and I've always been told that's a sign someone is trying to protect themselves.

"Can I tell you what I think?" I ask, hoping he'll hear me out.

"Nope," he pops his lips and drops his foot from the wall, "get your fucking clothes on so I can walk your ass home."

I can't help the smile on my face as he walks away. He doesn't have to walk me home. But he is, and I think it's because he wants to. Today was a breakthrough with us, and a big part of me is actually excited to see what tomorrow brings.

FOR THE PAST two days I've been walking around on cloud nine. My time with Lev at the cabin was eye-opening. It's strange, but I feel special in a way. Like I'm seriously the one who is going to save Lev from himself.

Yesterday, I returned to this cabin with the essential cleaning products, and I spent four hours out here washing walls and appliances. Today, I've enlisted help.

"Eww," Scar grumbles as she picks up an old cup full of a thick moldy substance. She brings it to her nose and gags. "This is disgusting."

"Just throw it out," I tell her as I scrub the kitchen floor on my hands and knees.

"Seriously, Ry. Why are you doing this?"

"Lev owns the place and he told me I could."

"Annnd?" she questions. "Why on earth do you want to?"

I kneel on the floor, my muscles stiff from the endless amount of scrubbing I've been doing. With the back of my arm, I wipe the rivulets of sweat from my hairline. "Don't you see the potential in this place? It's so beautiful and serene here."

"Beautiful, yes. But this place is owned by a psychopath. Aren't you concerned that he's being so nice to you because he wants something in return."

I could tell her Lev does want something in return, but I couldn't tell her what it is and she'd likely press until I spilled the whole truth. Then, I'd be backing out of my deal with Lev, and I'm not ready to do that. Things are finally going smoothly. He hasn't kidnapped me or threatened death in, like, three whole days now. He hasn't exposed my secret, or done anything to make me question if he's sticking to our deal. So, for now, I have to trust that I'm doing what's best for myself.

"For one," I tell her, dropping the rag into the bucket full of murky water, "Lev isn't nice to anyone. I simply asked if I could fix this place up a bit and he said yes. No strings attached."

"All right, Mrs. Clean. What's your plan after you fix this place up? You'll just walk away from it and never step foot inside again? Sounds to me like you're the one doing Lev a favor."

"Actually," I say, "I was sort of thinking I might stay out here sometimes to work on my poetry."

"And you think Lev, the guy you claim is not nice to anyone, is going to allow that?"

I shrug my shoulders as I stick my hand back in the water, squeezing the rag. "We'll see."

I think I could get Lev to agree to just about anything if I keep giving him what he wants.

"All right," Scar sighs as she tosses more trash into the black garbage bag, "I'm just here to help." She pauses for a minute. "And I also have every intention of forcing you to spill your guts about what's going on with you and those three guys."

"Hmm." I smirk. "Seems we've been down this road before."

Scar laughs. "Only it was me on the receiving end of *your* interrogation. So what's going on, Ry. You catching feelings for all these boys?"

There once was a sicko,
who watched me day and night.
His invisible leash,
never let me out of his sight.
His friends were unlike him,
one a monster I feared.
The other bled crimson,
with a heart that was pure.

With my gaze facing down, I say, "Maybe a couple of them."

I push the rag to the floor and try to scrape up some sticky goo stuck to a floorboard. Digging my nail into the fabric, I put all my strength into it.

Scar crouches down in front of me, a sign that this conversation is about to get serious. She wants to read my expression. She *always* has to read my expression when we're talking about matters of the heart. "I already know you and Maddox are seeing each other. So who's the other one?"

I inhale a sharp breath and keep scrubbing, hoping she doesn't notice the pink in my cheeks. "Ridge."

I gulp, giving her a second to process what I said before sliding my eyes to hers. Her eyebrows have hit her forehead and I can't imagine how far they'd ride up if I'd said Lev too.

Then again, Scar knows very little about Lev and so much about Ridge.

"Ry," she says in exasperation. "Why Ridge? He's insanely obsessed with you. The guy gives me the creeps."

"One could say the same about Neo."

"Neo was never obsessed. He was just very…"

"Cruel."

"Cruel, but oddly sweet, and only to me. It makes me feel special."

"Well, Ridge is similar in that aspect. He might go about things in a fucked-up way, but I really think he does it all in the name of love. Ridge would never hurt me, I know that. He cherishes the ground I walk on, for heaven's sake."

"I can definitely see that. What's going on with you and Maddox then?"

Chewing on my bottom lip, I look away again.

"Riley Cross! You're fucking them both, aren't you?"

I stare into the air and whistle, pretending I don't hear her.

"You totally are!"

I have to tell her. I just have to. I won't go into detail, but it's on the tip of my tongue and I can't bite it any longer. "All three of them."

"Nooo," she drawls. "Maddox, Ridge, *and* Lev? You little whore."

I laugh at the name she pegged for me because it's the same thing I called her, teasingly, when she admitted she was screwing Crew, Jagger, and Neo, all at the same time.

"I am a whore." I toss the rag across the floor and drop to my ass. "I'm a dirty fucking whore, Scar. And I have no idea what I'm going to do."

"Then do nothing."

"Come again?"

"Are you happy?"

"I mean, today I am."

"Then, be happy. No one says you have to make any decisions, or choose. If they're cool with it, then keep doing you."

"But I feel like I'm playing games with their hearts. It feels so...wrong?"

"You're not, though. If each one of those guys offers you something different, then just consider yourself lucky and accept what they have to give. I'm doing it, and there is no way in hell I could ever choose between my guys. The thought alone makes my heart hurt."

"And if they make me choose?"

"Then you stand your ground and you tell them no. That gives them the option to walk away, and if they stay, then you know how much you really mean to them. Just be honest with them and take it one day at a time, babe." She flings an arm around my shoulders. "That's all you can do."

One day at a time. I can do that.

———

I'm covered in grime and yuck and all I can think about is how nice a hot shower sounds. Going straight for my room, I halt when I see that the door is cracked open. Scar said she was meeting Crew at the library, so I know she's not inside, and I'm certain I locked the door before I left for the cabin.

That leaves only one person.

I push the door open. "Ridge?" My eyes go right for my bed and I see him lying on his back, one leg hanging off the side, and his eyes closed. He looks so cute and peaceful when he sleeps. Taking care not to wake him, I tiptoe to my dresser and shuffle through my drawers, pulling out a pair of gray sweatpants and a cropped pink tee.

Creeping like a mouse, I make my way to the door.

"Going somewhere, Angel?"

My eyes shoot over my shoulder, and I smile. "Showers."

Ridge pats the bed beside him. "Can it wait a couple minutes? Need to ask you something."

I set my clothes down on the floor beside the door and cross the room to my bed. "I'd ask how you got in here, but I already know. Question is...*why* are you sleeping in my bed?"

"Been waiting for you." He scoots up, both feet now on the bed.

"I'm just glad to see you kicked your shoes off before climbing onto my nice comforter." I smooth my hands down the fabric and take a seat on the edge. "What's up?"

He side-eyes me, eyebrows raised. "Wanna go on a date?"

"A date?" I chuckle. "You wanna take me out on a date?"

"Hell yeah, I do. Was thinking we could take Maddox's car, leave campus and have some fun."

That actually sounds amazing, but... "Wait. Maddox has a car? I thought vehicles were prohibited on campus?"

"They are. He stores one close by, off-campus."

"Weird. He never mentioned it."

"That's because he doesn't use it often. Obviously you know students don't leave campus much, considering anywhere that matters is a good thirty-minute drive. Now, back to this date. Are you down?"

Giddiness washes over me. The idea of going on a date with Ridge is a thrilling thought. I'm curious to see what someone like him would plan. "And what exactly did you have in mind?"

"It's a surprise." He claps a hand to my upper thigh. "Just say yes, then go get your cute ass ready."

"Yes!" I beam, all too eager to get the hell out of here and have some fun. I jump off the bed and head back to my dresser, changing my clothing choice. Being that Ridge is a hopeless romantic with such a soft side, I know this is going to be a dress kind of night.

CHAPTER 21
RIDGE

RILEY GAPES at the building in front of us, her eyes wide with wonder, or maybe it's confusion. I can't be certain. "A destruction depot?" She turns her head slowly. "This is our date?"

"Sure is. You ever been to one?"

Her head shakes and her eyes move back to the building. "Can't say that I have."

I take her hand in mine and lead her to the front double doors. "Well, you're about to find out just how liberating this place can be."

Opening one of the doors, I allow her to enter first, still holding tightly to her hand. "Ridge," Tito, the doorman says, slapping his hand into mine, "long time no see."

"Yeah. School and shit. Keeps a guy busy."

"No doubt." He pats my shoulder. "How the hell have ya been?"

"Not too bad. Just living life."

"Cool, cool. And who's this pretty girl?" Tito looks at

Riley and my jaw clicks when his eyes drag up and down her body.

"None of your concern, man. Just get us a room."

"Of course. Anything for an old friend. We've got a room opening up right now."

I pull Riley close to my side, keeping my arm wrapped snug around her waist as we follow Tito to the back of the building.

He hands us a couple pairs of goggles and leather gloves, then pushes open the door. "Enjoy, kids."

I've known this guy for almost three years now and I'd never refer to him as a friend. He's a scumbag, to say the least. The six-foot-ten beast not only owns Tito's Depot, but he's also the recruiter for a dark web app that coerces girls into sharing live footage of them doing just about anything. He's already gotten to a couple girls at BCU, and if he thinks for a second he's going to groom Riley, he's got another think coming.

We enter the room—my haven for de-stressing. It's been a good six months since I've been here, and the lingering aroma of rubber from the tires sitting against the back wall is a familiar one. Two outdated televisions sit on old stands in two separate corners, and there's a cluttered desk in the center of the room that I intend to clear. All four walls are covered in graffiti, and sitting on a shelf is an array of paints in various forms and colors. Though, I have no plans to make art here today.

Maddox, Lev, and I frequented this depot our freshman year, because the first year here was by far the hardest.

The door closes behind us and Riley walks deeper into the room. I stroll beside her, watching her expression while she takes it all in.

"Choose your weapon," I say, and her eyes widen when they land on the rack of golf clubs, baseball bats, and wooden boards.

Riley opts for a golf club, which is a good choice, but not as good as mine, which is a metal bat. I pat the tip of it to my palm a couple times. "Ready to break some shit, Angel?" I slip her goggles over her head and hand her a pair of gloves.

Once she's got the strap adjusted, and she's looking sexy as hell with those big plastic bug eyes, she gushes. "Let's do this."

When she put on a dress for our date, I couldn't keep the smile off my face. Watching her destroy shit looking every bit of the angel she is, is going to be my undoing. I can see the slight hesitation in her eyes now, and it's cute as fuck, but I take the lead, so she feels confident to enjoy herself.

Walking over to one of the televisions, I bring my bat back and swing it forward like an avenging angel. It smashes into the screen with a satisfying crunch, and the sound is music to my ears. Pieces of glass crash to the floor, shattering into a thousand shards at my feet. Then I swing the bat back and do it again, already feeling the weight of the world lifting from my shoulders.

Once the screen is completely dismantled, I step aside so Riley can partake. "Give it your best shot."

Her nose scrunches, as if she could potentially get in trouble for this. "I just hit it?"

"No, you don't just hit it. You smash the fuck out of it." I raise my bat and smash it down onto the top of the screen. The vibration of the hit reverberates through my hands and up my arms.

Riley comes up beside me, takes a deep breath, then

swings her club at the TV. Her eyes widen with glee, and she smiles back at me. "Damn, that felt good."

"Right? Do it again."

Next thing I know, she's swinging the club left and right. Beating the fuck out of everything around us, and the sight is everything I could have ever dreamed of and more. If I thought I was swinging with the force of an avenging angel, she looks like one.

"Get mad at it, girl. Yell, scream, kick!" I egg her on, hoping she uses this opportunity to get rid of all the shit she's been holding in.

Doing exactly what I said, she beats the TV off the stand and it crashes to the cement floor. Once it's down, she doesn't stop. She kicks and hits and screams. "Fuck you, you stupid TV. You're old and ugly and I don't like you one bit."

Not exactly what I had in mind, but whatever works for her.

I toss my bat down and grab a tire, looping it around my arm, then I swing it back as far as I can and chuck it at the wall. "We can't be stopped," I scream at the top of my lungs. "We will fucking reign over The Society. Fuck every one of you Elders and your rules and your money."

We go to town, tearing shit up. Screaming and beating inanimate objects, as if they were our own worst enemies.

"You deserved to die, you sick bastard," Riley roars. "I'm not even a little bit sorry."

Now we're getting somewhere.

Before long, I'm no longer breaking shit, and I'm just watching Riley instead. She doesn't even notice I've stopped, just beats the hell out of anything in her path. Somehow, she's ended up at the desk with an old adding machine under the head of her club.

"...this one's for you, Lev. You think you have the power when you order me around, but I'm the one with the power. You need me so much more than I need you."

I walk closer, drowning out the smashing sounds, while listening to her truth spill from her mouth.

"You should be thanking me. You said so yourself, I'm the only person who can make you feel anything at all."

Suddenly, she stops. Her head turns slowly, sweat accumulating on her forehead. Her entire body is shaking as she tosses down the golf club.

She gulps. "How much of that did you hear?"

My eyes blink rapidly as I process her confession. "Enough." I take a couple steps toward her when she braces herself on the desk behind her. "Did you have some sort of breakthrough with Lev?"

Saying it out loud makes it seem that much more impossible. *That's what he's been up to.* No one has been able to get through Lev's barriers. His walls are stacked so high around him, Maddox and I were positive he'd die before he even saw the sun.

"I...I think I did."

This changes everything. Every-fucking-thing I thought I knew about the two of them, not that I really knew anything at all. I was prepared to go to war with Lev over Riley. Because, of course, I'd choose her. I'd choose her over anyone. I thought whatever he had going on with Riley came from a place of anger—just to hurt her.

Now, standing right in front of her, I sweep her sticky hair out of her eyes. "Has he been good to you?"

"No," she says exasperatedly. "It's Lev. But he hasn't been all that bad. There are moments where I feel like I can see into his soul, and it's not as dark as I'd expected it to be."

Lev's my boy. Aside from Riley, he and Maddox are the most important people in my life. If there is hope for him, then who am I to stand in the way.

"Don't give up on him. Okay?"

Riley's head jerks back and her mouth falls open. "Are you for real right now? You're encouraging me to hang out with Lev?"

"I guess I am." I slide up to her, feeling the rapid beat of her heart against mine. "But I'm not going anywhere. Don't think I'm gonna let you forget about me in the process."

Her arms wrap around my head and she pulls my mouth to hers. "Couldn't even try."

AS MY GAZE dances around the moonlit area, I take in every exquisite detail. The fragrant scent of white roses from a crystal vase in the center of a small wrought-iron table set for two. Little flickers of light from tiny white bulbs strung along the tree branches that surround the garden. It's breathtaking, and I'm rendered speechless.

"Well," Ridge says as he joins my side, "what do you think?"

I steal a glance at him, expecting him to be dressed in some fancy suit because this is most definitely a fancy scene. But I'm actually happy to see he's dressed in his normal attire because it's him. He doesn't dress to impress or say the words he thinks someone else wants to hear. It's one of the things I admire most about Ridge. He's unequivocally *him*.

"It's...wow. Absolutely amazing. I can't believe you did all this."

"Eh. It was nothing. Got a little help from some freshman football players, and had it set up within the hour."

After the rage room, I was caked in sweat and in dire need of a shower, so Ridge walked me back to my dorm and said to meet him here—in the botanical garden, just a short walk from The Square.

It's so beautiful here, and I'm not sure why I haven't visited this place more often. Every shrub imaginable lines the pathways, spilling over into the grass. Flowers of all different sizes sway in the breeze and the scent of their petals fill the air. There's a small man-made pond tucked in a corner with a fountain in the center that is constantly running. Everything here is so perfect—like something right out of a movie.

At the start of our date, I was certain we'd be having muffins in the student center or eating junk food on the steps in front of the library, which would have been completely fine with me. I'm easily impressed and not hard to please. But this...this is spectacular.

I turn to look at Ridge, my heart nearly in my throat as tears prick at the corners of my eyes. "No one's ever done anything like this for me before."

Ridge tucks my hair behind my ears and his eyes travel down to my mouth. "That's because you've been hanging with all the wrong men. I have every intention of making you feel special, every single day, from here on out."

"You already do," I tell him honestly. "You have no idea how much of a terrifying blessing you've been."

We both laugh because it's all so true.

"Well, who else would take you to a rage room to unleash all your anger, as you scream your secrets out at the top of your lungs?"

I slap my hand to my face in embarrassment. "In my

defense, my adrenaline was pumping so fast, I didn't know what I was doing, or saying."

"That's the whole point, Angel. I always knew you were a tough girl, but tonight proved just how tough you are. Remind me to never take you golfing when you're pissed, by the way."

I swat his shoulder playfully and push him back. "Are you gonna feed me, or what, smartass?"

Pivoting on his heel, Ridge takes my hand and leads me to the table. In the center, beside the flower vase, is a large silver platter with a lid. Beside that are two smaller platters and a clear bottle of some maple-colored liquid. "Paper plates, huh?" I giggle as Ridge pulls out my chair.

"Options are limited in these parts. However, I did have a couple guys from the culinary program whip us up something delicious for dinner." My chair slides in and Ridge rounds the table to his seat.

"You really thought of everything, didn't you?"

I watch him from across the table as he speaks, using his hands to really punctuate his points. But I don't hear the words coming out of his mouth. All I hear is the steady beat of my heart as it accelerates with each passing second. And all I see is him. A guy who, months ago, had me convinced he was unhinged when he said, with the utmost confidence, that one day I'd fall for him just as hard as he fell for me. My cheeks flush with warmth when I realize that's exactly where I'm at. Falling faster, and harder, than I ever knew possible.

You came with no warning,
as my soul heard your cries.
My heart begged me to run from you,
but now I'm lost in your eyes.

"Brace yourself," Ridge beams, snapping me out of my

slumber as he lifts the lid on the larger platter, "because I doubt you ever expected..." His voice rises in pitch. "Pancakes for dinner.

"Oh my god, Ridge," I laugh, covering my mouth, "you did not!"

"Oh, I did. Because I know how much you love pancakes. And, of course, we have lemonade for our beverage tonight." He lifts the lids on the smaller platters. "And bacon and eggs."

"This is...amazing. Really," I tilt my head to the side and stare at him adoringly, "I couldn't ask for a better dinner."

"Knew you'd like it." He jabs one of the pancakes with a fork and drops it on my plate.

"Syrup." I pick up the clear bottle. "That's what this is. I was wondering."

"Not just any syrup. That's lukewarm maple syrup."

His excitement for all of this makes him that much more adorable. I can tell he put so much thought into tonight, and he is one hundred percent getting laid when we get back to my room.

We get our pancakes ready in silence, every once in a while making eye contact. I take the first bite, and it's heaven. A deep hum of pleasure vibrates from my chest. "So good," I tell him, licking the thick syrup from my lips as I stick another bite in my mouth.

Ridge jabs his fork in the air. "Knew you'd like it."

"You can never go wrong with pancakes."

Biting another piece of pancake off his fork, Ridge asks, "What are some other things I can't go wrong with?" He taps the side of his head. "I'm taking notes for the future."

"Hmm." I think about it, trying to pull from memory all

the things I love. "Poetry. Sweet little notes." I nod toward the flowers. "Absolutely love roses."

"And what is it you love that isn't a thing or an object?"

I take a big bite, chewing while I think. "Rain. I love the sound and the smell, and watching it fall from the window."

"You ever danced in the rain?"

"Can't say that I have."

"We're gonna have to change that. Now tell me something you hate?"

"Easy. Silence. There's just something about being alone with my thoughts that makes me anxious. Unless I've got a pen and paper handy to jot down my thoughts, I prefer to be surrounded by noise."

"I could argue that silence is beautiful if you're in the right company." He lifts a smile. "So many times I've sat in silence while watching you, and it was my most favorite sound."

I can feel my cheeks blushing. Ridge compliments me all the time, and I'm not sure his compliments will ever stop making me feel giddy. I hope they don't. The feeling I get in my stomach—that tingling butterfly flutter—it reminds me of the feeling you get in a new relationship. That 'can't eat, can't sleep, daydream of him' sort of feeling. Now that I think about it, I've been getting that a lot with both Ridge and Maddox. And a couple days ago, I felt it with Lev.

"You're turn," I tell him. "Start with something you dislike."

"So many things. But most of all, lies."

"Same. The true colors of people begin to show through their lies. Okay. What's something you love?"

"You," he says without hesitation.

I reach across the table, my elbow landing in a pile of

syrupy goo, but I don't even care. I take his hand, thumb grazing the calloused skin on the top of his knuckle where one of his tattoos is. "You make me feel so special, Ridge."

He locks our fingers together and stares down at them. "You have no idea how much I needed to hear that." His eyes lift to mine. "It goes to show that everything I did, everything I'm doing, is all worth it."

"Thank you," I tell him. "For not giving up, I mean."

"Never, Angel. Every time I see you, it feels like I'm taking my first breath. Every time you would walk away, I feared it would be the last. I was suffocating without you. My entire world, all of my existence, rides on us. So now I'm asking you not to give up."

My heart pangs. It's an agonizing feeling when it's being called in so many different directions. But I know my heart is safe with Ridge, and I'd be crazy to walk away from this, even if I'm sharing it with someone else. "I'm not going anywhere."

We finish eating, while talking about more of the things we love and hate. Turns out, Ridge likes pineapple on his pizza. Never saw that one coming, because I do, too. I actually argued the topic in my debate class my sophomore year. Another thing Ridge loves...snakes. That I can't agree on because snakes freak me the hell out.

This night has been enlightening. I've been looking at Ridge with new eyes for a few days now, and after this evening, I can only describe what I'm feeling as euphoria. With every passing minute, my adoration for him grows. He illuminates a darkness inside me, and I meant it when I said I'm not going anywhere.

"WHAT'S on your mind today, Lev?"

I glower at Dr. Edmonds, my hatred for him burning into the depths of my soul. He always does this shit. Tries to dig deep and pull out my demons.

"Nothing," I snap back.

I know it's his job, and I know he's the best at what he does, which is exactly why I continue to talk to him—only him.

The truth is, I don't really hate him at all. But I do hate the way he tries to make me feel.

"Do you think it's time to go back to that night yet?"

"Don't," I grit out. "Don't you fucking dare even try."

I changed my mind—I do hate him.

His hands go up, landing softly on his crossed legs. "All right. You're the one in control. I'm just here to listen."

A few moments of silence pass, but a nightmare I had is sitting heavy on my mind today. I can feel the words climbing up my throat, a dire urge to get them out, but I fight it. I fight it so damn hard because once I unleash them, I can't take them back.

"I dreamt about them last night," I spit out on impulse. I didn't want to. The words just shot out of my mouth and now they're free. I jump to my feet, my entire body ready to break out in a cold sweat as I pace in front of the loveseat.

"Care to tell me about it?"

Fuck no. But instead, I say, "Maybe."

Dr. Edmonds's eyes grow wide in surprise, and I'm sure it's because this is the first time I've ever agreed to anything he's asked. As he said, *I'm the one in control,* and I've kept it that way since I was fourteen years old.

"Have you been taking your medication, Lev?" The seriousness in his tone unsettles me—confuses me, rather.

"Why the fuck are you asking me that? I told you I had a nightmare and you ask me about my damn medication?" Dr. Edmonds must be off his rocker today, because he's been grasping at the opportunity to get inside my head for years.

"I'd just like to be sure. I assume that's a yes?"

"Yes." My voice rises and the irritation I'm feeling becomes obvious. "Yes, I've been taking my fucking medication." It's a boldfaced lie because I haven't been taking it.

"Very good." He crosses his legs tighter and sinks back into the chair with his pen pinched between his fingers. "Now tell me about this dream."

"Nightmare," I correct him. "It was a fucking nightmare. And you know what? I don't wanna talk about it anymore. You ruined it. Good job, Doc." I head for the door, ready to kick my foot through it, but instead, I pull myself together and open it the proper way. Doesn't mean I don't slam the shit out of it behind me, though.

As soon as it latches, I draw in a deep breath. My hands

jab straight into the front pockets of my jeans, and I pace. Back and forth, over and over again, in front of the door.

Dr. Edmonds won't come out. We do this every meeting. Sometimes I go back in. Sometimes I don't.

But fuck, I gotta tell someone about this nightmare or it's going to live rent-free in my head every time I'm awake. And when I sleep, it's going to slither back in like a snake in the grass.

After fifteen minutes have passed and I've calmed myself down, I jerk the door back open again.

"I'll call you back," Dr. Edmonds says into his phone before tapping the screen and setting it on the round end table beside him.

I stop in the doorway, glowering at him. "Who was that?"

"My wife. It was just a short call." He chuckles. "She asked me to pick up dinner on the way home."

"What are you doing right now, Dr. Edmonds?"

His expression goes stoic. "I'm here. In a meeting with you."

I step farther into the room and swing the door closed behind me. "And how much do I pay you hourly?"

The level of intimidation he feels at this moment is crystal clear. He clears his throat and straightens his back while casting down his eyes at his notebook. "Two hundred dollars an hour, plus extra for the inconvenience of the drive here."

"That's right. Two hundred fucking dollars an hour. And I don't pay it to you so you can make dinner plans with your wife."

"You had stepped out, so I assumed—"

"Assumed what? That the time clock stopped? Or that I was simply wasting your precious time?"

"Not at all. I apologize if you feel that way."

"I dreamt that I shot them," I shout. "Okay? That's what my fucking nightmare was. I dreamt that I pulled the trigger and I was the one who murdered my whole family." My words crack and splinter and I choke as the words leave my mouth. "I looked into Alana's sweet eyes and I shot her in the chest."

"Lev..."

"Do you even fucking care at all, or is this just a paycheck to you?"

I can't help the unstoppable force that comes over me as I trudge toward him. Grabbing his phone that's plugged into the charger on the wall, I rip it off. "You have a fucking family to bring dinner home to! I don't!" I slam his phone on the floor then grab the round table and swing it around, letting it fly from my hands and into the wall. "I have nobody!"

Dr. Edmonds shoots to his feet. "Lev." His hands rise then lower. "Have a seat and we will talk this through. This is your safe space."

I side-eye him, snarling, "Is it, though? Is it really safe? Because I'm starting to think you don't really want to be here and if you don't want to be here, you can't help me."

"Of course I want to be here. I'd come for free, you know that. I've told you so many times. You're like a son to me. This is more than just a job."

A calmness washes over me. "But you have a son. You can't really tell me you care about me in the same way you care about him." I feel like a child who is making a parent choose. Not that Dr. Edmonds is my parent, but there's a part of me that needs to hear him elaborate on that. A part of me that needs to feel cared for.

"Yes," he says. "Julian is only six years old. I've known you since my wife was pregnant with him. "I care deeply for you, Lev."

I drop down on the couch and rest my head back. Eyes closed, I allow the calm to wash over me. Dr. Edmonds gives me the time to decompress and when I'm ready, I lift my head. "I'm ready to talk," I tell him.

Even I'm surprised as the words just spill out of my mouth. I tell him all about my nightmare and how it made me feel. Then I tell him about Riley, and how she makes me feel.

"Ridge calls her Angel, and I'm starting to see why. She's changing me, Doc. I can feel myself getting better."

Dr. Edmonds cautions me against jumping into a relationship while I'm still working on myself, but I make it clear I am *not* looking for a relationship.

"What's the endgame with this girl, then? Where do you see this arrangement going?"

"Honestly, I have no plan. Each day I take it wherever the fuck I want it to go. And she follows. Because I give her no choice."

"SILENCE IS BEAUTIFUL," I repeat the words Ridge said the other night as I fight to see the beauty in the quiet around me.

I sink into the comfortable plushness of the old couch I cleaned. Yesterday, I toted all the cushion covers to the dormitory laundry room and washed them—twice. Then, I used carpet cleaner to scrub the back side of the couch.

The sun is shining through the windows and I make use of the light source while I've still got it. With my pen pressed to the paper in my notebook, I write...

Silence sucks.

My thoughts scream in my head.

My heart beats faster.

Louder.

Harder.

And it's silent no more.

Ugh. I slam the notebook shut with my pen wedged between the pages. For the last few days, I've had a terrible time expressing my thoughts on paper. It's as if I can only write when I'm down and depressed. Guess I should be happy I'm not living in that headspace anymore.

I look around the dainty space. A lilac-scented candle on the small table in the kitchenette flickers, the flame dancing off the walls. My entire day was spent here yesterday and I'm pretty proud of the work I accomplished.

When I started cleaning up this place, I planned to use it as my own little reprieve. A quiet place where I could go for solitude. Although, I seem to have forgotten how much I dread being alone with my thoughts. But they're not drifting into the darkness like they have for the past year. Instead, I keep seeing them—Ridge, Maddox, and even Lev.

Times like this, when I'm all alone, I remember the way my body felt with each of their hands all over it. My eyes close, picturing each one of them in awe as they fucked me. I see them individually, then I see them all at the same time.

Bending my knees, I separate my legs, my heels positioned so that they rest just beneath my ass. My fingers graze over the soft curve of my stomach before dipping below the elastic band of my sweatpants. Bristles of hair poke at my palm as I smooth my hand down, dragging my fingers up to my clit.

The air brushes against my skin as I sink farther down into the couch. I know I'm alone, but the thought of anyone looking in a window and seeing me touch myself is terrifying.

With two fingers, I massage my sensitive nub. A wave of pleasure courses through me and I chase the feeling, rubbing faster and faster. My head falls back, chin up, and I open my mouth, allowing the sounds to climb up my throat. No one can hear me. I'm all alone. *Maybe being alone isn't always so bad.*

I slide my fingers down and angle my hand just right, so I can push two fingers inside myself. Then I drive them in and out, in and out. My fingers are short, so it doesn't feel nearly as good as when one of the guys does it.

Hand still down my pants, I lift up and look around the room in search of something to aid in my pleasure. I wasn't a total prude before the guys and I do have toys, but they're not here and I'm so desperate for this release.

My eyes land on the foot-long Maglite I brought with me, just in case the sun has set already when I go back to campus.

Pulling my hand out of my pants, I jump up and hurry across the room to grab it. I unscrew the back and quickly pop the batteries out, letting them drop onto the table. The length is intimidating, but I have no plans to use even a quarter of it. I wrap my fingers around the end of it. It's only got about an inch girth, but it'll definitely get the job done.

I go straight to the kitchen sink and wash it really good.

Once I'm sure it's clean, I go back to the couch and take off my sweatpants and panties.

Completely naked from the waist down, I lie back again. Legs spread, I position the opposite end of the reflector at my entrance. The cold metal sends a chill down my quivering thighs.

Feeding myself more, I slide it in inch by inch until I feel resistance from my back wall. Then I pull it out slowly, only to push it back in again. Using my other hand, I massage myself softly, feeling a sweep of adrenaline rush through me. I work the object faster, relishing in the way the grooves of the flashlight feel inside me.

Spreading my lips with my fingers, I lift my head and

watch. My muscles tighten around the flashlight and I gasp as it slips out of my hole, only to go right back in.

I feel so nasty—so naughty. But this is another secret I plan to keep.

I run my fingertips in circles and press them harder against my clit, feeling the sensation grow as I move in deeper, creating more insistent movements. My breathing quickens and I increase the pressure, until a wave of warmth spreads through me.

Rocking my hips in the same rhythm as my hand, I watch again, the visual forcing me to cry out in pleasure.

My nipples pucker against the fabric of my bra as I drag my hand up my stomach. Sliding my fingers under the loose fabric, I caress the peak. I roll my nipple between my thumb and index finger—pinching it. I imagine it's Ridge's fingers instead of mine. I imagine it's Maddox's cock inside me. And it's Lev's mouth tasting my skin. The thought arouses me further, and another whimper slips through my lips as my hips jerk off the couch.

The sound of a creaking board sends my heart into my throat as I quickly pull the object out of me and remove my hand from my breast. I jump up, into a sitting position, and all the blood drains from my face when I see Lev.

He comes strolling toward me with his mouth tugged up in a grin.

"I...I wasn't doing anything," I lie. There's no way Lev didn't see what I was doing, so there's no point in lying. Still, I hold true to it because I will never openly admit I was getting myself off with a flashlight.

"Lie down," he demands, now towering over me while I shrink into the couch in humiliation.

When I don't comply, and continue to question him with dopey eyes, Lev retaliates with a forceful shove.

He pins me against the couch with his hand around my throat. My chest heaves as he stares me down. His heavy gaze lands on mine before he climbs between my legs, snaking his way up my body until his hot breath reaches my neck.

Moving his hand, he snares the flashlight off the floor while he hovers above me. Bringing it to his mouth, he smirks as he drags his tongue down it. "Mmm. Nothing like the taste of sweet lies."

I swallow hard, feeling my throat bob. My heart is hammering inside my chest and I can't even think straight right now. *Is this really happening? Did Lev really just see me use that thing?*

"It's not what you think," I tell him. Another lie.

He smiles as he moves down my body, his breath fanning over my dripping center. "Don't be embarrassed, Trouble. We all need a release every now and then. It just makes me think your boys aren't getting the job done right, that's all."

It's not that. I am fully satisfied; sex with Maddox and Ridge is amazing. I just needed my thoughts to stop. I needed the quiet to go away. But I can't tell him that because every time I open my mouth to speak, I choke on the words.

He slides the slender object between my legs, causing me to shiver. "What...what are you doing?" I ask him, though I'm well aware of his intentions.

"Just giving you a hand." He slides the tip of it in me then lowers his head. I fall back against the couch, my treacherous body aching for him to put his lips on me.

My tense shoulders draw back and I inhale sharply as his

mouth kisses my pleasure spot. "Lev," I say his name, unsure what I intended to follow it with.

"Just relax. I've got it from here."

Two fingers part my lips and his tongue drags up and down my sex, my entire body trembling.

He gently pushes the cold object deeper inside me, the pressure increasing with each inch.

"Jesus Christ, Lev. That's enough," I shout, as I try to lift my body from the couch.

With effort, I manage to pull away slightly and look down to see half of it already inside me. But he's not stopping.

His eyes bore into mine, and he gives me a small mischievous smile before pushing it all the way inside, until every single one of its twelve inches are engulfed by my body.

I gasp and scream, my cries so loud I wouldn't be surprised if the students on campus heard me. The pressure is too much, but it also feels so good.

Ignoring my pleas, Lev keeps going, sliding it in and out while sucking on my clit. I watch as the object raises my belly button with each plunge. My breaths are ragged and unfulfilled as immense pleasure ripples through me with each deep stroke.

"Holy shit," I whimper, digging my nails into the cushion of the couch. My head falls back and my eyes roll into the back of my head. "Don't stop," I beg, barely recognizing my own voice.

He sucks and licks, using the pad of his tongue to force pressure on my sensitive spot. I start to move with his thrusts, needing more. The discomfort turns to pleasure with every stroke of his tongue and I relax into the feeling.

My mind is in a whirlwind, unable to even fathom

what's going on. This is degrading, to say the least, but I have no intention of letting it end until I've come.

Lifting my hips, I force more pressure. Lev growls into me, giving me everything I need. His tongue laps harder, before he starts a pulsating suction that has my eyes crossing.

"Oh god, Lev. I'm gonna come." I arch my back, hold my breath, and clench my muscles. The intensity of my orgasm hits like a shock wave, rippling through my body. My toes curl and my fingertips tingle as I cry out, using sounds I didn't know I could make. My breaths come in short gasps as I come down, still in a state of ecstasy.

Lev slides the flashlight out of me, but the empty feeling is short-lived. The next thing I know, he's naked on top of me. His dick slides in, filling me back up. His body rides up and down mine, writhing against my clammy skin.

Rolling his hips in slow circles, he works himself inside me, pushing deeper with each thrust. We both look down as he pushes himself all the way in, watching in rapture at the pleasure we find in each other.

Sometime between the start and now, my hands end up on his back, fingers grazing his skin. I grab his biceps as I work my hips to meet his, heading toward another release.

Lev's rapid breaths tickle my ear as he groans and shifts his hips against me, sending sparks of revelry through my body. My hands move to wrap around his neck and I force his body taut with mine as I dig my heels into the couch to create more pressure.

"Riley," he moans as he wraps his arms around me. The sound of my name on his tongue ignites something inside my chest. His scent floods my senses. A mix of spice, sweat, and desperate lust so potent I can almost taste it.

They say the line between love and hate is thin, and while I know I don't love Lev, being this close to him as we both find pleasure in each other definitely has me testing that theory.

Warmth spreads through me, and my heart rattles against my rib cage to the same beat as his. "Oh, Lev," I cry into the air.

As if my saying his name has the same effect on him, he moves faster as his pants grow heavier.

"Fuck," he bellows as his entire body trembles. He jerks and jolts, his cock as far in as it'll go as he pulses inside me.

His thrusts gradually slow, until he stills on top of me. The heat of his body seeps into mine as I run my fingers down his sweaty back. Pleasure and confusion knead inside me. I drop my hands to my sides, unsure if I want to make this moment more than what it is.

Lev just fucked me with a flashlight, then fucked me for himself. It shouldn't feel like this was more than sex, but there are emotions inside me I can't define or understand.

With gentle ease, he pulls out of me. It's a one-eighty from the briskness of his exit in the past.

Lev gets on his knees, and our slick arousal slides down the length of his cock. "Well, Trouble," he murmurs, his voice low and husky, "now I know why you wanted to fix this place up."

My face burns as I realize what he's implying—that I wanted to use his cabin as a sanctuary to get myself off.

"I don't know what you're insinuating, but that's not why I wanted to come here. This is a peaceful place for me to clear my head," I say through clenched teeth.

He chuckles, a smug look on his face. "Sure, whatever you say," he responds, his tone dripping with sarcasm.

I spring up and plant my hands to his chest, shoving him back. "Why do you always have to ruin things for me?"

He falls onto his back laughing, and all I want to do is slap the sound out of him.

"Hey," he holds his hands up, "I'm not judging. Watching you push that thing inside you may have been one of the sexiest things I've ever seen in my life. The expression you had on your face is a close second."

"Fuck you, Lev."

"Later, babe. I'm sure your pussy needs a rest after that beating."

I scowl, looking down at his crotch. "Your dick is dripping. Might wanna go clean it up."

I scramble off the couch, my skin hot and tingling as I search the floor for my clothes. Gathering them in a disheveled bundle, I hurry to the bathroom as fast as I can, slamming the door shut behind me with a loud thud.

With my hands braced on the porcelain sink, I lean over it, looking at myself in the clouded glass mirror. I can pretend to hate Lev and what he does to me, but that was one of the best orgasms I've ever had. I'll never admit that to him, though.

A minute later, Lev is pounding at the door. "How am I supposed to clean myself up if you've locked me out?" He jiggles the handle, but it doesn't open, because he's right, I did lock him out.

"Open the damn door. I've got shit to do."

"Oh yeah," I holler back. "Like what?"

"I gotta help Maddox pick up some booze in town for the party."

Party? Why didn't I hear about this?

"What *party*?"

"That stupid fall ball shit the Delta Chi chicks throw every year. Don't act like you didn't know. I saw you helping those bitches decorate The Square."

But I didn't know.

No one told me about a party. In fact, I helped them decorate for fall and not a single girl mentioned it. There's a pang in my chest and I can't help but feel like they intentionally left me out of this because I'm not one of them.

"Right," I say softly. "Guess I just forgot."

I slip on my clothes, quietly questioning what I could have done wrong for them to all of a sudden leave me out of this. It's an awful feeling, not being accepted. My confusion turns to pain, then my pain turns to anger, and...*fuck those sluts!*

I rip open the door, now face to face with Lev, who's got his hands on either side of the doorframe, still naked. My eyes drag down his chest to his semi-erect dick, then back up to his face. "Can I go with you?" I ask him. It's a risky question, but I don't wanna show up alone. I could ask Scar, but she's always so tied up with her guys.

His eyebrows pinch together. "To pick up booze?"

"No, dumbass. To the party."

"Well," he scoffs. "Not now that you called me a dumbass."

"Don't be such a baby." I push past him, still fuming over my wandering thoughts. How dare those girls fail to include me in this after I helped them decorate?

"You sure are pissy all of a sudden." It isn't until the words leave his mouth that I realize he's following behind me. He slides the zipper up on his jeans with his shirt hung around his neck. One arm slips through the sleeve, then the other.

A mixture of humiliation and anger stab at my chest. "Forget that stupid party. Didn't wanna go anyways."

Truth is, I only have an interest in going because I wasn't invited. It's a student-affiliated party and I'm a student. Not like I even need an invitation. Still, it would have been nice.

"Good," Lev quips. "You'd probably just be a drag like you always are anyways."

Fuming, I spin around. "Screw you, asshole!" I shove him back then whip around and head to the door with every intention of dragging Scar to this party with me. Once I'm out, I attempt to close the door, but Lev steps through just in time and closes it himself.

"Go away," I tell him. "I'd prefer to walk back to campus without your constant insults chirping in my ear."

"Don't be such a baby, Trouble. It's just a party."

"See," I huff. "That's exactly what I'm talking about." I mock him, "*You're a drag, Trouble. Don't be such a baby, Trouble.* God," I shout. "You're so damn insufferable."

"Dramatic much?" he mumbles under his breath, but I hear him. Oh, do I hear him.

My adrenaline is rushing, my thoughts are racing, and I'm beyond livid right now. I'm not even sure I have any control of my body when my fist flies to his face. His head jerks back and I immediately clap my hands over my mouth. "Shit, Lev. I'm so sorry."

He smooths his fingers down his cheek with an unaffected expression on his face. "You fucking hit me."

"I know..." I stumble over my words, still surprised at myself for doing that. "And I shouldn't have. I'm just so fucking pissed right now."

He takes a step toward me, tapping his cheek. "Do it again."

"What?"

"Punch me again, Trouble. You know you want to."

Sighing heavily, I shake my head and turn and keep walking. "You're insane."

"If you're pissed, make it known. You wanna hit me, hit me. You wanna scream, scream. That's the problem with people today. Everyone holds in all their damn anger until it boils to the surface."

"As opposed to you, who goes around making his fury known to everyone in its path without a care about the repercussions."

"At least I don't pretend."

"Is that what you think I'm doing, pretending? Pretty sure I just punched you." My hands fly up in the air and I drop them fast, smacking my sides. "Because I'm fucking normal. When someone does something they regret, or feel bad about, they apologize."

"Do you regret hitting me?"

"No," I deadpan. Because it's true. I'm about to do it again if he doesn't shut up.

"I hate to be the one to educate you, but an apology means you either regret it, or feel some sort of remorse. And if you don't—"

"Okay. Would you shut up?" I snap. "I take back my apology. I'm not sorry. Now leave me the hell alone."

"Why the fuck are you so pissed over a party?"

"Because," I blurt out, "I helped those girls and they never once mentioned it to me."

"Sounds like they're the ones you should be hitting. Not me."

"Maybe I will," I mumble.

A couple minutes pass in our silent walk until Lev's

frame fills my line of sight. "Meet me outside your dorm in an hour," he says before he heads up the walkway toward his dormitory.

My eyes widen and I raise my voice. "Thought you said I couldn't go with you."

With a quick glance over his shoulder, he says, "Then you hit me. Now I sort of wanna see how this night plays out."

I keep walking, biting back on the smile that threatens to spread across my face.

Lev is softening for me. I can feel it in my bones.

"YOU HAVE no idea how glad I am you're coming," I tell Scar, who's sitting cross-legged on her bed folding a week's worth of laundry that sits next to her. "The thought of going to this party with a bunch of people I barely know terrifies me."

"Oh, come on, Ry. You know people."

I skeptically glance at her. "Not well enough to call them friends."

When I got home a half hour ago, Scar was here and I was so happy to see her. I needed to vent to someone about the Delta Chi girls and this stupid party they left me out of. Needless to say, Scar changed her plans last minute and she's meeting me out there later.

"Shit," I panic when I glance at my phone on my end table and see the time, "Lev's gonna be here soon and I haven't even gotten ready. What should I wear?"

"Hmm," Scar taps her chin sarcastically, "a party outside in the dead of fall. How about something warm and not one of those skimpy dresses you like to flaunt your ass in."

"Ugh," I grumble. "There is absolutely nothing cute about warm clothes."

Scar rummages through her overflowing pile of laundry and tosses a pair of jeans at me. I catch them in midair before a hoodie smacks me in the face. "Problem solved," she says with a satisfied grin.

I hold both articles of clothing up before tossing them back at her. "No thanks." Then I rummage through my own drawers and decide on a pair of beige leggings, a black crop top, and an oversized black-and-beige checkered flannel. I lay them out on the bed, pleased with my choice. "How's this with a pair of knee-high boots?"

"Your stomach's gonna freeze."

Scar and I are polar opposites when it comes to fashion. She's more goth, and I'm more chic. Naturally, we like to give each other shit, even though we both look hot as fuck no matter what we wear.

I scoff at her remark. "Such a pessimist."

"I prefer realist."

"Either way, it's a mood killer."

Twenty minutes later, I'm twirling around to show off my outfit and bouncy curls. "Cute, right?"

"You look great, babe."

"Thank ya." I bow. "Now get your ass ready."

Scar drops back on the bed and grunts. "I'll be there as soon as I finish this never-ending pile of laundry."

"Wish I could help you," I tell her as I look at my phone in my hand. "But Lev's probably down there now." I head for the door, stopping in front of it. "See you soon?"

She nods against the mattress. "See you soon."

As I slowly pull the door closed, a feeling of dread begins

to take hold. I can't stop thinking about how those girls had the opportunity to tell me about the party, but instead just bossed me around like their own personal slave. I never wanted to be part of their little gang, but I helped out because, as a Guardian, it's what's expected of me. Not to mention, I like decorating. So to know I helped them and they didn't at least have the courtesy to ask me to come to the party or even tell me about it, doesn't sit well with me.

What a bunch of fake bitches.

I've thought about all the words I'll say to them when I see them. What I'll do to get my point across, that it's rude to use people. But my resolve starts to falter as I walk through the halls alone.

My hand slides down the banister and I'm dragging my feet when I see Lev through one of the glass panes beside the door. A strange feeling stirs inside me—one I didn't expect. It's a combination of nerves and giddiness.

I never thought Lev would have such a profound effect on me. Everything with him has been going by in a blur. I started out hating him, then had hate sex with him, and now I get this rush of excitement whenever we're together. Sure, there's still some anger and resentment that lingers beneath the surface. But they tend to fade away when I'm around him...at least, until he makes a stupid comment and they come back again.

Before I even make it to the door, it opens. Standing in the frame is Lev, wearing a pair of black jeans that hug his ankle-high combat boots. He's sporting a black BCU hoodie and looks really fricken hot in it. His hair is a disheveled mess, but it only adds to his appeal.

I stop on the bottom step, drinking him in, while he does

the same to me. His gaze drags up and down my body. The cold gust of wind is no match for the heat of his stare.

The moment Lev's eyes finally reach mine, I can see the shift in his demeanor. No longer engulfed in me, he's quickly snapped back to his own reality. "Are you fucking ready or what?"

"Yeah, Lev." I chuckle. "I'm ready."

I slide past him in the doorway and he pulls the door closed. "What's so damn funny?" He huffs in irritation.

"You and your cocky attitude." I jog down the stairs and keep moving when my feet hit the sidewalk. "If I don't laugh it off, then I plot your murder in my head. Therefore, you're welcome."

"Now you plot them? Thought you murdered on impulse."

"Only yours." I press my lips into a tight smile. "When it happens, it's going to be the most perfect, agonizing death."

"I'm not even surprised, Killer."

"Oh. It's Killer now? What happened to Trouble?"

"One for each of your personalities."

"Wow. You're really on a roll tonight. All this because of a laugh."

"Just getting myself mentally prepared for a torturous night by your side."

"Whoa," I hold up my hand, "no one said you had to stick by my side. I just wanted someone to go with so I'm not walking in there alone."

Lev claps his hand over his heart dramatically. "Ouch."

"Don't even pretend you have feelings. I know better."

"Watch out!" Lev shouts, just as my body is yanked recklessly to the left. My feet stumble on a loose stone, but Lev's arms catch me before I fall. When I look up, I see three guys laughing their asses off as they barely dodge us on their skateboards. They keep going, the wheels clattering against the pavement.

"What the hell!" I holler at them, as they steal cheeky glances over their shoulders until they disappear in the night.

"You stupid motherfuckers," Lev roars. "Just wait until I get my hands on you."

It isn't until I've steadied my heart rate that I realize Lev's hand is on my side. I glance down at it and he notices the gesture, immediately jerking his arm back and sticking his hand in his pocket.

"Thank you," I say softly. "Death by a skateboard stampede would be a terrible way to go."

Lev waves his free hand in the air and keeps walking down the sidewalk. "Don't mention it. Besides, do you really think I'd let you go out that easily after you've spent so much time plotting a meaningful death for me?"

I chuckle inwardly. "Guess not."

Lev clears his throat, his voice now brash and masculine. "I'm gonna fucking strangle them, though. No thought process behind it. If I see them, they're dead."

"Uh-huh. I'm sure you will."

"What's with the sarcasm, Trouble? You don't think I'm capable?"

I shrug my shoulders. "I think anyone is capable when pushed far enough. I just don't think almost getting hit by a couple dumb-ass guys would justify being pushed to that level of insanity."

"Says the girl who just told me I have no feelings."

I pinch my thumb and index finger and hold my hand up. "You might have a little bit of feelings. Barely there. Hardly even noticeable. But there *might* be a sympathetic bone in your body."

Lev stops walking, covering his heart. "Why, Trouble. That's the nicest thing anyone's ever said to me." Then he drops the sarcasm and fake smile and keeps walking.

"Don't get all pissy, Lev. We both know..." *Dammit. I'm not sure how to say this without totally ruining the night.* "You're not exactly the endearing type."

"You don't have to beat around the bush, because we both know it. I'm fucked up. But I'd like to see any fucking person go through what I did and come out sane."

I'm still not sure what happened to Lev, but it has me wondering what he was like before this traumatic event. Out of respect for him, I don't dare ask. I've learned that people who experience trauma never truly return back to who they were before. So, to ask wouldn't make a difference because he's no longer that person, and he never will be again. Not that he'd tell me anyway. I'm not even sure Ridge or Maddox would.

Instead, I stay silent for the remainder of the walk, imagining a kinder Lev in my head. A boy with a bright future ahead of him. One who probably cracked jokes and fought with his siblings. If he even has any.

The sounds of laughter and chatter from the partygoers rings louder and louder as we approach The Square.

Before we reach the roaring crowd, I decide to see if he might open up to me about this one thing. "Hey, Lev. Do you have any brothers or sisters?"

His eyes snap to mine, the icy blue orbs glowing under

the lamppost above us. "We're here. I did my part. Now get lost, Trouble."

I gulp, hating that I said anything at all. The truth is, I don't want him to walk away from me. But he is. And a minute later, he's submerged in a group of girls and I'm all alone, yet surrounded by a hundred people.

SITTING on the branch of a tree on the outskirts of The Square, I don't take my eyes off Riley. I could be down there, mingling with the crowd, or even following her around. But up here, I get the best view. It's the only way I can be certain she's safe. Cade might be gone, but eliminating one bad guy doesn't mean they all just disappear. There's a whole slew of horny men down there, just waiting for the opportunity to worm in on my girl. She's hands down the most gorgeous girl here, and probably one of the most vulnerable.

Her sad eyes dance around the crowd as she hugs tightly to her woven plaid jacket. She looks lost, even though she knows exactly where she is. I'm not sure why she even came to this party. Riley is too good for all these people.

Fuck it. She needs me.

My ass slides off the branch, fingers wrapped around it, and I'm ready to drop my feet to the ground, when someone approaches her. Shifting back up on the branch, I straighten my back and watch the situation play out.

It's a guy. He's wearing a slate gray hoodie with Marvel

across the center, and a pair of blue jeans. When I spot the slip-on Hey Dudes on his feet, I'm certain he's harmless. Pretty sure the dude's a sophomore named Parker, and I'm also certain he's been simping Melody Higgins.

Walk away, Riley. Last thing you need is another mud wrestling match with that bitch.

Riley's gaze flickers over his shoulder as she talks, never looking him in the eye. She's trying to find an out. Suddenly, her hand lifts and she points past him, then smiles and walks away as if she's just spotted her best friend in the crowd.

But she didn't.

She walks about ten feet in front of her, tucks into a group of people, then pokes her head out to see if he's looking. A smile spreads across my face.

That's my girl.

And that's exactly why I'm up here. Had that been a guy like Cade, she'd be getting coerced into walking away with him right now. Then I'd be forced to follow and I'd likely murder the guy.

No one fucks with my angel.

I watch intently as she approaches the coolers of booze Lev and Maddox brought. Flipping the top, she reaches in and pulls out a skinny can. After careful inspection of what she's about to drink, she cracks it open and takes a long sip. Pleased with the taste, she grabs another and stuffs the spare in the pocket of her jacket.

Riley is always thinking ahead.

"Dude."

It isn't until Maddox's voice hits my ears that I realize he's standing beneath me. He jumps up and slaps my boot. "What the fuck are you doing up there?"

"Watching. Waiting. Contemplating."

"Have you seen Riley?" He looks over his shoulder, searching the crowd. "I can't find her anywhere."

"Have I seen Riley?" I mock him. "Do you even know who you're talking to?"

"Right. Right." He spins around, facing the party. "So where is she?"

An airy laugh climbs up my throat. "I might let you get down with the girl, but don't think for a second I'm making it easy for you. Go find her your damn self."

Reaching into my pocket, I pull out my mini binoculars. These wasted thirty seconds of talking with Maddox has me losing sight of her.

"All right. I see how it is." Maddox scoffs. "But keep watching because I'm about to find her and I have every intention of giving you a show."

Ignoring him, I press the binoculars to my eyes and sweep the crowd. *Where the hell did she go?*

I keep looking, and each minute that passes has my heart beating faster and faster.

"Come on, Angel," I whisper. "Show me your face so I know you're okay."

I'm prepared to jump off this branch in thirty seconds if I don't see her. With one leg hanging low, I teeter on the edge.

Fifteen. Fourteen. Thirteen.

My heart jumps when I finally spot her. *About damn time.*

"Who the fuck is that?"

I lean outward, watching through my binoculars as she takes a bottle from the same guy she just walked away from. "Parker," I grit out. "Give the bottle back, Angel. Don't you do it. You don't know what's in that thing."

Fuck. She drank it.

She's *still* drinking it.

Inching forward just a tad more, I try to read the label on the bottle, but I lose my balance and slip off the branch.

Dropping a good six feet, I crash to the ground, landing on my back. "Son of a bitch," I grumble, rubbing a sore spot on my ass.

Rolling my shoulders, I sit up and snatch my binoculars out of the thicket and stick them back in my pocket.

With no time to lose, I get on my feet and search for her on foot.

Love can be brutally painful—physically and emotionally. But I'd withstand a thousand wounds and fall from a hundred trees just to be certain she's okay.

With thorns stuck in my jeans and an arm-length scratch from the branch, I trek through the weeds and keep walking once I'm on the pavement.

Five minutes later, I see her. She's laughing with a group of people, one being Parker and another being Maddox.

The second I see Maddox bump his chest into Parker's, I barrel through the crowd, heading straight for them. I don't stop until I'm grabbing Parker by the head and throwing him forward like a bowling ball.

"Ridge!" Riley gasps, one arm spread between me and Parker, and the other between Maddox and Parker. "For the love of God, would you two stop? We were just talking."

My gaze slides down her shirt, but it's not her shirt. "What the hell is that?" I nod toward Parker's Marvel hoodie wrapped around *my* girl's body. "Get that shit off right now!"

Maddox and Parker continue to spew vile words at each other, but my focus is solely on Riley.

She peers down at the horrid shirt she's wearing. It probably smells like him. Now *she's* gonna smell like him. "I spilled a drink on my jacket and Parker was kind enough to let me wear his sweatshirt."

"Take it off."

"What?" She scoffs. "No. It's cold."

Without hesitation, I rip my hoodie off my head and throw it at her. It rolls down her stomach and drops to the pavement. "Take his fucking shirt off."

When she still doesn't, I take it upon myself to grab the hem of the shirt and lift up. She resists and squirms, trying to fight me but I don't give in. "Dammit, Angel." My voice rises in pitch. "Take the fucking thing off, now!"

Finally, she's free of it, but not after a fight.

"And didn't you learn your damn lesson about accepting drinks from strangers? Don't fucking do it!" Still fuming, I kick up my hoodie at her, but it falls back to the ground. "Put that on so you don't freeze."

"You're unbelievable!" she snaps, obviously pissed. But that's okay. She'll calm down and when she does, she'll understand why I don't want her wearing some douchebag's cologne-scented hoodie. And it's the good smelling shit at that. Now I'm gonna inhale this fucker's scent for the rest of the night.

Riley aggressively snares my hoodie off the ground and pulls it on, the scowl on her face never faltering. While she hates eating her pride like this, I'm thoroughly enjoying it.

Maddox's voice rises behind me and I spin around just as his fist lands on Parker's nose. "Damnnnn," I drawl. "Fucking go, Maddox!" It's not often we see Maddox's feisty side and it's definitely one I think he needs to display more often.

Parker cups his nose in his hand and curses a few times before backing away and retreating.

Riley grips the sides of her head as fury radiates from her in waves. "I cannot believe you guys. How dare you!" She pivots on her heel and pushes her way through the crowd that's gathered around us, her head hung low in embarrassment.

"You or me?" Maddox asks, referring to which one of us should go after her.

"Think this one might take us both. She's pretty fucking mad."

As we're following behind her, I ball Parker's sweatshirt in my arms, bringing it along with me.

A few minutes later, she finally stops when she sees Scar. Instantly, she throws herself into her friend's arms. Just when I think she's crying, I'm proven wrong when she lifts her head up and a wide smile is on her face.

"I'm so glad you're here." Riley hooks her arm around Scar's and shoots Maddox and me a death glare before pulling her away.

"Let her go," I tell Maddox. "She needs some time, and she's in good hands for the time being."

"YOU HAVING FUN?" Scar asks as she zips up her black sweat-jacket.

"I was," I grumble. Just thinking about the way Ridge and Maddox behaved has me furious again. "All I was doing was talking to a guy—"

"Let me stop you right there." Scar puts a hand on my shoulder. "Lemme guess. They both lost their shit and the poor guy you were talking to ended up licking his wounds as he was forced away?"

"How do you even know that?"

"Ry," she deadpans. "Have you forgotten who my boyfriends are?"

My forehead creases prominently and my shoulders sulk. "It's not normal, though. Is it?"

"Well, hello there." A man's voice comes from behind me. I glance over my shoulder to find two guys I've never seen before. One pair of eyes undressing my body, while the other does the same to Scar. "Why don't we go fill those empty hands with drinks?"

Out of nowhere, Neo and Crew appear, forcing their bodies in front of us like a shield. "Not a chance in hell," Neo barks, shoving one of the guys away, while Crew does the same to the other.

"Walk away while you still can," Crew says as the guys turn and practically run away.

Scar and I share a look as we burst out laughing. "You see," she says. "I'm right there with ya, babe." Her eyes dart to Neo before she slithers up to him and presses her lips to his.

"And no, it's not normal," Scar says, still looking at her men. "But I wouldn't change it for the world."

I stand to the side and watch as Jagger approaches, crowding Scar from behind and asking about what happened. They all surround her and I smile as I see my friend getting the kind of love she deserves. I've always been a tad envious of what she has while I sit on the sidelines. They all worship the ground she walks on and stand as guard dogs, willing to do anything to protect her.

There's a qualm in my stomach at the realization that Ridge and Maddox are doing the exact same for me. A sweep of contentedness washes over me—giddiness, even. Then suddenly, I'm hit with a wave of guilt. I treated them so awful when they were only trying to protect me like normal boyfriends do.

Oh my god. Is that what they are?

No. That's crazy. I don't even have one boyfriend, let alone two.

But maybe...maybe that's where this is headed.

"Hey, I'll catch up with you all in a bit," I tell Scar and the guys.

"Eh," Crew makes a noise. "Probably best if you don't wander around here alone, Ry."

"It's The Square." I chuckle. "I'll be fine."

"That's what they all say," he croons. "Right before they're dragged into the woods, raped, and murdered."

"Whoa." I raise my hand and lower it slowly. "Calm down on the dramatics. I'm going to find Ridge and Maddox, and I can guarantee they won't let anything happen to me."

As I step away, a smile plants firmly on my face and my stomach pools with warmth. I could credit it to the shots I've taken tonight, but I think it's more so the epiphany I just had. The staggering steps, though, now that's the booze. Regardless, I'm feeling pretty damn good. That is until an invisible force sends me flying forward. Before I can catch my balance, I crash into none other than Melody Higgins.

"Watch it, whore," she snickers.

I cackle back at her, mocking her tone. "Gladly, *whore*." I go to step past her, but I'm halted by her hand being tossed out in front of me.

"Why are you here?"

My eyebrows cave in and I plant my hands on my hips. "Excuse me?"

"You heard me," she leans in with a nasty smirk on her face, "why are you here?"

"Why wouldn't I be here, Melody? It's a party."

"It was supposed to be a Delta Chi party, yet here you are. Then again, you always seem to end up everywhere we are. Just like you always seem to end up bouncing on a new dick every week."

Then it hits me. It was Melody who orchestrated this little ploy to keep me out of the loop.

"You bitch!" I lunge at her full force, aiming for her soft

midsection. My fist swings out to knock the wind out of her, but she sees me coming and raises her hands between us. My fist connects with the air, but I'm not stopping. I lunge again, this time going straight for her weak spot, tangling my fingers in her pretty blonde hair. I jerk her head back and plant my knuckles into her jaw. "How'd you do it, Melody?" Her eyes widen as she flaps her hands all over, trying to hit me back.

"Did you tell your Delta Chi sisters not to mention the party to me when we were decorating?"

"I didn't have to say shit, because no one likes you. Can't blame us for not wanting to associate with a dirty slut."

Her fingers are like claws in the air. If they do get a hold of me, I know they'll do some damage. But she misses every time because I continuously jerk her head back. "Probably because you filled their heads with a bunch of bullshit lies!"

"The company you keep is telling. Trust me, girl. No lies were necessary. Speaking of..." She reaches out farther and manages to slap me across the face. It's a petty slap and doesn't faze me in the least. "Have you talked to Cade recently?"

"What the hell is that supposed to mean?"

"Oh," she seethes. "You know exactly what I mean."

"Actually, I don't. Care to elaborate?" I push her head away and yank my hand free from her now very messed-up hair. I back up a few steps, keeping my eyes locked with hers, while creating space between us.

Melody combs her fingers through her locks and glowers at me. "No one has seen or heard from Cade for days. Seems a little coincidental, considering what happened to Zeke after your boy went all psycho on him in class just for talking to you."

I tsk. "You're delusional, Melody. Have you considered

the possibility that Cade left BCU because he's the one who killed Zeke?"

"Nope." She twists her wrist and draws a circle with her finger in the air. "Because all of this bullshit has your name written all over it."

"I've got better things to do than listen to your speculations right now."

"Of course you do. You're entertaining three men. That's gotta be exhausting."

"Fuck you!" I shout, my fists ready to strike again in an instant. But before I can swing, two strong arms wrap around my waist and pull me back.

"She's not worth it, Trouble. Just walk away." Lev's grip is ironclad, and I don't even attempt to break free.

"Oh, it'll be so worth it. Just let me knock her stupid ass out."

"Not happening." He scoops me up with my back to his chest before I can take another step. My feet leave the ground, dangling in the air, and I resist my instinct to flail.

"I can walk, ya know?" I mumble into the night air.

"I know you can. And I'll put you down as soon as I'm sure you're not gonna go after her." He clutches me tighter, as if this is more than just him pulling me out of a sticky situation.

I let myself relax in his arms as dead weight. "Why do you even care?"

"Because I need you, in case you've forgotten. And you're no use to me if you're lying in a hospital." His voice is soft, with an edge of determination.

My cheeks burn with annoyance at his words. "So you think Melody would win the fight? Gee. Thanks for the vote of confidence, Lev. Don't know if anyone told you, but I've already beat her preppy ass once. I know I could do it again easily."

"No." He pauses briefly before continuing. "But I do think her posse would be gunning for you, so it's best this way. You can thank me later."

"Just tell me you care and we'll end this conversation." There's a bite of snark to my playful tone, but deep down, I think Lev really does care about me. And I think it goes beyond my help. Even if he won't ever admit it.

"Don't care. Not even a little bit."

"Liar."

We reach the library, which is beside The Square and away from the crowd. Lev finally sets me down. "Why would I lie?"

"Because your pride won't allow you to admit it. Consider this my way of helping you. Just admit you care what happens to me."

"Fuck that." He sweeps his hand in the air and averts his gaze.

"Come on, Lev," I poke his side and he jolts. Liking the reaction, I do it again. "Say it. Tell me you care."

"Knock that shit off." He jumps back. "I'm not saying it because I don't fucking care."

"Fine." I scoff. "Guess I'll just go back to the party and get even more drunk. Maybe I'll jump Melody and beat her ass. Better yet," I waggle my brows, "maybe I'll find a guy to take me for a walk in the woods." I start walking back toward the party, knowing—or hoping, rather—that I won't make it far.

"Oh no, you don't." His arms envelop me from behind again, sweeping me off my feet. I can't even fight the millions of wings fluttering inside my belly. "You've had enough fun for tonight. I'm taking you home."

Lev sets me back down with a cocky confidence that I won't run off. Which I won't. I got the reaction I wanted.

"Wait up," I hear Maddox holler from behind us.

Lev and I both turn around to see him jogging in our direction. "Leaving so soon?"

I steal a glance at Lev before responding. "Yeah. I think the alcohol is starting to get to my head. Should probably call it a night."

Truth is, I'd be more than happy to stay if it weren't for Lev wanting to take me home. It's not even home I want, it's the walk with him.

"Ridge is looking for you," Maddox says to Lev, shooting a thumb over his shoulder. "Says it's a 10-33 situation."

"You've gotta be fucking kidding me?" Lev says, sounding annoyed.

"Nope. Why don't you go see what he needs and I'll take Riley home?"

Next thing I know, I'm being pulled away by Maddox, leaving Lev behind.

When I toss a glance over my shoulder, my gaze lingers on Lev longer than planned. He's watching me, too, and I can see disappointment in his eyes. There's undeniable chemistry between us and I know he feels it, too. As happy as I am to be leaving with Maddox, I'm also yearning for Lev. It's an unexpected desire, but one I can't wait to explore even more.

"Did you have fun tonight?" Maddox asks, tangling his fingers around mine. He brings our clenched hands to his mouth and kisses my knuckles. Those butterflies return and my legs turn to jelly.

"It was short-lived, but it was all right. Not quite the night I anticipated, but I got a good buzz and I'm looking forward to lying in my bed."

"About that," he drawls. "What if I told you I have no intention of taking you back to your room?"

I look at him, watching his eyes narrow as he bites the corner of his bottom lip. My eyebrows dance in excitement. "I guess I'd ask what it is you have in mind?"

"How about my bed, instead of yours?"

"In that case, I'd say, I like the way you think."

WE MAKE it back to the room I share with the guys in record time. I'd credit our near run to the rapid drop in the temperature outside, but really, it's because I've been waiting all night to peel off all of Riley's layers and blanket her naked body with the warmth of mine.

As soon as we're both in the room, I close the door with Riley's back to it. "Mmm," I hum into the crook of her neck as I push her into the frame, "I've missed you."

"I've missed you, too." Her fingers trail up my shirt, delicately dancing as they move down my chest. Goosebumps run down my spine as I grind myself against her perfect form. "Fuck me, Maddox."

"Damn, baby." I press my lips to hers, speaking into her mouth. "You don't have to tell me twice."

My heart beats rapidly in my chest as I sink to my knees, my hands trembling with anticipation. I let my palm wander northward, tracing the delicate skin of her leg until I reach the apex of her thighs. Pausing at her crotch, I massage gently through the fabric of her skin-colored leggings until she quivers in response.

Continuing upward, I run my fingers along the waistband of her leggings and slip them down slowly as I peer up at her. She stares down at me, her baby blues wide as saucers as she gnaws on her bottom lip.

Once her pants and panties are down, settled around her ankles, I remove one of her boots, then the other. My hands caress her legs, leaving a trail of goosebumps behind. I smile inwardly, loving the effect I have on her. It's like she was made for me and my touch.

I look up to see her bunching the bottom of Ridge's hoodie in her hand. She gathers her shirt underneath and lifts both over her head, tossing them to the floor. My breath catches in my throat when her cleavage bounces free. Her tits still covered by the cups of her pink lace bra leaves very little to the imagination.

One of the many things I adore about Riley is her self-confidence when we're together. Even as she stands here, naked from the waist down, she doesn't show an ounce of unease. And I can't help but think that this is all for me.

My eyes travel down her body, captivated by her smooth curves and the tautness of her skin, resting on the petal-soft flesh between her legs. She's so beautiful and I plan to make sure she feels that way, too.

I brush my fingertips lightly between her swollen folds, tracing around them while she shivers in anticipation. Gradually, I increase the pressure, massaging her clit with my fingertips. When I move my fingers lower, slowly dipping them into her wet entrance, she gasps and her back arches in response. I watch keenly as my fingers slide in and out of her, coated in her slick arousal.

My heart hammers in my chest and I'm overcome with a fierce desire to replace my fingers with deep thrusts of my cock, burying myself inside her tight, wet pussy.

Her head rests back against the door, eyes closed and a soft expression on her face. Slowly, I pull her leg over my shoulder and angle her hips so I get a perfect view of my fingers entering her. I watch as they slide out and she instantly whimpers for more. Using both palms, I spread her open and lean in to inhale her scent.

I swallow hard and lick my lips before dragging my tongue up her slit, while moving my fingers back into her. I pump them fiercely, loving how she reacts to everything I do.

Her leg trembles and a raspy moan slips through her lips as her fingers root in my hair. "Maddox," she exhales feverishly.

I feast on her as if she's my favorite dessert, which I'm pretty damn certain she is. The salty, acidic—but sweet— taste of her arousal seeps onto my tongue and I keep going, wanting more. "You taste like a dream, baby."

She moans in response, tugging my hair harder and harder, before she pins me to her pussy. "Oh god," she cries out, now rolling her hips and fucking my face. She takes all control, her body dictating the movements, commanding me to work her with my tongue and fingers.

With a resounding cry of pleasure, she tenses up then shudders against me. I feel her walls clench my fingers as she comes, and I force them in and out, dragging out her climax as long as I can.

Proof of her orgasm spills down my chin and hand as I continue to move in and out of her. Every few thrusts, I pause and drag the tip of my tongue up her slit, savoring the flavor of her arousal.

When she relaxes and I'm certain she's coming down from the dizzying high of her orgasm, I slowly pull my fingers from her quivering cunt. In a swift motion, I stand up and lift her by the hips, hoisting her up until she's straddling my waist. With the weight of her legs around me, I keep my balance as I carry her to my bed. Her lips crash into mine, still needy for more. I kiss her back before admiring every inch of her post-orgasmic bliss. Her sweat-infused skin glistens under the light on the ceiling and her breaths come in ragged gasps as she clings to me tightly.

At the edge of the mattress, I lay her down on the soft comforter then I strip down. She watches with rapt attention, her eyes never leaving my body.

I crawl on top of her, pressing my naked body against her warm skin. "That feel good, baby?" I ask, my tone thick and husky.

Her response is a subtle nod and a tight smile.

"Good," I hum. "Because I'm about to make you feel even better." I slide my cock inside her, watching her face the whole time. At first it pinches in pain, then pleasure takes over her features. She's as tight and as warm as I remember.

"You have no idea how bad I've wanted to fuck you again, Riley. You've hooked me from my very first time. You're like my own personal drug," I say breathlessly as I push in deeper. "I'm addicted, baby."

I stay fully seated inside her and watch as her chest rapidly rises and falls in anticipation, while mine does the same.

Grabbing her leg, I lift it over my shoulder, then the

other, until both are spread wide. I lift up slightly, my knees pressed firmly to the mattress while grasping her hips.

Her doe eyes peer into mine and I watch as her mouth falls open and her nostrils flare with each rapid thrust.

The smacking sound of our bodies connecting rings in my ears and arouses me further. I squeeze her hips harder, pushing deeper inside her. "Yes, Maddox," she screams as she pushes into me.

"Fuck, baby," I growl. "You feel so good."

A bead of sweat pools on my hairline, dripping down until it lands somewhere between us. My pace quickens and each plunge has her riding up farther and farther on the mattress. Her dampened hair clings to the headboard as she gasps for breath.

Her body shakes with pleasure—her hands squeezing my biceps, while using my arms for leverage as waves of ecstasy ripple through her.

I move my hands firmly around her hips, making sure to keep my rhythm as I thrust in and out of her.

Just when I feel like I'm ready to come, the bedroom door flies open, casting a shadow across the room. My gaze travels to the door and my shocked expression meets Ridge's.

Riley's head shoots up, but she doesn't stop me. Her wide, cautious eyes land on Ridge and her cheeks flush red.

"Well," Ridge begins as he trudges toward us, removing one shoe and tossing it at the wall, "if I'd known the party moved here, I would have come sooner." He takes off his other shoe, kicking this one behind him. "Mind if I join?"

I look at Riley, hopeful she'll shoot down his idea before I have to, but instead, she looks at me and says, "Is that okay with you?"

Fuck. I wanna say no, it's not okay. Dammit, this is my

time. But keeping her happy and satisfied is the only thing on my agenda tonight.

"Have at it, brother," I tell Ridge as I lower Riley's legs to the bed on either side of me. "But I'm not moving."

He drops his pants in a split second and begins pumping himself while I return my attention to Riley and her pussy that's dripping around my cock.

IS THIS REALLY HAPPENING? I lean forward, studying Maddox's face for any hint of anger as he thrusts into me. His sterling gray eyes appear dark, almost animalistic with desire, but I can tell from the way he's moving that he isn't mad.

I could have told Ridge no, that he couldn't join us, but the truth is, I want him to. This is a fantasy of mine I've been dreaming about for weeks now. I might be slightly intoxicated, but I'm grateful for the boost of courage the drinks gave me tonight. I'm also levelheaded enough to know I'll have no regrets tomorrow.

"Come here," I say to Ridge who's on his feet beside the bed, stroking his big cock.

He leans in and softly parts my lips with his. His free hand slowly grazes over my breast. He removes my bra with one hand, while the other presses gently in circular motions as he deepens our kiss.

My fingers eagerly reach out, wrapping around his thickness as he gracefully moves closer until he's kneeling beside me on the bed.

A sudden thrust from Maddox has me squealing. "Fuck her harder," Ridge orders him. "I love it when she makes those sounds."

My chest quivers in delight and the next thing I know, Maddox is slamming his pelvis against me, pushing my thighs apart and shoving his cock upward. Each movement is so powerful, it has my toes curling into the mattress. I can't contain the sounds that slip between my lips. I pull Ridge closer, so I can trail my tongue down his length. I take him in my mouth, the vibration of my moans rumbling against his shaft.

Ridge's fingertips lightly caress the arch of my breast as he rolls the bud of my nipple between his finger and thumb. Waves of pleasure surge through my body, and I arch my back in response. His lips curl into a devilish grin as he pinches again, then he flicks it with precision, igniting a fire deep inside me.

"Do you like that, Angel?" Ridge asks as he keeps pinching and rolling the sensitive nub between his fingers.

"Yes," I finally manage to respond with a gasp as I pop him out of my mouth. "I like everything you're both doing to me."

My hips rise and fall with each thrust. Every time Maddox rams into me harder, I cry out around Ridge. My teeth drag down the curve of his hard shaft, from base to tip, as I suck and lick. With each pass around his head, I flick my tongue and his body trembles before stilling again.

"You suck dick so good, Angel." Ridge wraps his fingers around my hair and lifts up, which helps ease the strain I'm putting on my neck. "You're missing out, Maddox. You see how good our girl is doing up here?"

His words give me a boost of confidence and I take all of

him, until he's hitting the back of my throat. When I look up, he's staring down at me with pure lust in his eyes. He wraps both hands around my head and holds me still while he savagely fucks my mouth.

"Fuck yeah, she's doing good. Feels pretty good down here, too," Maddox says in a husky voice.

I let my legs fall wider, an invitation for Maddox to go deeper.

My entire body is overstimulated and I'm on the brink of exploding when Ridge says, "Let me get a feel for that tight pussy. Switch spots."

My eyes shoot to Maddox, while my mouth is still stuffed full of Ridge's cock, and I'm certain this isn't going to end well. But, once again, I'm taken by surprise.

"All right," Maddox looks at me, "wanna taste yourself, baby?"

The thought of sucking Maddox off after he's been inside me is both repulsive and intriguing. I pull Ridge out of my mouth and lick my lips. "Okay."

As soon as Maddox takes himself out of me, I already miss the feeling. I was sore at first, after what Lev did to me earlier with the flashlight, but the pain ended up only adding to the pleasure and now I can't seem to get enough. My chest heaves with eagerness. Ridge leans down and kisses my forehead. "Promise it'll be worth it."

Just as Maddox's feet hit the floor, Ridge's hand closes around my hip and he flips me over so I'm face down on the bed. Then he's behind me, yanking my hips toward him until I'm on all fours. One hand presses to my back, creating an arch. A yelp is thrust out of me when he slaps my ass cheek, really fucking hard. The sting left behind only excites me for what's to come.

Maddox joins me in the front, kneeling in the same position Ridge was. I get one look at his sopping cock before he fists it and pushes it into my mouth. I'm taken aback at first, but the taste isn't quite what I thought it would be. It's actually...sort of sweet. The more I suck, the more it diminishes, and when Ridge rams his cock into my cunt, the thought of tasting my own arousal completely eludes me.

Ridge's hands tighten around my hips as he slams into me from behind, in quick and relentless thrusts. I gasp for air as I feverishly suck on Maddox, whose strong hand holds my head firmly in place—the other fondling my breasts. Part of me thinks this is wrong. I shouldn't be this turned on by two men, who are like brothers, fucking me from each end. I shouldn't want this. But I do, and the more they move, the less I care what everyone might think. All thoughts of a normal life left me the day I let Ridge fuck me in that theater room, and I believe I'm so much better for it.

An audible gasp climbs up my throat, spilling out of my mouth and echoing off the walls. "Holy fuck!"

My muscles tense and tremble and shake as pleasure shoots through me. I pinch my eyes shut, taking it all in. Suddenly, Maddox is fucking my mouth hard and fast. The next thing I know, warmth spreads quickly down my throat. He pushes in deeper until his head is pressed against my tonsils, and I feel every pulsating ripple through his length. When his shudders subside and every last drop is released, he reluctantly pulls out and I swallow the thick fluid that's clinging to my tongue.

Ridge is still going, riding me out through my orgasm, as every cell in my body is hit with a rush of adrenaline. I drop my head to the pillow, digging my teeth into the plush fabric, while I shovel my claws into Maddox's thighs. "Oh god. Oh god," I repeat before screaming, "oh my god."

Ridge's breathing grows unsteady and shallow as he pounds himself into me, my stomach almost flat on the bed. Finally, with one last thrust, his movements halt, and I feel the warmth of his release inside me.

"Fuck, Angel. That was incredible." He leans forward, resting his chest on my back, and I collapse with him on top of me, his dick still holding in every drop of his cum.

I'm rendered speechless. My head is in a fog and I feel like I'm on the biggest high of my life.

When Maddox lies down beside me and Ridge wraps his arms around my stomach, I feel more content than I even knew possible.

AS I STIR AWAKE, my eyes flutter open, and I glance over to Ridge's bed. The blanket is perfectly smoothed out and there's no sign of him in sight. Moving my gaze to Lev's bed, I see his large frame tucked underneath the covers, sleeping peacefully. My heart races when I recall what happened last night, and I can't help but wonder what Lev thought when he came home and saw me here—in Maddox's bed.

"Good morning," Maddox says from beside me.

I rest into him, wrapping my arms and legs around his core. "Is this a dream?" I murmur into his ear as my body curls tighter around him. One arm is thrown over his waist while my leg entraps his lower half. My exposed breasts crush against his side and my nipples pucker against his warm skin.

"Feels like it, huh?" He strokes my head with his fingertips. "You were incredible last night."

"I still can't believe that all happened." I lift my head up to get a look at his face. "Are you sure you're not mad that I let Ridge join in?"

"Nah." He exhales audibly. "It's not like I'm unaware of what's going on with you and Ridge."

My mouth draws back, the cords in my neck tight. "But at the same time?"

"This is gonna sound weird, but it almost felt normal sharing you. Maybe it's because Ridge has ingrained it in my mind that you're his girl, while at the same time, I've convinced myself you're mine, too." He lets out a long sigh. "Does that make sense?"

"Yeah," I tell him honestly. "Because that's sort of the way I see it, too." I rest my head on his chest again, that content feeling I had last night returning.

So this is what it feels like to be adored by two men. Wonder how it would feel to have three men here with me. Fucking me, even loving me.

My mind wanders to Lev. The enigma in my life. The one who pushes me away but keeps me at arm's reach. The one who violently assaults my body in a way that has me craving more.

I shouldn't be sprouting feelings for Lev, but I am. They're growing rapidly and out of control, and I can't even begin to wonder what I should do about it. Probably nothing, if I have any sanity left in me. Getting involved with him would be reckless. A recipe for disaster. But, oh my, what a thrill it would be.

The thought gets me excited and there's a sudden desire to see his face. Even though he's just across the room, sleeping, he feels so far away. Like he's in another world than the one I'm existing in.

I unpeel my sticky skin from Maddox and roll to my back. "I gotta pee," I tell him. It's true, I really do, but I also can't resist the urge to look at Lev. Just a peek. "Think the guys in your dormitory will freak if I walk in there?"

Last night everyone was asleep when I used the bathroom. Being nine a.m. on a Saturday morning, I'm sure the bathrooms are flooded with testosterone.

"Probably, which is exactly why I'm coming with you." Maddox springs out of bed in just a pair of black boxer briefs.

I pull myself up to a sitting position, my eyes darting around the room in search of my clothes. I spot them lying in a crumpled pile on the floor beneath the windowsill. Shivering as I leave the blanket, I swing my legs over the edge of the mattress then quickly pad across the room, my bare feet slapping against the hard surface.

I'm not sure where Ridge ran off to this morning, but I'm sure he stayed here all night. When I woke at 3 a.m., I saw him in his bed while Maddox slept soundly beside me. Hopefully he's out getting coffee, because that sounds really damn good right now.

I'm crossing the small space to my clothes when I look over to Lev's bed and see him—arms folded under his head, heavy-lidded eyes that are filled with hunger and something else I can't quite place. A smile spreads across his face and his eyebrows rise.

My entire body fills with heat from his stare and I pick up my pace, swiping my clothes up in a hurry. With my shirt in one hand, trying to hide my breasts, I use my other to try and spread the waistband of my leggings so I can step into them. It's a sticky situation that has me stumbling to the left and dropping the shirt. I swiftly sweep it back up to cover myself and manage to get one leg in.

"Trouble," Lev croaks and my gaze snaps to him, "you're trying too hard. I've seen it all before."

Giving up the attempt to shield my body from him, I ascertain that he's right. He has seen it all before, and while it doesn't feel appropriate at this moment, I really don't give a damn.

Dropping my shirt, I glare at him as I step into the other leg of my pants then I pull them up and snap the waistband as my eyebrows cave lower and lower. Then I slowly snare my shirt off the floor and jam one arm in, then the other, before pulling it over my head—braless. My nipples pucker against the fabric and a sheath of my stomach is exposed since it's a crop top.

Lev waggles his brows and scoots himself up an inch and I'll be damned, his jumbo dick is poking straight up, raising the fabric of his black satin sheet.

Air catches in my throat and I clear it before steadying my breaths. Quickly, I avert my gaze and try to get a grip.

Now that is exactly what would make this morning even better. Hopping on top of Lev and riding that big, bad cock.

Oh my god, what has gotten into me?

Ready?" Maddox asks, snapping me out of the sexual fantasy I fell into.

"Mmhmm," I mumble.

I follow behind Maddox, head hung low as I fight not to look back at Lev, but the desire is stronger than I am. So damn strong. And before I step out the open door, I shoot him a glance. Frozen. Stunned. Speechless. I gape as he pushes his sheet down, revealing his erect cock.

My heart might have literally stopped, or it's resting somewhere in my stomach.

Look away, Riley.

But when his hand wraps around his girth and he fists the fuck out of that thing, I can't stop watching.

"Baby," Maddox nudges me, "you coming or what?"

There's no doubt Maddox saw what I saw. He also saw my reaction. The way my body tensed. The continuous stare I held with Lev's cock, while he was staring back at me.

In an instant, I push past Maddox and step into the hallway. Unable to look at him out of sheer humiliation, I walk briskly down the hall to the bathrooms.

To my surprise, there's only a couple guys in there. Tucking myself behind Maddox, I try to hide as I slip into one of the stalls.

"Chick in the stall," I hear someone holler, but Maddox immediately shuts them down before chaos ensues.

"Mind your fucking business," he snaps at the loudmouth.

I finish up then step out of the stall and rush out as fast as I can. As my feet hit the hall, laughter ensues, and I feel like a child. When Maddox laughs along with me, I'm reminded of why I'm so drawn to him. It's so easy to be myself with him—effortless even.

We get back to the room and Maddox leads me through the door with a lax hand on my hip. I halt, shooting Maddox a nervous look, and it's like he's reading my mind.

"Fuck Lev. He was just trying to make you uncomfortable by being an asshole."

But what if that's the problem? What if I *do* want to fuck Lev?

I'm happy to see that Lev is now standing at his dresser with his back to us and his pants on, but when he turns around, showing his bare chest, my heart jumps into a frenzy. *What the hell has happened to me and since when am*

I such a hornball for this guy? Or all of them, for that matter?

"Morning, Angel," Ridge says as he jumps up from his bed. I didn't even know he was back, but his presence brings a smile to my face as the memories of last night infiltrate my mind.

"Good morning."

He crosses the room, wearing a pair of gray sweatpants and a black hoodie. "Sleep well?" he asks as he presses a chaste kiss to my cheek.

"Very well. Thank you."

Suddenly, I'm the center of attention. All three guys are just silently staring at me, and my body feels like it's caught on fire.

I draw in a deep breath, hoping someone says or does something soon because this is awkward as hell. Are Ridge and Maddox thinking about last night in Maddox's bed? Is Lev contemplating his next plan of action to assault my body? *God, I hope so.*

"All right then," Ridge finally says, and I exhale my pent-up breath. "Got you breakfast on the table, Angel. Maddox and I have to head out."

"We do?" Maddox asks, unaware they had plans.

"Yep. 10-33. A real one this time."

"What's a 10-33?" I ask, assuming it's some sort of secret friend code, but curious what it means. Maddox said it last night at the party to Lev, but I was too caught up in the moment to question what it meant.

"Important shit," Lev chimes in, his face lit up with a mischievous grin. "And while they're out doing that, you get to have breakfast with me." He plops down on his bed, arms crossed as he leans into the headboard.

"Oh, joy," I sing, a bit of sarcasm in my tone. When in reality, I literally feel like jumping for joy. I'm a masochist, plain and simple. A glutton for punishment.

"I'm trusting you, man," Ridge says, eyes narrowed on Lev. "You fucking hurt her in any way, shape, or form, I'll light your bed on fire with you tied to it."

"Well, fuck." Lev scoffs. "You just ruined my plans for the day."

Maddox steps in front of me, takes my hands in his and looks softly into my eyes, while Ridge and Lev toss insults back and forth. "Call me if he starts getting too...Lev."

I give him a reassuring smile and kiss his lips softly, letting the warmth of the moment linger for a few seconds before I pull away. "Don't worry about me. I'll probably just eat then head back to my room."

"Just keep your guard up. Still don't trust him with you." Maddox's hands shimmy down to my ass and he smirks. "You were incredible last night. Did I tell you that already?"

My cheeks warm and my lips curve in a smile as I chuckle. "You did, actually."

With a mischievous glint in his eye, he steps closer and gives my ass cheeks a firm squeeze as he whispers seductively in my ear, "Good. And I'm going to keep reminding you until I get you in my bed again."

"Can't wait," I mumble back, feeling faint and weak in the knees. I lean my head back to look at him as I bite the corner of my bottom lip. "Cancel your plans for the day and we can do it right now."

He grumbles, "You're killing me, baby."

"Right," I drag out the word, "10-33 and all."

"Exactly. But I promise you, it won't be long. I'll swing by your room when I get back. Maybe we can get dinner?"

"Sounds like a plan," I say as I bat my eyelashes at him.

He kisses my lips again, holding our mouths together momentarily to savor the moment. When suddenly, he's nudged out of the way by Ridge.

"Get a fucking room," Ridge barks as he slithers up to me. "Angel," he says, peering down into my eyes. "You call me if Lev fucks with you, got it?"

I laugh because it's the same song and dance I just went through with Maddox. "I'll be fine, guys."

"Jesus Christ," Lev growls. "You assholes act like I'm some sort of feral animal who will chew her body up and fuck her lifeless corpse."

"Wow," I gulp, eyes rolling. "Pretty descriptive, Lev."

Ridge pinches the bridge of his nose and sighs, shaking his head as he glares at Lev. "Ignore him," he says, his jaw visibly tensing. He glances down between us and intertwines our hands, brushing gentle circles along my knuckles with his thumb. His eyes soften as he looks at me, and a small smile tugs at the corner of his lips. "I'll see you later?" he asks in a low voice.

Smiling, I nod. "Of course."

Then I realize that I just made plans with both him and Maddox. *Oops. I guess I'll deal with that later.*

Ridge kisses my lips then steps back and hooks an arm around Maddox's shoulder. "Let's go, fucker."

The sound of the door closing is comparable to a jail cell locking. They've only just left and I already miss them both so much.

I inhale, filling my lungs completely as I spin around to face Lev. On the exhale, I say, "Looks like it's just you and me."

He just sits there, all cocky-like with a grin on his face,

staring at me. My eyebrows rise, questioning his awkward glare.

When he doesn't stop, or say anything, I drop my tense shoulders and walk over to the small table that has a large grocery bag on it. I assume it's the breakfast Ridge brought, so I unfold the top and look inside.

A smile immediately raises my cheeks when I see a clear container holding pancakes. I pull it out and see another container with bacon. And on the bottom of the bag is a baggie with butter and syrup.

My heart swells at Ridge's sweet gesture. There's something about the way he treats me, and only me. It makes me feel adored—as if I'm the most precious thing in the world to him.

I feel Lev's presence behind me before I hear him. "What a kiss ass," he gripes, his voice thick with disdain. He's so close that his warm breath on my neck sends an involuntary shiver through my body.

The urge to turn around is high, but I know at that point we'll be face to face, and I'm not sure I'm strong enough to refrain from kissing him. Which would be a huge mistake. My eyes will travel to his lips, and he'll notice. Then he'll call me out on it and make me feel an inch tall, which I often do in his presence. After some heavy banter, and likely some defamation on both our parts, I'll either wind up on my knees sucking him off, or he'll lay me flat on this table.

The thought of how this will end has me spinning around. Sure enough, his mouth is the first thing I see. Those soft, pink lips, almost too soft for a man so brash.

"Those are your friends," I say. "Why are you always ready to attack when it comes to them?" My eyes blaze with intensity, daring him to argue with me.

"Not always," he quips, his eyes now dancing across my lips. "Only when it comes to you."

My chest visibly heaves. No matter how hard I try to steady my breaths, they come in unfulfilled gasps and fleeting exhales.

"But why?" I manage to choke out as I feel a bead of sweat roll between my breasts. *Is it hot in here? It feels hot.* If he weren't so close, I'd be fanning myself with my hand. Then again, if he weren't so close, I might not need to.

"Because," he scoffs, "don't you see how they fucking cater to your every need like you hung the damn moon just for them? They try too damn hard and you drink it up like a thirsty dog."

The temptation to call him out on his jealousy is agonizing, because I know that's what it is. He won't admit it, though. Because being jealous would mean admitting he has some sort of feelings for me, and that, he will never do. Instead, I'll use some of the reverse psychology tactics we learned in class. "And that bothers you, why?"

"It's sickening. It's obvious they're both insecure as fuck to go to these extremes to keep you. And there's only one person to blame for that." He raises an eyebrow and the accusing look makes all the giddiness inside me dissipate.

"Are you saying I'm to blame for Maddox and Ridge... wanting me?"

"Not wanting. Obsessing, Trouble. They fucking obsess over you. And they try so damn hard because you've pinned them against one another as competitors for your heart."

"Whoa," I drawl, hand raised as I step around him. My shoulders go taut, nostrils flaring with each rapid breath. "Ridge and Maddox like me. And I like them. They see the real me. All you see me as is an object." My hands flail in the air as I express how downright pissed I am. "You've gotta be kidding me right now?"

Lev turns around and presses his hands to the table behind him, while wearing a cocksure expression on his face. "Nope." The popping sound he makes has my fingers twitching.

"You asshole!" My voice rises in pitch until I'm nearly shouting. "If anyone's to blame for any insecurities either of them are feeling, I'd say it's you. If you weren't forcing me to fuck around with you, maybe they wouldn't feel the need to try so hard."

"Forcing?" He laughs, the one sound that grates on my nerves. "You can call it that, but I know damn well you want it just as bad as I do." He pushes himself off the table and struts two steps toward me.

"I should have never turned around," I mumble under my breath.

He taps his ear, leaning in. "What's that?"

"Nothing," I blurt out as I reach around him and grab the bag off the table. "I'm taking my food back to my room before you and I kill each other."

As quick as I grabbed it, Lev pulls away. "Hey!" I snap. "Give that back."

When I go to reach for it, he holds it behind his back. "You can eat...after I do." His eyes drag down my body. From my mouth to my nipples that are threatening to cut through the fabric of my thin shirt—down to my crotch.

"You ruined my mood, Lev." I go for the bag again, to no avail. "Just let me leave."

"Nope."

There's that annoying popping sound again. I swear it's like nails on a chalkboard, only because it's so damn arrogant. Lev is so sure of himself. So certain I'll comply. Part of me feels like he pushes my buttons on purpose, just so he can order me to do sexual favors for him.

"Fine," I huff, arms now crossed over my chest to hide the chill on my breasts. "Have at it. Eat *my* food that Ridge bought *me*. I'll just grab something on my walk to my dorm."

"Trouble," he roars. "I don't wanna eat your fucking food." He tosses the bag behind him, likely cracking open the containers inside, and ruining my breakfast. One final step forward has his chest flush with my knotted arms. He reaches his hand down and cups my crotch, sending a thrilling pulse between my legs. "I wanna eat this."

My jaw drops, eyes wide in surprise. His mouth is so fucking dirty, but damn if I don't love the way his vile words make me feel.

"What?" I gasp. "No."

"I wasn't asking permission."

He drops to his knees and swiftly tugs down my pants. Suddenly, I feel very exposed. So vulnerable but so desperate for his mouth on me.

I could put up a fight, which he'd enjoy, or I can stand here and let him give me all the pleasure, while offering him nothing in return.

Lev runs a hand up my leg, leaving a hot trail of excitement in its wake. He separates my thighs, and I feel his lecherous gaze searing me with intensity. He slides one finger inside me, then shifts his attention to his own hand, watching closely as he works it. His head lowers until I can feel the weight of it between my legs, and when his tongue flicks out, tracing my delicate folds, a shiver runs through me.

Starting at my inner thigh, he works his way up to the apex of my legs, then settles his tongue around my clit. His mouth works expertly—licking, sucking, and flicking. The combination of that and his fingers delving deep inside me have me panting. I find myself gripping his hair tightly, holding him firmly against me because if this is a game and he tries to stop just as I'm about to come, I will literally shove him down and ride his face until I squirt in his mouth.

Damn. That thought turns me on.

My head falls back, mouth agape, and I moan in pleasure, relishing the way he's working magic on my body. Feral sounds escape me and just as I fill up with an insatiable urge to release, he pulls his fingers out and pulls his head back.

"Oh, hell no," I mutter, slamming his face back into my pussy. "You finish what you started."

"Fuck yes," he growls as his mouth lands on me again. He clamps his teeth on my clit, with little pressure, but enough to have me crying out in ecstasy. I roll my hips, working them against his face.

"Let me fuck you," he says between sucks and licks.

"Okay," I whimper. "Get up."

The power dynamic shifts suddenly. It's an exhilarating feeling, me being the one barking orders. It feels good to be the one in control for a change.

Lev stands in front of me and immediately drops his pants. Before he can turn this around and start barking orders, I jab a finger to his bare chest and force him to take steps back toward his bed.

His eyes never leave mine as he yanks my shirt over my head in one swift motion. Once he tosses it over his shoulder, I shove him down on his bed and straddle him, pressing my hands firmly to the sheet on either side of him.

I've never ridden a guy before, and I'm not even sure if I

know what to do, but the moment I lower myself down on his dick, everything seems to fall into place.

Lev pinches the skin of my waist, guiding me as I bounce up and down on his cock, letting it fill me up completely. He moves one hand to my breast, squeezing with tenacity, but the pain only arouses me more. I shift, so I can grind down on his pelvis, and the sensation has me trembling.

"God damn, Trouble," he croaks as he watches my tits bounce up and down. "Work that pussy, baby girl. Come around my cock."

His words light an inferno inside me and I lean forward, letting my chest rest against his. I trail my mouth down his neck and arch my back as I rock myself into him.

He firmly slaps a hand to my ass and I yelp in response. With his hand still on my ass, he massages the flesh between his fingers, while using pressure to coax my movements. With every thrust and arch of my hips, I feel the fire of plea-sure build inside me.

"Fuck, Riley," he roars, and the sound of my name on his tongue sends me over the edge.

A dizzy wave of ecstasy hits me out of nowhere. "Oh god, Lev. I'm coming." I clench his cock, feeling a bolt of lightning jet through my body.

Lev grips my hips again as his breathing quickens. His thrusts from beneath me grow faster and harder, sending my body in the air, only to drop back down on his cock. With a deep groan, he stiffens and releases.

I still my movements, resting my head in the crook of his neck. His arms spread wider before wrapping around me completely. The thumping of his heart against me is elec-trifying.

It's a strange sensation and not one I thought I'd ever

feel. Being held by Lev isn't comparable to any emotion I've ever experienced. Not even with Maddox or Ridge. It's different. Everything with each one of them is different, but in all the best ways.

I don't dare move out of fear of ruining this moment. So I lie there as long as he'll allow it.

A minute passes, maybe two, and I can feel him softening inside me. I move my hips just slightly and he slips out. I wish I could take that movement back, because the next thing I know, I'm being flipped over on my back.

Only this time, Lev doesn't retreat. He hovers over me for a moment, looking deep into my eyes as if he's searching for a reflection of himself. I hope he sees it. I hope he sees what I see right now.

"Go get yourself cleaned up," he says, peeling his eyes off me and getting off the bed. "Bathrooms shouldn't be too busy right now."

I close my eyes for a minute, letting the image of him linger in my mind a little longer.

Then I get up.

Once I've cleaned up in the shared bathroom down the hall, I hurry back to the guys' room and *finally* dive into my breakfast. It's good, but the food mixing with the alcohol in my stomach suddenly makes me feel nauseated with a slight headache.

"I'm going out," Lev says as he snatches his jacket off the hook by the door. "Lock up when you leave."

"Okay," I say in a hushed tone. Oddly enough, I don't want him to go. Lev and I are always two breaths away from killing each other, but then those other ones, they're the ones I hold on to. Those moments when I see a fleck of humanity in his eyes. Or the smile on his face when he doesn't know

I'm watching. He makes me feel things that I don't want to feel, but I do, regardless. I shouldn't want him. Shouldn't desire him. But I do.

Stopping in the doorway, Lev glances over his shoulder with his hand still tightly wrapped around the handle. "Hey, Trouble."

My eyes jerk to him. "Yeah?"

"For what it's worth, if you could see yourself through my eyes, you'd know why I chose you. It was always you. Only you."

My mouth opens to speak—to tell him I want him to keep choosing me. *A hundred times. Choose me.* But before the words leave my mouth, he's gone.

She was rainbows and brightness,
all things that glittered.
Her dreams could touch mountain peaks,
until her heart withered.
Stepping into the darkness,
her world, now black.
She saw no way out.
There was no turning back.
Then he came along,
and another one followed.
Soon there were three,
Her heart no longer hollowed.
They each offered something,
That brought back the girl who once was.
And the rainbows appeared again,
Because of him.
Because of them.
Because of love.

. . .

For the first time in so long, I feel like me again. These past few weeks have been a whirlwind, but I wouldn't change a thing because it brought me here. My relationships with all three of the guys are still a work in progress, but all relationships are.

I continue eating my breakfast, while the ache in my head continues to grow to the point of a constant pounding. I'd swear off drinking, but I know it'd be short-lived.

I wonder if any of the guys have any pain reliever?

Unable to take another bite, I toss the containers back in the bag and fold it up so I can drop it in the dumpster on my way out.

I go to Ridge's side of the room and pull open the drawer on his nightstand, only to find a bunch of crumpled papers, a lighter, and a half-smoked cigarette. *Gross.*

I close the drawer and go to Maddox's corner, opening and closing his dresser drawers. In the bottom one, I find a bunch of old photos. I pick one up and look at it—it's Ridge, Maddox, and Lev on Halloween. They can't be any older than ten. They all look so happy wearing their matching Batman costumes. My heart swells at the sight. Just seeing this proves how close these guys are, even if they don't always show it.

Sometimes friendships—or love, rather—are strange like that. It's not easy. You don't always see eye to eye. And the arguments sting worse than one with an enemy ever could. But they are the ones who are there. Day and night. Good and bad. They never leave. I can see that with Ridge, Lev, and Maddox. What they have is solid and it's an everlasting bond.

Dropping the picture in the drawer, I shuffle through a

couple more, smiling at each one. Then I close it and continue my quest to get rid of this headache.

Next, I try Lev's side of the room. If any of them came in here and saw me going through their shit, they'd probably lose their minds, but they're not returning anytime soon.

Opening the top drawer of his dresser, I move around some papers. One of which is an assignment that was due in class last week. *Such a slacker, he is.*

There's a bottle of meds that I snatch up, but I don't think it's the meds I'm looking for. I hold it up, reading the prescription, but it's not what I'm reading that catches my eye. It's the contents inside. I quickly twist the top off and dump a couple in my hand. These match the pill I found on the rug in my room. But Cade is the one who dropped that. Why would Lev have the same pills Cade did?

Brushing it off as a strange coincidence, I put the top back on and place it in the drawer. There are no other meds in here but being the nosey shit I am, I keep rummaging. A folded-up piece of paper throws me for a loop. Not the paper itself, but the name on the front of it—*my name.*

I quickly unfold the paper and hold my breath as I read...

Riley,

This is probably a bit odd, considering we barely know each other. But our first encounter wasn't a pleasant one. Truth is, I've been under a lot of pressure with the team and trying too damn hard to impress them, so I made you the butt of a joke. It was dumb. I know this and I want to apologize. I know I should do it in person, but I know you won't give me the time of day, and I don't blame you for that. I'm slipping this note under your room door in hopes that you'll allow me that opportunity.

I'm sorry for being such a jackass in class. You didn't deserve that.

Talk soon,

Zeke

As I let go of the paper, it hangs in the air for a moment before fluttering softly back into the drawer. My mind is in a whirlwind, spinning in circles, lapping around thoughts that make no sense.

That's why Zeke was in my room, or at the door, at least. He was leaving a note. Zeke didn't drug me and take advantage of me then jump out my window. *No. I already came to that conclusion.* It was Cade. But why does Lev have the note Zeke left.

I pick up the bottle of pills again, then snatch the note and walk briskly to the door, not even bothering to hide the evidence of my ransack.

A ball lodges in my throat, my stomach twisting in knots. I have to compare the pills and I fear that when I see the ones in this bottle match the one I found on my rug, I'm going to realize, it wasn't Cade who came in my room that night.

It was Lev.

CHAPTER 31
LEV

I GLANCE at my phone to see twelve missed calls from Cade's father. The man may be my uncle, but he's no one I've ever been able to rely on.

After everything that happened with my family, he pretended to generously take me in. That was until they couldn't handle my mood swings. Cade was always making me feel worse, while his father only added to the grief I was feeling at the time.

Eventually, they gave up on me and sent me into foster care. From that point on, things only seemed to get worse for me. Not a single person I was placed with wanted me there, and I was bounced around from one abusive home to the next until the day I turned eighteen. My only constant was Dr. Edmonds, who always made sure I had access to my medication.

I've never needed much, but those few years of being homeless really taught me things. Maddox and Ridge have no idea how bad it was because I didn't let them see. But if it weren't for the sleepovers at Maddox's house every weekend, there are nights I probably would have frozen to death on a park bench.

When I finally received access to part of my family's funds, I knew what I wanted to spend my money on, and it was finding a way to get better. I want to feel. I don't want to be this person who everyone looks at as fundamentally broken, even if I may be.

My phone buzzes in my pocket and I take it out to see another call coming in from Cade's father. I press the end button, letting it go to voicemail. If he wants to know what happened to Cade so badly, he can come down here and investigate it himself. Even if I didn't know what happened to the son of a bitch, I wouldn't be helping him. Not after the way he treated me.

Pushing the intruding thoughts aside, I embrace the new emotions that have been surfacing lately as I trudge down the gravel road to the warehouse. I shove my hands in my pockets, watching as the clouds drift lazily apart, opening up the sky.

The sun makes an appearance—a bright orange ball of fire, and I feel the scorching heat wash over me. I've been numb for so long that even this small comfort feels like a gift. I know it's because of her. Riley has given me a reason to live again.

A smile creeps slowly across my face as I kick up small stones, sending them flying through the pressed blades of grass. Shuffling my feet, I take long strides toward the main doors. Today's meeting with Dr. Edmonds is going to be different. I can feel it in my bones.

Walking briskly, I go straight down the hall to the room where all our meetings are held. I push open the ajar door and step inside to find the good doc waiting patiently with his hands folded in the lap of his khaki pants. His exposed socks show a blue-and-black checkered pattern that match his blue button-up. After our last meeting, I doubt Doc will ever touch his phone in this building again. I don't regret my outburst for a second. He's on the clock when he's here and I'm paying him damn good money.

"Good morning, Lev," he says with a broad smile on his face as he pushes up his glasses.

"Morning," I respond as I make a beeline for the sofa. I plop down on it, legs spread and arms rested out on the top of the couch. "And how do you plan to invade my brain today?"

"Well," he begins, leaning forward and picking up his notepad on the glass table in front of him, "I was thinking we'd just talk about the present today. How are you handling your social anxieties with your peers and the pressure of your classes?"

I tug on the collar of my shirt, loosening it, then scratch the side of my head. "I'm still alive, and so are my peers, so I'd say I'm handling it quite well. Thanks for asking."

I can feel my temperature rise as I speak. I'm hyperaware that any second, he's going to shift this conversation and force me to talk about feelings. The thought alone gets me heated.

"I'm glad to hear that. And your roommates? I assume things are going well with them?"

"Eh," I tilt my head from side to side, "they're my boys, so everything is fine." I sit forward with a grin on my face as I continue, "I mean, we are all fucking the same girl, so there's that."

Dr. Edmonds's eyes widen. "Really? That's...interesting. And how does that make you feel?"

I lean forward, resting my elbows on my knees. "She's got a smoking hot body, Doc. If you saw it, you'd wanna tap that ass, too. Tight pussy." I jiggle my hands at my chest. "Perky tits and legs for days. Feels pretty fucking good."

Just thinking about it has my cock twitching.

Dr. Edmonds clears his throat. "I meant, how does it make you feel knowing your friends are having sexual relations with her, too."

"Oh. That." I draw my fingers around my mouth, grinning. "Don't really give a damn, to be honest. Ridge and Maddox are chasing feelings, while I'm just milking my cock in her."

"I see." He scribbles something in his notepad, then lifts his eyes again. "At any point in time when you've seen your friends with this girl, have you experienced any twinges of jealousy, pain, or anger? Anything at all?"

I drag in a deep breath, contemplating how I want to approach this. I try my best to be honest with Dr. Edmonds by telling him the truth, but I'm not so sure I want him to know what Riley really does to me. He'll push and make me explore feelings for her that I'm not yet ready to explore. "Let's just say, this girl is changing my whole life."

"Really?" He shifts in his seat, eyes wide with surprise. "That's great news, Lev."

In an attempt to downplay the situation, I sweep my hand through the air then slap my knee. "It's all right, I guess."

"How are you doing with your meds?" he asks, and I'm a bit surprised he's changing gears so abruptly. For years, he's pushed me to open up and I've said more positive words in this short session than I have in all the time we've been meeting. Yet, he's asking about my meds.

"My meds are fine. No changes needed. Why the fuck are you asking about the meds? You've had me on the same one for years."

"I just want to be sure no adjustments are needed at this time. I'm happy to hear they are working well for you." He scribbles in his notebook again and I move forward, stretching my neck.

"What the hell are you writing?"

Quickly, he closes the notebook and sets it back on the table. "Tell me more about this girl. What's her name?"

I settle back on the couch, feeling a wave of serenity pass through me. She's definitely woken something inside my soul. Even just the mention of her mollifies me lately.

"Her name isn't important," I tell him. "It's what she's doing to me that matters."

Tilting his head slightly to the right, Dr. Edmonds studies me. "And what is it that she's doing?"

I inhale sharply, speaking on the exhale. "Making me feel things that I didn't think I'd ever feel again."

"Such as?"

"Jesus, Doc." I huff. "You really are a nosey son of a bitch, you know that?"

He smirks, lifting his shoulders. "Just doing my job. We can skip the feelings, though. Let's talk about the intimacy between you and this girl..."

"That's a big fuck no."

"It wasn't long ago you struggled to—"

"I said no," I snap, rolling my hand through the air. "Next topic."

"Very well. How about your cousin, Cade, and your aunt and uncle?"

"Fuck those greedy bastards." I abruptly get to my feet,

suddenly feeling the urge to get out of here. Walking toward the door, I pause when I get to it. My neck arches back, and my eyelids fall shut. Normally, I'd be rapidly firing insults at Doc while I'm on my way out the door. There's a familiar impulse to rip it open and slam it shut with an almighty bang. But this time, I surprise myself by turning back around to the conversation. It's a reminder that I'm a work in progress. "I think Cade left campus. Must've gone home. As for his fuckwad parents, I don't care if I never see them again for as long as I live. They aided in my misery and they're dead to me. Next topic."

Eyebrows raised, Dr. Edmonds nods slowly, pleased with my response. "That was good, Lev. Very good."

"Don't patronize me, old man." I scoff on my way back to the sofa. "Next topic."

"How's your grades?"

Easy question with a quick response. "Shit."

"And your plans for the impending holidays?"

"Fuck this." I jump back on my feet and haul ass toward the door. I was able to refrain from escaping with the previous question, but not this one. I jerk open the door. Gripping the handle fiercely, I slam it shut, but it bounces back open and I'm forced to slam it again.

Sweat protrudes on my hairline as I pace the hall for what feels like minutes.

Plans for the impending holidays.

How fucking dare he go there. Dr. Edmonds knows how I feel about the holidays. Much like every year, as Thanksgiving and Christmas approach, the realization hits me that I have no family to go home to. Everyone around me will soon prepare to travel home to be with their families—except Ridge, who now considers Maddox's family his own. They'll beg me to come with them, but I won't because I don't accept pity handouts, and that's exactly what it would be.

I've got nobody.

But I could have her.

I can see it now—as vivid as a picture in my head. Riley has a family of her own, but with enough persuasion, maybe she'll stick around campus with me, while everyone else goes home. With how quickly things are changing between us, it's a possibility. That thought has me smiling as I go back into the room where Dr. Edmonds is waiting.

CHAPTER 32

MADDOX

I GLANCE around the empty space in front of the Kappa Rho House impatiently. Ridge stands in front of me, thumbs drumming against his phone's screen, oblivious to the task at hand. Frustrated, I step closer and push him forward. "Clear!" My voice is low but sharp, but when he doesn't budge, I shout, "Fucking go!"

Ridge growls. "Chill out, man," he says with a huff as he stuffs his phone in his pocket. "I was checking to see where they were. They're going to the hot springs, so we've got all afternoon."

"We're about to raid a dead man's room. I don't wanna be here a second longer than necessary."

"No one knows he's dead, though," Ridge says all too casually.

"Not yet. But eventually they will. People are already asking about him around campus. It won't be long until an official missing person's report is filed."

Ridge walks around to the back of the house, where he says a ground-level window is unlocked. I'm beginning to think he's done this before. When he pushes up a sill, I'm more than certain he has. I don't ask questions because I don't want to know. I just follow behind and hope like hell we can find what we came here for.

"Maybe this isn't such a good idea," I tell Ridge as we trail down the hall. "You do realize once Cade's deemed missing, it's my ass The Elders will be after? If anyone catches us here, they'll for sure list us as suspects."

"Fuck them." He scoffs. He's ahead of me, so I can't see his face, but I can tell he doesn't give a shit about this whole thing. "Just say you were doing your job and keeping an eye on the Kappa Rho guys. We're here on official business."

He has a point; I can just claim I was doing my duty. Sure would make my father happy to hear and no one in The Society would think twice about it. We walk farther into the kitchen and a chill runs down my spine. "Something's not sitting right with me, man."

"Then let's hurry our asses up, search his room for his phone, and get the fuck out of here."

It still blows my mind that Cade didn't have his phone on him. What twenty-year-old doesn't carry their cell phone with them at all times?

We ascend the stairs and I can't help but reflect on the last time I saw Ridge here. The fury in his eyes as he beat Cade's half-naked ass was unparalleled to any anger I've ever seen him express. The thought of that incident alone has me looking over my shoulder as we enter Cade's room.

If it ever comes out that Cade is dead, we will likely be the first suspects. So it's important we keep a low profile and keep ourselves off The Society's radar. Just as that thought crosses my mind, I look over to see Ridge raiding Cade's drawers without a second thought about things looking suspicious. "What the fuck, Ridge? Do you want the whole fucking fraternity to know his room was raided?"

"Don't really give a shit, if I'm honest."

I follow behind him, attempting to put stuff back in Cade's drawers, while Ridge continues tossing everything without a care in the world.

Ten minutes later, Ridge comes to a halt and I exhale heavily as I say, "It's not here."

He runs his fingers through his hair, eyes scouring the small space. "Where the hell could it be?"

"Well, he was at the main campus building when you kidnapped him. Could he have dropped it?"

Ridge's eyes widen as if a light bulb just came on in his head. "He had weight training that day. I bet he left his bag and phone—"

Reading his train of thought, I finish for him, "In the gym lockers."

"Bingo."

I hurriedly scoop up any remaining evidence of us being here, tossing the random junk into one drawer. Once I slam it shut, we leave in a hurry. This time, we opt for the front door instead of the window, since we're sure no one is here.

"Should we call for a shuttle?" I ask Ridge as we close the door behind us.

"Nah. We don't want anyone tracing us back here, or to where we're going."

I nod in agreement, then we turn on our heels and race away from the house, down the trail that leads to the school. We dodge trees and leap over roots as we make up for lost time, both panting heavily by the time we make it.

Pushing open one of the heavy double doors of the main building, I step inside and Ridge follows. The large foyer is deserted, but the muffled conversations coming from the student center can be heard. An eerie stillness hangs in the air and I can't help but be afraid of what we will find when we actually do get Cade's phone.

"Dude," Ridge nudges me. "Get a grip. We're not doing anything wrong. You look like you saw a fucking ghost."

He pats my shoulder and waves me along. With little choice given, I follow his lead.

Bypassing the student center, where a couple tables are filled with students studying, I keep my head down, avoiding eye contact.

I hate this shit. Hate what happened. Hate what's to come. I've royally fucked myself by getting involved in any of this shit with Cade. I should've just stayed away, then none of this would've happened.

A few minutes later, we're on the other side of the building, walking into the boys' locker room. Ridge goes straight for one locker in particular, and once again, I'm thinking he's done this before. "Were you fucking stalking the guy?"

"Fuck off. I was doing your job, watching those shithead frat boys, while you were having panic attacks over your dad's constant texts."

I still haven't told Ridge about my dad and how he suspected Riley killed those guys who used to work for the governor. At one point I planned to, then the next day, we found out it was Cade who did all that shit to Riley and I figured it didn't matter anymore since we knew the truth.

"Got it," Ridge beams, holding up Cade's phone. "It's dead, but after a quick charge, we will know all that rotten fucker's dirty secrets." He fishes a charging cord out of Cade's drawstring bag and rushes over to a nearby outlet on the wall. Once it's inserted into the slots, he sets the phone on a bench and we both watch impatiently as the phone gets a charge.

The screen lights up and Ridge immediately snatches it off the bench, still leaving the cord attached.

I hover over him, watching every tap and swipe. He taps on his Instagram and I scoff. "Seriously? His social media?" I snatch the phone from his hand and the charger is forced out.

"Instagram has important shit. What if he had messages in there?"

"From who? His fucking nonexistent fans?" I roll my eyes as I tap into his actual text messages.

I scroll down, saying the names out loud as I see all the unread messages, "Mom. Dad. Mel. Katie. Ashton. Lori. Sara. Amanda. Gail. Jesus, how many fucking girls does this guy talk to?" The next one has me stopping. I look at Ridge before saying, "Doc Eds."

"Doc Eds? Who the hell is Doc Eds?"

"Edmonds," I exclaim. "I bet you fucking anything it's that dirty doctor. Remember how you found his card in Cade's wallet?"

"Well, read the damn thing," he says as he leans into me to get a better view.

I tap into it and begin with the message that was received one hour ago...

Doc Eds: Your dad has been trying to reach you. I'm in town for a meeting with Lev today. We need to talk about his odd behavior lately. Call me or your dad as soon as you can so we can meet up and discuss this. Delete this message once it's been read.

"That's it," I tell him. "That's the only one. What the fuck does that even mean?"

"Something's going on between Cade, his dad, and Lev. That's what it fucking means. Go to the texts from his dad."

I scroll down and tap, then read the messages out loud...

> Dad: I'm not sure what happened to you, but you need to call me ASAP.

> Dad: This is very important, Cade.
> Call me.

> Dad: Where the hell are you?

> Dad: This is important. Respond or call me. Eugene said if Lev completely weans himself off his meds, he will revert back to feeling normal and all of this will be for nothing. We need you to intervene.

"Who is Eugene?" I ask Ridge, hoping he knows.

"I bet it's that damn doctor's name. Makes sense. But why are they discussing Lev's meds?"

I clear my throat and continue...

> Dad: Eugene said something is up with Lev. He's got the feeling he's cut back on his meds. Possibly self-weaning. Said the numbness is wearing off. His temper is decreasing slowly. He's more rational. More levelheaded. Also noted that shouldn't happen with such a heavy dose of Arcadulan. He wants to know if we want his dose increased, but I need to know what the hell is going on out there. Call me, dammit.

> Dad: We need to talk about your cousin.

I stop there for a minute, giving myself time to process this fuckery.

Pinching my lips, I shake my head in disbelief. "What the actual fuck."

"If I'm hearing what you read in those messages right, that fucking doctor was keeping Lev numb."

I swallow hard, still not believing what I just read. "And Cade and his dad—Lev's own flesh and blood—were behind it. But why? Why the hell would they do that to him? And for how long? It's been years since Lev was himself. Has this doctor been giving him a larger dose of that Arcadulan medicine all these years, just to purposely keep him from feeling anything?"

As we hash this out, I do a quick Google search of the med Lev's been taking. It's an antipsychotic med and in large doses, it causes emotional numbness, lack of empathy, loss of autonomy, decreased sexual function, and a sense of resignation. May also cause patients to enter a catatonic state.

"None of this makes any damn sense," Ridge roars as he slams his fist into a locker. "What the hell did they do to him?"

"Think it might have something to do with the murders? Just a hunch, but maybe in Lev's uncle's mind, he was helping him."

"No. Fuck that!" His voice rises to a near shout. "They hate Lev. Wouldn't surprise me if they blamed him for the death of his own family. Lev's the one who found them. Maybe they think he killed them."

"Not a chance in hell," I retort. "The Lev back then had the biggest heart of anyone I knew, and he fucking adored his dad. They were so close."

I keep reading, hoping answers are given further back.

"This one's from two weeks ago, just after Cade went missing..."

> Dad: How's Lev been? Any changes. Keep me updated.

> Dad: It's almost time, son. We're so close. Keep an eye on your cousin and you let me know the minute he fucks up so I can record it for the attorneys. One more year until he graduates and he gets the remainder of his inheritance. It won't be long until all that money is ours, as it should have been in the first place.

My entire body breaks out in chills. Ridge and I both stand there, looking at each other, completely stunned by what we've just uncovered.

"We've gotta go tell him," I say, feeling as if all the blood has been drained from my body. "We gotta tell him right fucking now."

CHAPTER 33

RILEY

> Me: I can't stop thinking about our time at the cabin the other night. How about we meet there in an hour and do it all over again?

> Lev: Maddox and Ridge sent me a 10-33. But fuck it. I'll be there.

I RE-READ the message exchange one more time before setting my phone on the couch beside me. It's been fifty minutes since Lev responded. It's also giving me fifty minutes to decide what I'm going to say and do when he gets here.

I've gathered some supplies I'll use if necessary—a rope, some duct tape, and some pepper spray. Let's hope it doesn't come to that. All I want is the truth, but if he doesn't willingly give it to me, I have every intention of torturing the fuck out of him until he does.

My heart hurts.

Nothing makes sense right now. After I left the guys'

room, I went back to mine and sure enough, Lev's prescription pills match the same one I found on my rug. This alone tells me he was there sometime within those couple days. I've gone over a few different scenarios: maybe Cade stole them from Lev. Or, maybe it really is just a coincidence and Cade just happened to be in possession of the same meds Lev takes. But the note doesn't lie. It's absolute proof that Lev was there. He took that note from my room the day Zeke died.

An innocent guy who was wanting to make amends lost his life, and for what? A cover-up?

The door to the cabin comes open and my back steels against the couch. I don't even turn around to look at him out of fear I'll break down in tears.

I have to be strong.

My mind is my armor,
I am not made of glass.
What once was a frail girl,
Is now a warrior at last.

"Sort of expected you to be bent over this couch, naked," Lev says as he emerges from behind the couch. His cold hands touch my shoulders, before his fingers slowly glide down, dipping into the V of my shirt. A shiver runs down my spine as he presses his palms against my breasts.

"Is that so?" I say, tone flat.

Leaning forward, he presses his mouth to my shoulder. "Mmhmm."

"Is it still snowing?" I ask him, feeling the need to manipulate this situation.

He chuckles. "Are you seriously asking about the weather?"

"Just curious. Is it?"

He pulls his hands out of my shirt and rounds the couch until he's standing directly in front of me. "Yeah." His eyebrows pinch together as he studies me. "It just started coming down pretty heavily. Which means we need to make this quick; otherwise, we won't be able to see going back to campus."

With an impassive look on my face, I say, "Yeah, that would be a shame."

"What the fuck is up with you?"

I roll my lips together and tilt my head slightly. "I don't know what you mean."

"This." He waves his arms at me. "Why are you acting like this? Since when do we have small talk about the weather, or anything at all for that matter?"

"You know what I'd like to talk about?" I pause for a beat. "I'd like to talk about Zeke."

He extends his chin, confusion on his face. "Why the hell do you wanna talk about Zeke? He's fucking dead."

"Yeah, he is. Because Cade came in my room, drugged me, took advantage of me, then pushed Zeke out my window. But there's something that just doesn't make sense to me."

"Oh yeah? What's that?"

"Why was Zeke even in my room? It's not like him and I were friends."

"Fuck if I know. Guess you'll have to ask Cade if you want those answers. But good luck with that."

"Right?" I drawl. "Because Cade is missing. It's so strange that he just completely vanished like he did. I mean, he killed a guy, and raped girls, yet one small threat from Ridge and he just takes off? Doesn't really fit his character."

"Look, Trouble. I think you're thinking too much." His hands run up my inner thighs as he positions himself between my legs. Bending down, he sweeps my hair over my shoulder and drags his teeth down my ear lobe. "I came here to fuck you. Not talk about a dead guy and his murderer."

Taking control of the situation, I push Lev back with a smirk, until he's catching his feet, towering over me. Then I stand up, grab his forearm and spin him around before shoving him onto the couch. "How about this?" I say, now straddling his lap. I arch my back and lean in close, my lips almost touching his ear as I hiss my ultimatum, "Confess what you did and I'll let you fuck me."

"You got it, Trouble. Tell me what to confess and I'll say the words. As long as this ends with you riding my cock."

Tempting as that is, I have no intention of ever touching Lev again once he admits he's the one who came in my room that night. I have the proof; I know it was him. As much as I want to deny it, the evidence speaks for itself.

My phone vibrates beside us, but I ignore it, putting all my attention on the task at hand. I've got two fists, and pepper spray within reach that I will use if Lev tries to fight me on this.

Forgoing the weapon, I reach between the two couch cushions and pull out the bottle of pills I stuffed in there minutes before he got here. I squeeze my legs around Lev, rooting him to this spot. My blood is beyond the point of boiling as I lift them up, showing him what's in my hand. "Are these yours?"

I should be scared when I see his jaw click and his nostrils flare. But I'm not. My fear has been channeled into rage, and I'm too pissed to be scared.

"Why the fuck do you have my pills?" he grits out. "Of course they're mine. They have my fucking name on them."

"I found these in your room—"

His face twists in anger, his fists clenched at his sides. "Yes, they were in my room! Because they're my fucking pills! Now tell me why the hell you have them. Were you going through my shit?"

"Let me finish!" I shout, overpowering his fury. "I found them in your fucking room then compared them to a pill I found in my room. And it's the same damn medication!"

Suddenly, I'm shoved off him, and I fall backward. Unable to catch my fall, I hit the floor with a thud. In two seconds, I'm back on my feet, shadowing Lev, who's pacing the room while gripping the sides of his head.

"Why was your pill in my room, Lev? Did you drop it? Is this the medication you drugged me with? I looked it up online. The symptoms I had match the side effects of this shit. It was you, wasn't it? You drugged me, then you killed Zeke!"

He stomps back and forth from one end of the cabin to the next while I follow. His eyes dart around the room like a caged animal. Every few steps he pauses briefly to stare at me before continuing to pace.

"Answer me, goddammit!"

When he doesn't, I walk steadfastly to the couch and pull the note out of the cushions where the pills were. I hold it up with a trembling hand. "I found this in your room, too. It's a note Zeke wrote me. Why'd you do it, Lev?" Tears sting the corners of my eyes and my whole body shakes. "Why'd you take advantage of me then kill him?"

His face twists in rage as he slams his fist onto the kitchen table. "Because!" he screams. "Because Cade needed to be taught a lesson. He needed to be banished from The Society. He doesn't deserve to be here, or even breathe the same fucking air as us!"

"So you decided to play God? You took an innocent man's life, Lev. When I was blaming myself, you encouraged it. You made me think I did something wrong. You would have let the whole world believe it was me that pushed Zeke when all along it was you." I can't stop the tears as they fall recklessly down my cheeks, and I don't even have the energy to try. "Why? Why do you hate me so much?"

"It was never about you, dammit!" He punches the table again and the impact causes me to jolt. "I would've never let it get that far. It was always Cade that needed to pay for this. And he has."

"You framed me for the murders, didn't you? All the evidence that was found in the ash of those men who died was put there by you, wasn't it? You killed them and framed me just to get me under your thumb. And I fucking fell for it. I fell for your games, then I fell for you, and I'm such a damn idiot."

He stops walking and turns to face me, his expression unreadable. His eyes search mine as if he's trying to find the truth in them. "You fell for me?"

After everything I've said, that's what stands out to him? "Are you hearing anything I'm saying?"

He strides toward me, each step bringing him closer. I stumble backward and feel my heart racing as the space between us grows smaller and smaller. "Answer my question, Trouble."

My breathing quickens and my palms grow damp as I curl my hand into a tight fist. I hold it at my side for a moment before thrusting it back and delivering a hard blow right to the side of Lev's cheek. "Fuck you!" I spin around and grab my phone and the pepper spray and quickly stuff them in the pocket of my cardigan. I swallow down the hard ball lodged in my throat and walk around him, knowing I need to get out of here fast because Lev would never allow me to get away with that.

But I'm not fast enough when he grabs me by the wrist. "Don't go."

Growling, I slap his hand down. "Don't touch me!" I grit out.

Lev's phone starts ringing, and it distracts him just long enough for me to make it out the front door. I have to talk to Ridge and Maddox. They need to know what happened, and that I plan to go to The Elders. I have to confess everything. The governor, how Lev killed all those men and set me up, and how he's the one who killed Zeke.

The snow is falling fast as I race toward campus. There's a constant white mist in the air, drifting slowly down and settling on everything below. Hugging my arms to my chest, I move as quickly as I can in my heels. It wasn't snowing this heavily when I left and I didn't even consider my poor choice of shoes.

"Riley!" I hear Lev shout from behind me as I reach the gravel road. "Don't go back to campus!" I glance over my shoulder to see him standing on the porch of the cabin with his hands cupped around his mouth. "Check your phone!"

I don't stop walking. In fact, I'm practically running as I reach into the pocket of my cardigan and take out my phone. I'm shocked to see so many text messages and missed calls—there's also a campus-wide alert.

I tap Ridge's name first and read his messages.

> Ridge: Where are you, Angel? Please call me.

> Ridge: Don't come back to campus. There are people here looking for you.

> Ridge: Did you get the alert?

> Ridge: Listen to me, Angel. I need you to go to the warehouse by the cemetery. Go inside and wait for me.

At this point, I'm just passing by the warehouse, so I turn around and move quickly toward the entrance.

As I'm walking, I read the campus alert.

> Campus Alert: Shelter-in-place. Homicide suspect at large.

I stop mid-stride, my feet pinned directly in front of the door. My breath catches in my throat as I put together the pieces of these messages.

Someone is looking for me?

Because I'm the suspect.

"SHE'S HERE!" I holler down the hall to Ridge. "Looks like Lev is coming down the drive behind her."

Ridge hauls ass down the hall, barreling past me as he pulls open the door. I'm right behind him when I see Riley standing there with snowflakes in her hair, and tears soaking her cheeks.

I step around Ridge, ready to pull her in for a hug, but he beats me to it. "It's gonna be okay," I hear him say.

"Is it me?" she asks. "Am I the suspect? Is it Zeke? Those other guys?"

Ridge pulls back, hands on her shoulders. "What other guys?"

Riley's eyes catch mine. "Does he know?"

I shake my head. "Haven't told him."

Ridge pivots around, his brow furrowed as his gaze shifts back and forth between me and Riley. "What the hell are you two talking about?"

"It was nothing," I say, trying to downplay the situation.

"It was Cade. He killed three other guys and framed Riley. My dad took the evidence and it's sealed. He kept me in the loop throughout the inside investigation, and I assured him Riley was set up."

"You assured him, or you think you assured him?" Ridge raises his voice. "Because Cade's fucking father—a Punisher—is on the hunt for Riley right fucking now."

"He sounded like he bought it, and it was the truth. He dropped the subject and we haven't discussed it since."

"Why the fuck didn't you tell me?" Ridge shouts. "Don't you think this is something I should have been made aware of? Anything that entails her is my fucking business!"

"I messed up, man. Should've told you, but I thought it was all under control."

"Well, you obviously thought wrong and now look at this damn mess."

Ridge is right. I should've told him and we could've worked together to prevent all of this. I've been so hung up on Riley and my own personal shit that I wasn't thinking straight.

Guilt begins to eat at me as I look at Riley and realize I wasn't there for her in all the ways I promised I would be.

I watch as her face transforms and the realization of what's happening sets in. Her eyes go wide in shock. Skin turning pale like a ghost. Her mouth hangs open slightly, stopping only with the occasional tremble. My heart breaks at the sight.

Lev steps up beside us wearing his own look of trepidation. It's obvious he read our messages about his uncle being here on an assignment, as well as the campus alert, but we still haven't told him why. He also doesn't know about Cade and the doc. Ridge and I agreed we'd hold off on that a little longer, until everything else settles down. But I'm certain once he knows, he'll be out for blood.

"So, what's going on?" Lev asks, breathlessly. "My uncle's on campus? Who's the suspect?"

Ridge and I both look at Riley as she gulps, choking down her tears. "Me," she whispers.

Lev's eyes shoot wide open. "No. That can't be right."

Riley turns around quickly and shoves Lev so hard he stumbles back a few steps. "Of course it's right. Because you did this!" she cries. "You killed people and framed me and now a fucking Punisher is coming for me!"

"What? No!" I reach out to grab Riley, pulling her sullen body to mine. My arms wrap around her and I hold her tight, stroking her head. "Lev didn't kill those people. Cade did."

"But he didn't." She cries into my shoulder. "Lev confessed that he killed Zeke." She takes a step back, but stays in arm's reach. "He's the one who came into my room that night. He drugged me. He assaulted me. Then he killed Zeke."

My eyes shoot over her shoulder, glaring at Lev with rage. "Tell me she's wrong," I beg through gritted teeth. He stares back at me, nostrils flared. His shoulders sag in defeat, but he remains silent. "Tell me, dammit!"

"It's true," he says. "It was me. But Cade—"

I charge at him before he can say another word. My arms wrap around his core and I take him straight to the ground. "You fucking did it! You killed him!" Words of pure wrath spill from my mouth and I scream in his face.

"I didn't fucking do it," Lev shouts, spitting in my face. "Get the fuck off me." He gives me a forceful shove, rolling me off of him and onto my back. I quickly get up and gun for him again, but he's faster and manages to stand up in time. "Yes, I went into her room, and yes, I killed Zeke. I was fucked up at the time. I was coming off my meds and my mind was a mess. I didn't give a damn about her then. But I do now. She changed me. She made me feel again."

"You should have fucking told us!" I shout at him. "When you started to feel like yourself again, you should have fucking admitted what you did!"

"Look. I'll handle my uncle and I'll pay for my sins by someone worthy of punishing me." He looks at Riley. "And I'll make this up to you. One day. Somehow. As for the two of you," he nods between me and Ridge, "you'll come around eventually. We're family, and family forgives."

"Not this time," Ridge tells him. "You went too far."

Lev's eyebrows rise. "And you haven't?"

Ridge's defenses kick in high gear. "What the hell does that mean?"

"You're not innocent here." He spins on his heel and walks toward the road. Once he's halfway there, he slows his steps and turns back. "I didn't kill those other men. So you might wanna check each other before you start pointing fingers at me. I'm not the only one who was keeping secrets."

Lev's words send a chill down my spine. The surety in his tone is unnerving. *Does he know?*

A text comes through on my phone that's now lying face up on the ground in front of me, covered in snow. I bend down, sweep it off and read it.

> Dad: Stay in your dorm, son. There's been another murder. This one is a member and student at BCU. They're searching for the Cross girl. With the evidence from the previous murders, her connection with the governor, and the boy who fell out her window, this one only adds to suspicion. Her trial has been set with The Elders. A Punisher has been assigned. Her fate will be sealed.

My gut wrenches. This can't be happening. I look at Riley crying into Ridge's shoulder. This sweet girl who stacked the odds against her by taking the governor's life, when all she was doing was protecting herself and the rest of the world from a monster.

Before I can respond to my dad, another text comes through.

> Dad: I just got word. It was Cade Pemberley whose remains were found.

My breath catches in my throat.

They think it was her.

I thought with Cade out of the picture, I was keeping Riley safe. I thought I could love her the way Ridge loves her. I wanted to protect her the same way Ridge always seems to protect her. But instead, I made everything worse.

She looks at me with tears in her eyes. "I don't know what's happening, but I didn't do this stuff I'm being accused of," she says, her voice sounding defeated.

I know she didn't kill Cade. Because I did.

The End

Coming this summer, the final book in the *Wicked Boys of BCU* series! You don't want to miss this finale. Everything wraps up and all truths are revealed! Preorder *They Will Fall* now.

ALSO BY RACHEL LEIGH

Bastards of Boulder Cove

Book One: Savage Games

Book Two: Vicious Lies

Book Three: Twisted Secrets

Wicked Boys of BCU

Book One: We Will Reign

Book Two: You Will Bow

Book Three: They Will Fall

Redwood Rebels Series

Book One: Striker

Book Two: Heathen

Book Three: Vandal

Book Four: Reaper

Redwood High Series

Book One: Like Gravity

Book Two: Like You

Book Three: Like Hate

Fallen Kingdom Duet

His Hollow Heart & Her Broken Pieces

Black Heart Duet

Four & Five

ACKNOWLEDGMENTS

Thank you so much for reading You Will Bow. I hope you enjoyed it!

A special thanks to my wonderful team for all the hard work you put into helping me create this book: My dedicated PA, Carolina Leon. All my girls for your support, friendship, and advice. My Street Team, the Rebel Readers for your help in getting the word out.

Thank you to my beta & alpha readers: Amanda, Taylor, & Drita. I appreciate you ladies so much!

A BIG thanks to...

Y'all That Graphic for the amazing cover and graphics!

Fairest Reviews Editing Service for the beautiful edit!

Rumi Khan for proofreading and being so flexible!.

Greys Promo for spectacular PR Services.

XOXO Rachel

ABOUT THE AUTHOR

Rachel Leigh is a USA Today and International bestselling author of new adult and contemporary romances.

She loves to write—and read—flawed bad-boys and strong heroines. You can expect dark elements, a dash of suspense, and a lot of steam.

Her goal is to take readers on an adventure with her words, while showing them that even on the darkest days, love conquers all.

Rachel lives in Michigan with her husband, three little monsters (who aren't so little anymore) and a couple of fur babies. When she's not writing or reading, she's likely lounging in leggings, with coffee in her hand, while binge watching her favorite reality tv shows.

facebook.com/rachelleighauthor

instagram.com/rachelleighauthor

bookbub.com/profile/rachel-leigh